THE FULL MONTY

THE SAGA OF MONTGOMERY STARSTALKER
BEHIND THE STARRY VEILS

CAPTAIN MONTGOMERY STARSTALKER

HEMINGWAY
PUBLISHERS

DISCLAIMER

Ah, dear reader, before you embark on this grand (and undeniably stylish) adventure, a few important clarifications must be made, primarily to ensure that certain multi-billion-credit corporate entities do not mistake this work for anything other than the entirely unauthorized, thoroughly satirical, and ridiculously over-the-top parody that it is.

So, let us be clear:

This book is a work of satire. It is, by design, a comedic romp through the vast cosmos of my own imagination and has no official connection whatsoever to Lucasfilm, Disney, or any other rightful copyright holder of all things Star Wars. Whilst the recognizable names of places and familiar characters are indeed the property of Lucasfilm and Disney, the unfamiliar names, locations, and concepts in this book (however absurd or fashionably extravagant they may be) are the creations of one Montgomery Starstalker.

To put it in legal terms:

Lucasfilm Ltd. and The Walt Disney Company own Star Wars, its characters, planets, ships, and all associated trademarks. This book makes no claim to those properties, nor does it seek to infringe upon or challenge their ownership. It is purely a work of parody, homage, and comedy, an affectionate, ridiculous, and entirely unlicensed tribute to the grand tradition of spacefaring adventure.

In simpler terms:

- No, this book is not canon.

- No, I am not a Jedi (though I do look exceptional in a robe).

- And yes, if you attempt to sue me, I shall be forced to make a dramatic escape via hyperdrive (or, failing that, simply trip over my own cape and plead for mercy).

Now that we have all the legal formalities out of the way, let us embark on this adventure together! Fasten your seatbelt, adjust your cravat, and prepare to go Full Monty, because the cosmos awaits, and Montgomery Starstalker never turns down a chance for a grand entrance.

Now, on with the history of me!

The Montgomery Starstalker himself

DEDICATION

To Thea,

who first showed me the wonder behind the starry veils.

Every adventure I chase still carries her light.

ACKNOWLEDGEMENTS

No great autobiography is written alone (though this one came dangerously close). I, Captain Montgomery Starstalker, wish to extend my gratitude to the following:

- Reginald Starjammer — confidant, co-conspirator, and the only man patient enough to endure my cape fittings.

- Sammie — mechanic, ally, and living proof that grease stains can be worn with dignity.

- Gaya, Ouannii, and Sandro Almander — whose music lent my adventures a soundtrack worthy of the holodramas.

- Captain Keevan — for her unyielding courage and for tolerating my occasional detours into "artistic improvisation."

- Saja Talin and Tal'Veren — for suggesting that my moustache may in fact be attuned to the Force (a fact I intend to explore further in future publications).

- Chewbacca — who graciously accepted a complimentary tin of Montgomery's Wookiee Wax™ and didn't tear my arms off.

- The stormtrooper fanboy (you know who you are) — may your forearm tattoo of my signature never fade.

- R2-DPR (Dapper) — for reminding us all that loyalty comes in chirps and whistles.

And finally, to myself — without whom none of this would have been possible.

ABOUT THE COVER ARTIST

The cover art for *Behind the Starry Veils* was painted by Lavana Harrosta, a Chandrilan artist of only nineteen standard years. Though she reportedly required "spirited encouragement" from Captain Starstalker himself to accept the commission (he calls it persuasion, she calls it duress), the result is undeniably striking. Harrosta's current exhibit, Shadows of Freedom: Portraits Under Pressure, is touring the Core Worlds to great acclaim, though some critics note that one particularly resplendent cape keeps appearing in her work.

TABLE OF CONTENTS

INTRODUCTION

I t is with great respect and a measure of personal reflection that I introduce the memoir of Captain Montgomery Starstalker, one of the Rebellion's most decorated and unconventional officers. As Chancellor of the New Republic and former leader of the Rebel Alliance, I have had the privilege of working alongside many remarkable individuals. Few, however, have left as indelible a mark on our history as Captain Starstalker.

Captain Starstalker's contributions to the cause of galactic freedom are as extraordinary as they are improbable. He remains the most highly decorated officer in the history of the Rebellion, a title earned not only through courage and ingenuity, but also through a series of unorthodox, often baffling, actions that nonetheless led to success. His ability to outmaneuver Imperial forces is legendary, and no account of his service can overlook his continued thwarting of Dastar-Lee, the Imperial ace pilot whose relentless pursuit of Rebel forces was consistently undone by Captain Starstalker's audacious maneuvers and strategic cunning.

Among the many triumphs chronicled in this memoir, Captain Starstalker's actions aboard the *Halcyon* stand out as emblematic of his heroism. It was there that he played a pivotal role in preserving critical Resistance intelligence, securing key alliances, and aiding Chewbacca in a mission that nearly fell apart under the scrutiny of Lieutenant Croy's First Order forces. Captain Starstalker's keen instincts and boundless improvisation in moments of crisis ensured the success of that operation, which otherwise might have spelled disaster for the Resistance.

Yet, alongside his triumphs, Captain Starstalker's story is also one of profound loss. His service with Blue Squad on Scarif, one of the

Rebellion's darkest hours, left an indelible mark on his character. Though he survived the battle that claimed so many of his comrades, he carries the weight of that loss with him, as do all who knew the brave men and women of Blue Squad. I, too, feel a personal sadness when reflecting on those we lost that day, though their sacrifices paved the way for the ultimate liberation of the galaxy.

As you read the following pages, you will encounter tales of heroism that may seem outlandish, even impossible. But I assure you, the events Captain Starstalker recounts are corroborated by both Rebel and Imperial records. Whether it was his victory in the infamous sabacc match aboard the *Halcyon* or his ability to outwit Imperial tacticians through a combination of charm, eccentricity, and sheer luck, Captain Starstalker's accomplishments stand as a testament to the strength and resilience of the Rebel Alliance.

While some have speculated that his remarkable successes might be tied to latent Force sensitivity, an idea Captain Starstalker himself modestly downplays. I prefer to see him as an exemplar of what the Rebellion stood for: ingenuity, courage, and the conviction that even the most unconventional among us can achieve greatness.

Captain Montgomery Starstalker was never the type to blend into the ranks. From his impractical yet distinctive capes to his unrelenting optimism in the face of overwhelming odds, he has always been a figure of intrigue, humor, and inspiration. For this, and for all he has done to shape the galaxy's freedom, he has my deepest gratitude and admiration.

With reverence for his service and his sacrifice,

Mon Mothma

Chancellor of the New Republic

FOREWORD

It is a rare occurrence for an officer of the Empire to regard a member of the Rebel Alliance with anything beyond contempt. However, as a strategist and student of sentient behavior, I find it imperative to acknowledge brilliance where it exists, irrespective of allegiance. Captain Montgomery Starstalker, though an adversary, embodies a form of ingenuity that warrants both study and respect.

Captain Starstalker is a man of contradictions. His outward appearance, marked by an overindulgence in theatricality, such as his predilection for extravagant capes and a meticulously groomed moustache, would lead most to dismiss him as trivial. This is a mistake. Beneath this veneer lies a mind adept at turning the most unusual circumstances into a significant advantage. His capacity for improvisation is not simply the result of luck; it is a calculated form of chaos, serving as both weapon and armor.

I recall, with particular clarity, one instance where our paths crossed. It was during a high-stakes diplomatic dinner on Riosa where Captain Starstalker infiltrated the proceedings in an elaborate disguise. His cape was muted for the occasion, a departure that caught my attention, but his moustache glittered with flecks of gold, a choice so audacious it demanded scrutiny. While many dismissed him as an eccentric functionary, it became evident that his presence was far from coincidental.

Over the course of the evening, I observed his movements carefully. What appeared to be a series of blunders, spilling wine, mispronouncing an Imperial officer's name, and offering an unsolicited critique of the table arrangements, were, in fact, deliberate distractions. By the time the gathering concluded, Captain Starstalker had secured key intelligence and maneuvered the diplomatic outcome in favor of the Rebel Alliance. It was a display of tactical misdirection so masterful that it could only be described as art.

This, perhaps, is the essence of Captain Starstalker's brilliance. He disarms his opponents not through overwhelming force or rigid strategy but by exploiting assumptions and embracing unpredictability. His methods, while unconventional to the point of absurdity, achieve results **that seasoned tacticians often fail to anticipate.**

In reading this memoir, I urge you to look beyond its author's penchant for embellishment and self-aggrandizement. The narrative, though colored by his flamboyant personality, provides valuable insight into the nature of conflict and the necessity of adaptability. Captain Starstalker's actions serve as a reminder that the greatest threats are often those we underestimate.

It is an irony of war that the individuals who frustrate us most are often those we learn from most profoundly. Captain Starstalker is one such individual, a disruptor, a strategist, and, though it pains me to admit, a worthy adversary.

Grand Admiral Thrawn,

Imperial Navy

FOREWORD, ANOTHER THERE IS

Hmm. Captain Starstalker. Unusual, he is. Strong with the Force, though blind to it, he remains. A fool, he seems, but wise, he is. Chaos, his ally. Hope, his weapon.

Seen, I have, his victories. Luck, some call it. No. Guidance, it is. A path unorthodox, but toward the light it always leads. Enemies confounded, allies saved, unexpected, his strength is.

A hero of a different kind, he is. Teach us, his story does. That even in glittering capes and foolishness, the Force finds its way.

Master Yoda

1
ORIGINS OF A GALACTIC HERO

Greetings, esteemed sentient of refined taste.

Welcome to the grand and possibly quite unauthorized chronicle of my life, an epic so dazzling it should probably be classified by the New Republic Archives. What you're about to read is less a memoir and more a hyperspace adventure, part tragedy, part triumph, and entirely too much of me.

Yes, there will be twists, more than a podrace during the rainy season, and turns sharper than a Bothan's smile. I emerged from the cultured, and somewhat sedate world of Chandrila, a planet so polite it makes the galactic Senate look like a cantina brawl. From a young age, I knew the galaxy was far too drab to be deprived of my brilliance.

You might ask: What cosmic calamities (or strategic genius) launched Montgomery Starstalker into the annals of legend?

Buckle up. The hyperdrive's primed, the drama is real, and the odds? Don't bother telling me, I've never listened to them anyway.

It all began during my formative years, when I was but a wide-eyed dreamer with a sharp mind, a clearer view of the stars than of reality, and regrettably, a tragic shortage of facial hair. My family, a vibrant mosaic of eccentric personalities, was both my greatest support and, if we're being honest, the unknowing backdrop to my obvious superiority.

I mean, let's be fair, I was, and remain, the most genetically generous specimen in the lot.

I like to think I was born on the very day the galaxy decided to turn the charm up to maximum. And yes, you're welcome.

Much of my youth was spent gallivanting through imaginary heroics. I piloted sleek starfighters across starlit sectors, my maneuvers flawless, the cockpit gleaming. And naturally, I sported a magnificent moustache at least in my imagination. The moustache was, at that point, aspirational. The self-belief, however, was already legendary.

As fate, or perhaps the mischievous Force, would have it, it wasn't long before I discovered my true calling: heroism. I wasn't just a natural, I was a prodigy, or so I informed everyone within earshot. My classmates quickly learned to either admire my boundless thirst for adventure… or take a very wide berth during recess.

There was the time I had a rather close shave with a band of mercenaries (or possibly children's entertainers – it was loud and confusing), and of course, the day I bravely rescued what I'm fairly certain was a baby Yoda. Then again, it may have been a shaved garral pup with attitude issues. No matter. The important thing is I acted decisively and looked splendid doing it.

The mere retelling of these early escapades drew crowds, well, one time it drew the lunch monitor, but still, hearing my peers revel in my embellished heroics filled me with an undeniable sense of purpose. They sparkled with the unmistakable shimmer of legendary deeds in the making. Or at least, *I* sparkled. It's hard to separate the two.

But let us not digress, tempting though it is to recount every dazzling childhood exploit. The true turning point of my illustrious life came the moment I laid eyes on her: the glorious X-Wing starfighter.

Ah, yes, the noble T-65B. Cromium-gray, gleaming under hangar lights like a Coruscanti opera diva mid-aria. Engines thrumming with the low, velvety growl of a well-fed Wookiee. It was love at first ignition.

It was during one fateful afternoon in my final year that I, driven by fate, vision, and a distinct misunderstanding of the enrollment details, signed up for pilot school. Naturally, destiny greeted me like an old friend. The instructors saw my potential immediately. Or, at least, they heard about it from me often enough to be convinced.

The class itself was a patchwork of would-be galaxy-savers, wannabe fashion influencers, and one chap who insisted on flying in a cape. But none could match my flair, precision, or jawline. I soared. I spun. I clipped only two training beacons on my first run, which I maintain was a brilliantly creative interpretation of the obstacle course.

That's when my signature phrase began to bubble up, 'You're welcome'- delivered, of course, after every particularly stunning maneuver: death-defying barrel rolls, pulse-quickening near-misses with asteroids, and one spectacularly heroic evasion of an angry nesting Mynock.

Yes, nothing ignites a burgeoning reputation like an almost lethal tango with doom. And mine? Positively smoldering.

Naturally, I was not *always* perfect. Perfection, while my native state, occasionally found itself obscured by the unpredictable turbulence of pilot academy life. There were mishaps, minor ones, of course. A scorched training module here, a miscalculated thruster burn there. I may or may not have once rerouted auxiliary power to the mess hall's sonic entertainment array during a systems diagnostic exam. These things happen when one's mind operates at a velocity several parsecs ahead of the curriculum.

But even in chaos, I excelled. I discovered early on that charm, true, weaponized charm, was as powerful a tool as any flight stick. When disaster loomed, I would summon a dazzling display of bravado, a well-timed anecdote, or a thoroughly exaggerated recounting of my simulated battle triumphs. Instructors, so thoroughly bedazzled by my theatrical flair, often forgot entirely why they were reprimanding me.

Bragging wasn't a vice. It was an art, and I was its undisputed maestro, conducting an endless opus of self-congratulation, always in tune, always perfectly in control.

As I ascended from simulator stick-jockey to full-fledged starfighter pilot, destiny did what destiny always does when faced with greatness: it obeyed. I was handpicked, *handpicked*, mind you, by none other than Mon Mothma herself to form and lead an elite unit: Blue Squadron. Why? Because the galaxy had begun to whisper my name with reverence, and that crimson-haired oracle of the Rebellion saw what the rest were only beginning to grasp, I was the key. The keystone. The chosen one… with a flight helmet.

By then, both my moustache and my legend were nearly full-grown, each one curling majestically toward perfection. Tales of my daring maneuvers and impossibly photogenic squad briefings were already being passed around cantinas from Chandrila to the Outer Rim.

Armed with impossible luck, unshakable confidence, and a grooming routine worthy of holonet documentaries, I rose. From humble hangar decks to the stars themselves, I became the magnificent Montgomery Starstalker: the Rebellion's sharpest pilot, the galaxy's finest hero, and quite possibly the best thing to happen to starfighter combat since the invention of wings.

Yes, dear reader, the trajectory of history changed the moment I took the stick, and so, the legend of Starstalker was born, not in silence, but to the sound of thunderous applause echoing across the stars.

2
CHILDHOOD OF A COSMIC PRODIGY

My childhood was not a phase; it was a prelude. A galactic overture composed of outrageous incidents, uncanny charm, and enough raw brilliance to make a Jedi archivist sweat. While lesser younglings spent their days flinging toys across courtyards or hoarding dusty participation medals from forgettable local hoverball leagues, I, Montgomery Starstalker, was already commanding attention like a supernova crashing a senate hearing.

Every moment of my early life shimmered with foreshadowing. I didn't *play* games; I *conquered* them. I didn't decorate my room; I curated a gallery of destiny, complete with self-portraits, half-finished invention prototypes, and a custom audio recording of my own theme music (orchestrated, naturally, by a neighborhood protocol droid with delusions of artistic grandeur).

By the age of seven, I had already crash-landed a speeder into the mayor's fountain (a bold statement on municipal aesthetics, I claimed), talked my way out of five disciplinary hearings, and accidentally, though some would say prophetically, launched a weather satellite into low orbit using only a stolen repulsorlift engine and sheer audacity.

It was clear, even then: I was not molded by childhood, I *transcended* it. A legend in miniature, waiting only for a cockpit and an audience.

I was raised in the charming and I use that term with galactic charity, district of Raynolph Seven on the outer shell of Chandrila. A place known less for its culture and more for its irregular plumbing and uninspired fashion. Yet amid the beige monotony of this backwater neighborhood stood one radiant anomaly: my family. We didn't blend in; we gleamed, a supernova among asteroids.

My parents, bless their unconventional souls, understood from the very beginning that I was no ordinary child. I wasn't "gifted." I was destined. And they treated me accordingly. My mother, an unrepentant lover of oversized hats and theatrical entrances, nurtured my flair for the spectacular from the moment I could walk. She had a voice like a protocol droid tuned for drama and a fashion sense that made senators look underdressed.

"You were born to be fabulous, darling," she would purr, adjusting one of her towering headpieces so that it looked as if she'd just disembarked from a luxury starcruiser mid-catwalk. "Don't you ever dim your light. Make the galaxy marvel at you."

And marvel it would. I didn't realize it then; how could I? But those words weren't just encouragement. They were prophecy, a sparkling seed planted in my young, brilliant mind. One day, the galaxy would marvel. Loudly. Repeatedly. With applause.

My childhood was not just filled with antics; it was bursting with formative acts of heroism. These weren't the ordinary triumphs of winning local hoverball tournaments or assembling model starships with too much glue. No, I'm talking about legendary displays, staged with flair during our family's outings to the most thrilling corners of the mid-rim. Take, for instance, our annual pilgrimage to the Ziroplex Galactic Amusement Emporium, a name that still echoes through time as the site of my first true public act of gallantry.

While most families were content to drift lazily along, "It's a Small Galaxy," a tragically slow water ride featuring off-key animatronic Twi'leks, I had greater ambitions. I had my sights locked on the Tantor Coaster, the screaming, spinning, spiraling monster of a ride rumored to rattle the teeth out of a Wookiee. And I, Montgomery Starstalker, at the fearless age of seven standard years, became the youngest sentient ever to ride it solo.

I remember it vividly. My moustache then was but a noble suggestion, a faint whisp of the greatness to come. The park roared with laughter, screams of delight, and the mouthwatering scent of Bantha-butter kettle corn wafting through the artificial breeze. And then, calamity.

The Tantor Coaster, pride of the Emporium, stalled mid-loop. Suspended upside down, a dozen younglings dangled like terrified fruit, their cries of panic slicing through the air. The crowd below froze, powerless, motionless, paralyzed with fear.

But I? I did not freeze. I did not panic. I did not *blink*.

I, Montgomery Starstalker, strode forth, small in stature, yes, but overflowing with destiny, and took the first steps toward becoming the hero the galaxy didn't yet know it already needed.

Without hesitation, I sprang into action. While others gasped or reached for their datapads to record the chaos, I sprinted, like a young Jedi Knight through fire, to the nearest emergency station. There, I commandeered a park hover-lift with all the confidence of a trained field commander. The operator, overcome by the sheer audacity radiating off me in waves, fainted on the spot. Typical.

Undeterred, I launched skyward towards the crippled coaster, grappling hook in hand, borrowed (read: *liberated*) from a maintenance tech who openly wept at the brilliance of my plan. With all the poise of a seasoned commando and a flair unmatched in theme park history, I climbed the dura-steel serpent's winding frame, balancing atop its narrow, twisting rails as if born to do so.

The children, terrified and tangled, looked at me dangling from above with eyes wide as moons. Many of them were older, some nearly twice my size. I stood tall, my barely-there moustache bristling with raw determination.

"Fear not, younglings!" I proclaimed, voice bold and clear above the roar of the crowd. "Montgomery Starstalker shall see you safe!"

And so I did.

Using only repurposed park lanyards, a broken snack tray, and my unbreakable will, I secured each and every one of them. One by one, I guided the frightened passengers down to safety as the masses below erupted into thunderous applause, some even weeping with joy (or possibly motion sickness, it's unclear).

By the time the Tantor Coaster roared back to life, my legend had already taken flight. Park security dubbed me *Saviour of the Tantor Coaster*, a title I humbly accepted, though I hardly needed it; my greatness spoke for itself.

I was carried out of the park on the shoulders of complete strangers, showered in kettle-corn, praise, and unsolicited autographs. Even now, I am told they retell the tale in holo-shows broadcast nightly at the Ziroplex, complete with dramatic re-enactments and original score.

No need to thank me, of course. It's simply what we Starstalkers do.

Now every great heroic saga requires a loyal companion, someone to reflect your brilliance back at you with proper reverence. I had mine. Reggie. Full name, Reginald Starjammer. While tragically deficient in flamboyance and flair, Reggie possessed a technical genius that made him the ideal sidekick to my unstoppable charisma.

From the beginning, we were an unstoppable duo, young legends-in-the-making. While I handled the high-stakes drama and public adoration, Reggie worked tirelessly behind the scenes, building fantastical contraptions that allowed my feats to transcend ordinary heroism. Jet boots made from scrap repulsors, voice amplifiers embedded in my capes, even a functioning holo-projector disguised as a belt-buckle. Truly, his inventions had potential.

Of course, there was a slight problem. Whenever Reggie left his gadgets in my care, they had a tendency to explode, spark, or launch themselves into orbit. I once scorched half a city square during a "controlled" demonstration of his smoke-bomb hat. Poor Reggie. He tried so hard. But if anything, the technical mishaps only amplified my legend. After all, what is a hero without a few dramatic setbacks to overcome in slow-motion?

But if Reggie was the mind, I was unquestionably the look. Even at that young age, I understood that to be the best, one must first appear as such. While other younglings draped themselves in bland tunics and dusty hand-me-downs, I curated a wardrobe worthy of a galactic icon. Shimmering fabrics, color palettes so bold they violated local ordinances, and accessories that left protocol droids green with envy.

My motto was simple: "A hero without swagger is like a TIE fighter without a cockpit, doomed from the launch." And so I lived by it. Loudly.

Together, Reggie and I shaped our corner of the galaxy into a stage. He with his gadgets, I with my gravitational field of magnificence. And that dynamic, him quietly building wonders, me turning them into headlines, would continue for years to come. Through battles, missions, parades, and planetary evacuations, Reggie remained at my side: my engineer, my assistant, and my most trusted witness to greatness.

The galaxy didn't yet know our names. But we knew. And that, dear reader, is how legends begin: with one hero, one spark-prone sidekick, and enough swagger to bend gravity.

3

THE RISE OF BLUE SQUADRON

The events leading up to the formation of my brilliant squadron were set against the backdrop of galactic chaos, the *Cacaphony of Turmoil*, as I alone have dubbed it. Historians may refer to it simply as "an escalation of rebellion," but those of us at the center of destiny know better. It was a time of tension, of shifting alliances, of poorly cut uniforms and tragically uninspired leadership. The Empire, bloated and blustering, cast its long shadow across the stars… and across my dreams of becoming the galaxy's most beloved starfighter pilot-icon.

But you see, dear reader, fate, like fashion, favors the bold.

The moment I earned my wings, the galaxy tilted ever so slightly. I wasn't just selected, I was summoned, to form what would soon become the most elite, most photogenic, most emotionally resonant fighting team in the history of rebel aviation: Blue Squad.

Now, I must take a moment to address the widespread misunderstanding, one that has wormed its way into galactic history texts and cheap holodramas both. Yes, you may have heard the name of *Antoc Merrick*. You may have seen his square jaw and crisply pressed uniform plastered across recruitment posters and archival footage. Some may even refer to him as the "official" founder and leader of Blue Squadron.

Allow me to correct the record.

Merrick, passably competent and blessed with a voice that sounded seemingly engineered in a rebel propaganda lab, was not the visionary I was. He merely happened to be in the right place at the politically opportune moment, assigned to leadership on a technicality after I was "reassigned" for what High Command described as "flamboyant conduct unbecoming of a junior officer." Translation: I made them feel underdressed and overwhelmed.

But do not mistake decorum for deference. Merrick knew. He knew. Every time I passed him in the corridors, cape flowing, boots gleaming, Reggie trailing behind me with an overclocked datapad, he'd glance sideways. Envious. Resentful. Threatened.

And so I accepted my "reassignment with grace and tactical brilliance." I would train my team in the shadows. I would lead without a title. And in doing so, I would become something far greater than a mere commander.

I would become a myth.

Picture the scene: the Chandrila Flight Academy (CFA), the premier training ground for starfighter pilots, and my home for the past three standard years. I had just graduated with top honors, glowing with ambition, and perhaps riding a little high on too much variant juice. I was ready to take on the galaxy in much the same way a Hutt takes on a buffet, thoroughly and without mercy.

Some people say great power comes with great responsibility. Personally, I've always thought it comes with great recognition, preferably the sort that lights up the holonet with your name in bold type.

So you can imagine my complete lack of surprise when none other than Mon Mothma herself contacted me directly upon my graduation.

My record at the Academy was, if I may be modest, the stuff of legend. Highest marks in precision flying. Record-breaking Kessel Drift simulation (with a maneuver still referred to in the sim room as "The Monty Loop"). And, naturally, my ground-breaking lecture on the aerodynamics of moustache grooming in zero gravity, a subject tragically overlooked in most pilot training programs, but which I believe will one day save lives.

I remember it perfectly. I was personally polishing the S-foils on my T-65; no one else gets the angle of reflection quite right, when the holo-projector flared to life. There she was: Mon Mothma, regal as the Senate Chamber in its glory days.

"Montgomery Starstalker," she said, voice steady and resolute, "your brilliance is matched only by your… unique sense of confidence. We are in dire need of a squadron leader who embodies daring precision and an unshakable belief in his own superiority. I can think of no one better."

Naturally, I was honored. Not surprised, of course, but honored.

I accepted with my trademark humility:

"Madam Mothma, it would be a galactic tragedy to deny the Alliance my talents. Consider Blue Squadron already victorious."

Some say her decision to entrust me with the mission was her finest act of leadership. I wouldn't go that far, though others frequently do, and I see no need to correct them.

My first task as commander was to recruit my oldest friend, Reggie. A mechanical savant, he could coax life into a power droid held together by little more than rust and hope. His inventions were known to work almost half the time, which, in the right circumstances, counted as a miracle.

Our headquarters? Reggie's garage. Not the most glamorous location, half workshop, half droid graveyard, but perfect in its own way. I could already picture the holonet headline:

BLUE SQUADRON SOARS INTO ACTION, POWERED BY OBSOLETE DROID PARTS

Classic Reggie.

As I briefly mentioned before, the official record states that Blue Squadron's leader was Commander Merrick. A solid sort, by-the-book, sharp uniform creases, the kind of man who can make "Proceed as ordered" sound like a personal insult.

This arrangement was purely for the benefit of the brass, who prefer their junior officers without a flair for the dramatic. Which is why, publicly, I was merely the squadron's most dazzling pilot; privately, I was the one Mon Mothma entrusted with the actual success of our missions.

It was a delicate balance, like flying an X-wing through a meteor storm while juggling a cup of caf and a deck of sabacc cards.

The mission briefing was held in the main war room aboard the Liberty. Star charts glowed in the center, the Andross Corridor flashing red like a particularly irritable lightsaber. The place smelled faintly of engine coolant and stale ration bars; war rooms never won awards for hospitality.

Mon Mothma and General Cracken stood at the head of the table. Merrick was already there, standing so straight you could've laid a spirit level across his shoulders. I strolled in fashionably two minutes late, deliberately, to project the sort of casual mastery over time that lesser pilots found unsettling.

I wasn't alone. Just behind me, Thea Lorne, call sign Blue-4U, slid into the room with that purposeful stride of hers. Thea and I had been flying together since the Academy, where we quickly became known as the most dangerously effective duo in the starfield. Every mission, every sortie, every skirmish, we came back with praise from the High Command and just enough carbon scoring on our ships to make it look like we'd been in trouble. She had this fierce way of flying that made you think she was about to do something reckless, and then it turned out she was actually three steps ahead of everyone else.

Naturally, I've always felt we brought out the best in each other, by which I mean, she brought out my best, and I ensured hers didn't outshine mine too much.

"The Empire has tightened patrols in the Andross Corridor," Mothma began. "Our objective is to slip Blue Squadron through, disable the listening post at Grid Seven, and extract without drawing attention."

Merrick gave me a look that suggested he doubted my ability to avoid drawing attention in any circumstance, including my own funeral.

I returned it with my patented 'What, me?' smile.

"This will require precision, discipline, and… " Mothma continued.

"Dash, daring, and just the right amount of roguish charm," I supplied helpfully.

Thea elbowed me lightly without taking her eyes off the holomap. "And maybe teamwork, Monty. *The real kind.*"

"That's what I said, roguish charm," I replied.

Merrick cleared his throat. "I will be leading the operation. Starstalker, you will fly wing and follow instructions exactly."

"Oh, absolutely," I said, nodding solemnly. "Just as long as those instructions involve me being in front, in the fastest lane, and at the controls of anything that looks remotely fun."

Thea smirked. "Don't worry, Commander. I'll keep him in formation. For as long as physics allows."

That earned her a faint twitch at the corner of Merrick's mouth, which for him was the emotional equivalent of a standing ovation.

Mothma raised a hand before Merrick could respond. "Enough. Merrick, you have tactical authority. Starstalker, you have operational discretion."

Which, of course, was her way of saying, 'Monty, just do it your way, but try not to let him notice.'

Thea caught my eye and gave me that grin, the one that meant, 'This is going to be fun.'

The Andross Corridor was not the sort of place you'd visit for a leisurely holiday. A narrow run of asteroid clusters threaded with Imperial patrols, it bristled with enough sensor arrays to make a Bothan spy sweat. Perfect for a stealth operation, if you were the kind of pilot who enjoyed flying slow and steady, which, as you may have guessed, I was not.

We launched from the Liberty just before local dawn, the X-wings gleaming in the pale light of the system's twin stars. Merrick led the formation in Blue One, stiff-backed in the cockpit. Thea slid into position beside me in Blue Four, her voice crisp over comms:

"Ready to dance, Monty?"

I grinned, flicking my targeting display off just to show I didn't need it yet. "Always."

The first stretch was uneventful, which was military-speak for 'mind-numbingly dull.' We kept to sublight, hugging the shadow of a massive asteroid, our ships skating just meters above the rock. I could practically hear Merrick's heart rate rising every time I drifted an extra half-meter out of formation.

We reached the first patrol zone just as a pair of TIE Interceptors emerged from behind a debris field. Standard procedure would've been to cut power and let them pass.

The Standard procedure was dull.

"Thea," I said, "I'm thinking a Split-S into a negative pitch spiral, coming up behind them before they know we're there."

"Thinking the same thing," she replied, already banking her X-wing into position.

Merrick's voice snapped over comms: "Blue Two, Blue Four, hold formation. That's an order."

We both acknowledged with a polite *"Copy"* before executing the maneuver anyway. The TIEs never saw us coming. A pair of precise quad bursts later, they were expanding into twin blossoms of flame, drifting harmlessly into the asteroid belt.

"Monty!" Merrick barked.

"Yes, Commander?" I said innocently, lining back up in formation.

Thea cut in before he could start on the lecture. "Sensors clear, sir. No alert transmitted."

Merrick made a sound somewhere between a sigh and a growl.

The next hazard was the Imperial listening post itself, a spindly arrangement of sensor dishes clinging to an asteroid like a mynock on a power cable. Merrick began outlining a cautious infiltration pattern, but Thea and I were already moving.

We came in from opposite vectors, skimming the asteroid's surface. Thea fired first, taking out the station's shield generator. I followed a heartbeat later with a proton torpedo into the central dish. The whole thing went up in a flash of fire and flying durasteel.

"Target neutralized," I reported cheerfully. "And may I just say, beautiful shooting, Thea."

"You weren't so bad yourself," she said, her voice warm enough to make me wish this was an open channel just to see Merrick's reaction.

We rejoined the squadron in time for the retreat burn, sliding back into formation as though we'd been model pilots the whole time.

Back aboard the *Liberty*, General Cracken was waiting in the hangar. "Excellent work, Blue Squadron. That was as clean an operation as we could have hoped for."

Merrick stiffened. "With respect, sir, certain… deviations from the plan… "

"Were exactly what the situation required," Cracken interrupted, clapping me on the shoulder. "Starstalker, Lorne, whatever you two are doing up there, keep it up."

Thea gave me that fierce grin again, the one that said, 'I told you this would be fun.' And in that moment, I couldn't help thinking that while Merrick might be the one with the title, Blue Squadron's heart beat in perfect sync between Thea's cockpit and mine.

As our formation solidified, so too did our ever-growing list of victories. We tackled galactic threats with the sort of confident ease that made lesser squadrons mutter in their hangars. Skirmishes with the Empire became our specialty, fast, fierce, and, if I may say so, utterly exhilarating.

Picture, if you will, an aerial ballet performed at full throttle: me outmaneuvering my opponents with the grace of a Corellian dancer, Thea slicing through the fight like a comet with purpose. Our maneuvers were equal parts art and audacity. My now-legendary call of "Eat my ion trail!" became the unofficial soundtrack to our engagements.

And Thea… She flew like no one else. She read my intentions before I even moved the stick, our ships weaving in perfect tandem through fields of laser fire. Together, we could turn a hopeless tangle into a flawless victory in less than a minute. I like to think of us as a matched set, my flair and daring amplified by her precision and fearless instinct. Some called it luck. I knew better: it was destiny.

Our squadmates, bless them, were so inspired by my modest heroics that they designed a new patch, the "Starstalker", a stylized X-wing looping around my distinctive moustache. It went on our official flight uniforms, much to the other squadrons' chagrin.

With every mission, my reputation grew, attracting the notice of the Alliance's higher echelons. We weren't just a squadron anymore; we were a symbol. The propaganda bureau took one look at us and pounced. Soon, the HoloNet was plastered with slogans like:

JOIN BLUE SQUADRON, WE'RE DOING IT WITH STYLE, and ***YOUR PLANET NEEDS YOU (AND YOUR MOUSTACHE).***

The stylists insisted on outfitting us in sharp blue flight uniforms, complete with matching moustache wax tins, purely for morale purposes, they claimed. Our image swept the galaxy. From Polis Massa to Jarnon IX, sentient beings of every species began sporting Blue

Squadron merch. Posters, patches, caf mugs, even bootleg bobbleheads of yours truly.

And through it all, Thea was there, sharp grin, steady aim, fearless heart. The galaxy might have seen me as the face of Blue Squadron, but I knew the truth: my most important victory had already been won, and she flew as Blue-4U.

4
KELVINAR PRIME

And now, dear reader, prepare yourself to bask in the unparalleled glow of true heroism.

It was the Battle of Kelvinar Prime, the engagement that transformed Blue Squadron from a ragtag assembly of Rebels into legends of the stars. And at the center of it all? Yours truly: Montgomery Starstalker, ace pilot extraordinaire, scourge of Imperial tyranny, and, let's be perfectly frank, the galaxy's most dashing savior in a flight helmet.

Picture it: Kelvinar Prime. A shimmering ice world, its frozen tundra bathed in auroras that curled across the sky like ribbons of the Force itself. Beneath all that beauty beat the mechanical heart of the Imperial war machine, a coaxium depot critical to their fleet in the sector. Destroy it, and the Empire's operations would grind to a halt.

A perfect opportunity, you might think.

Except for one tiny detail: six full squadrons of TIEs, two Star Destroyers, and enough laser turret emplacements to make even the boldest pilot double-check their will.

A trivial challenge for me, naturally, but enough to make more cautious types, such as Merrick, mutter about "acceptable loss projections" in tones best left to accountants.

Blue Squadron had been tasked with spearheading the attack. This was our moment to shine, and by the Force, I wasn't about to let history forget the name *Starstalker*.

We dropped out of hyperspace into immediate chaos, TIE fighters swarming like mynocks on a power conduit. Over comms, Thea's voice cut sharp and bright through the din:

"Monty, you're on my six."

"I was hoping you'd be on mine," I shot back, already twisting my X-wing into a climb.

She laughed, a sound that always hit me like a proton burst, and rolled to cover my flank. We moved in perfect sync, a seamless weave of speed and precision. If I were the showman, she was the steel spine of the act.

Merrick's orders came crisp and controlled. "Form up. Maintain strike vector. Stay in formation."

Naturally, I obeyed… with modifications.

"Let them come," I told the squad, my voice dripping with the kind of confidence that could charm a rancor. "I'll handle the first wave."

And handle them, I did. I spiraled through the black, impossible turns, spinning through green lances of blaster fire. TIEs burst apart behind me, each explosion a stroke in the mural of freedom I was painting across the void. By the time my tenth kill blossomed into debris, I heard Merrick's voice, tight, incredulous:

"That's impossible… he's flying circles around them!"

The Star Destroyer moved into firing range, its turbolasers locking on. Thea's voice came through calm and fierce. "Monty, time for it?"

"Oh, it's time," I grinned.

The Starstalker Special, dear reader. A maneuver requiring the nerves of a Jedi, the reflexes of a Corellian smuggler, and just enough theatrical flair to make your enemies question their career choices. The idea was simple: convince the largest ship on the field to focus every gun on you, then dance through the explosions while your squad moves in for the kill.

With the Destroyer's gunners fixated on my weaving silhouette, Thea led the rest of Blue Squadron in tight, clean strikes on the depot's shield generators. The shields collapsed, and my proton torpedoes followed, slamming into the coaxium reserves in a chain of fire that lit the frozen skies like a galactic Life Day display.

The Imperials broke. TIEs scattered. And in a story I will continue to insist was entirely factual, several Imperial pilots defected on the spot, citing "psychological shock" after witnessing my flight patterns.

Back aboard the Liberty, the hangar was electric. Merrick strode over, his face unreadable.

"Monty," he said at last, "you're… the best pilot I've ever seen."

I chuckled, ever humble. "You're welcome, Merrick. But don't forget, it's not just about skill. It's about heart… and looking spectacular while you save the galaxy."

Thea was there beside me, helmet under her arm, that fierce smile tugging at the corner of her mouth. "Don't let it go to your head, Starstalker," she said, which, between us, I interpreted as something deeply romantic.

And so, the legend of Blue Squadron was cemented. We were no longer just a collection of pilots. We were the ones the Empire whispered about in briefings, the ones the Rebellion toasted in cantinas from the Core to the Rim.

And I, Montgomery Starstalker, was their brightest star.

***

The hangar had finally settled. Mechanics swarmed over battered X-wings, the clang of tools echoing against the bulkheads. Somewhere in the background, Merrick was probably filing three separate incident reports on me.

I found Thea by her ship, leaning against the hull with her helmet tucked under one arm. Her hair was damp from the ice crystals that had melted in the cockpit heat, and she had that look, the one where her eyes were a little distant, like she was still flying somewhere in her head.

"Well," I said, strolling up with the casual grace of a man who had just saved an entire planet, "another glorious chapter in the ongoing saga of Starstalker and Lorne."

She smiled without looking at me. "Funny, I thought it was *Lorne and Starstalker.*"

I made a show of considering this. "Alphabetical order? Perhaps. But in the legends, my name got top billing. Purely for marketing purposes."

That earned me a laugh, low and warm, and for a moment, the hangar noise faded into the background.

"You ever think," she said, running a hand along the scorched plating of her X-wing, "that one day… we might not come back from one of these?"

"Of course," I replied instantly. "I think about it all the time. And then I remember that we're far too good-looking to die young."

She gave me a look that was equal parts exasperation and affection. "You can't joke your way out of everything, Monty."

"True," I said, stepping closer, lowering my voice. "But I'll joke my way out of most things. And I promise you this, wherever I am, whatever mess we're in, I'll have your six."

For once, she didn't have a quick comeback. She just held my gaze for a long moment, and I felt something shift, like a targeting computer locking onto its mark.

Then she grinned, that fierce, brilliant grin. "And I'll have yours. Always."

We stood there for a moment longer before the bustle of the hangar returned to full volume, and we were pilots again. But somewhere, deep down, I knew I'd just made a promise I could never afford to break.

I don't know what possessed me, maybe the adrenaline, maybe the auroras of Kelvinar Prime still dancing in my mind, but I leaned in and kissed her right there in the hangar, between the smell of coolant and the hum of cooling engines.

Now, I've heard it said that in all the star systems of the galaxy, there have been only a handful of truly perfect kisses, the kind sung about in cantinas, written into holodramas, and whispered about by smugglers on long hyperspace runs.

I am proud to report, dear reader, that ours left them all behind.

When we broke apart, she smirked and said, "Top billing, huh?"

And I, being a gentleman, replied, "For you, Thea, I'll make an exception."

We went back to our ships then, because that's what pilots do. But if the Empire had attacked that hangar at that moment, I swear to you, Blue Squadron could have taken them down without even taking flight.

5
THE STARRY VEILS

T he call came, as such calls often do for the galaxy's most indispensable operative, during a moment of both romance and heroism. I was on the *Dashing Resolve's* observation deck, arm around Thea "Blue-4U" Lorne, watching the twin moons of Praxil drift past while we shared a vintage Corellian starfruit fizz. I had just reached the part of my anecdote where I single-handedly negotiated the surrender of a pirate armada using only charm and an improvised limerick, when the comm pinged with a private encryption key I hadn't seen since the Siege of Brentaal IV.

"Who even has that code?" Thea asked, tilting her head toward the console.

"Only the most mysterious and discerning patrons of the Rebellion," I said, brushing an imaginary speck from my impeccably pressed jacket. "In short, Luthen Rael."

Moments later, the holoprojector flared, revealing Luthen in all his calm, calculating glory. He glanced at me, then at Thea, then back at me as if weighing exactly how much trouble he was about to cause.

"Starstalker. Lorne," he said with the kind of gravity one usually reserves for discussing black holes or galactic treaties. "I have an assignment. You were… recommended."

Thea arched a brow. "Recommended for what?"

"A traveling Imperial cultural exhibition is touring the Mid Rim," Luthen explained. "Among its artifacts is an item stolen from the Rebellion, an encryption module hidden inside a piece of Alderaanian sculpture. We need it back before they reach Coruscant."

I nodded with the solemnity of a man receiving the keys to the galaxy's most exclusive speeder. "Naturally, you've called me for my unparalleled skill in high-society infiltration."

"You've also been paired with Captain Cassian Andor," Luthen said, which I took to mean I would be mentoring him in the finer points of social elegance.

"Andor's expertise is infiltration," Luthen continued. "Yours is… being seen. Thea will cover you both, inside and out."

Thea smiled, that fierce, brilliant smile that could make a TIE pilot surrender mid-chase. "So I'm the one actually keeping you alive," she murmured to me.

"Darling," I said, squeezing her hand, "you make everything worth surviving."

Luthen's lips twitched, the closest thing he ever came to amusement. "Your cover identities are as follows: Count Aurelius Starstalker of Serenno… "

"Finally, someone gets my title right," I interjected.

"… and his co-investor in rare Core World art, Lady Thea Lorne," Luthen finished. "Cassian will pose as your valet, and your technical attaché will be Reginald Starjammer. You'll also have a K-series security droid… as an interactive art installation."

An offscreen voice, dry as a Jakku sandstorm, chimed in: "You couldn't afford me otherwise." K-2SO stepped into view, his photoreceptors narrowing as if sizing me up for a particularly sarcastic remark.

"This will require coordination," Luthen said. "Cassian will secure the module. You will… ensure the room is watching you."

"My dear Luthen," I said, moustache at a curl so perfect that it could've been classified as a minor miracle, "when am I not?"

Thea laughed the kind of laugh that, if bottled, could fund the Rebellion for a year. "Force help us all." Her laugh, bright, unguarded, and slightly dangerous, still echoed as Luthen's holo fizzled out.

I turned to her with my most heroic grin. "Well, darling, looks like we've been summoned to the stage once again."

She leaned against the console, arms folded, eyes glinting. "Summoned to cause a distraction so Cassian Andor can do the actual work."

"Semantics," I said. "You say distraction, I say commanding the narrative. Besides, I have the moustache for it."

From somewhere in the engine room, Reginald's voice floated up the comm tube. "If this involves me wearing a suit again, the answer's no."

"Oh, you'll look dashing," I called back. "And if you don't, you'll at least look clean, which is nearly as good."

Thea shook her head, smiling despite herself. "Where's the rendezvous?"

I brought up the nav chart Luthen had transmitted. "A lonely little freighter dock in the Wobani system. We'll meet Cassian and his… valet."

"Valet?" Thea asked, eyebrow arched.

"That's what Luthen called him. I suspect it's his towering murder-droid, dressed as modern art."

Twenty minutes later, Reginald had grunted his way through final checks on the *Dashing Resolve*. As we lifted off, I felt that familiar thrill, the kind that you feel just before a new adventure unfolds, when the galaxy feels like it's holding its breath.

By the time we dropped out of hyperspace, the dock was visible: a battered orbital platform clinging to a small asteroid, half its lights flickering, the other half presumably stolen. And there, leaning casually against a freighter's boarding ramp, was Cassian, all dark coat and narrowed eyes.

Beside him, towering and gleaming, stood K-2SO, who gave us the kind of assessing once-over usually reserved for malfunctioning equipment.

Thea descended the ramp first, every inch the poised ace pilot and covert operative, and I followed, adjusting my cape for maximum dramatic sway in the recycled dock lighting.

Cassian Andor didn't move from where he leaned against his freighter's ramp, arms crossed, expression as warm as a Hoth sunrise. K-2 stood beside him, the very picture of looming disapproval.

"Starstalker," Cassian said in a tone that suggested he'd already regretted this arrangement.

"Andor," I replied with my most winning smile. "You look… exactly as serious as your reputation suggests. And this must be your valet."

K-2SO tilted his head. "I am not his valet. I am his partner, his superior in wit, and in this moment, the one wondering if you were chosen for your skills or because they couldn't find anyone else with a working ship."

I grinned. "Oh, definitely the skills. Though the moustache helped."

Thea stepped in smoothly before the taunts could escalate to something more serious. "What's the job?"

Cassian gave her a nod of acknowledgment, a subtle recognition between professionals and then keyed a small holoprojector. The image of a grand starliner shimmered into the air. "The Impeccable Imperial Cultural Exhibition. High security, high-profile attendees, and one very particular artifact Luthen wants."

I leaned closer, studying the holo. "Stunning lines. Terrible name."

Cassian ignored me. "We can't just take it. It's in a sealed vault on the upper deck. The plan is simple: you and Thea draw attention in the main hall. Keep the officers, dignitaries, and security eyes on you."

I spread my arms. "In other words, do what I do best."

"Yes," Cassian said dryly, "except this time it has to last long enough for K-2SO and me to slip into the vault and get out without the entire ship locking down."

K-2SO leaned forward. "So your task is to be loud, flamboyant, and distracting. Which, judging by your cape, is the one mission you've been training for your entire life."

"Flattery will get you everywhere," I said.

Cassian cut through the banter. "We board in disguise. You two as wealthy patrons. I'll be crew. K-2 will handle… logistics."

"Logistics," K-2SO repeated. "I prefer the term mission salvation."

Thea's eyes met mine. "Force help us all."

Cassian deactivated the holo. "One more thing, we're not taking your ship in under her real identity."

I straightened, scandalized. "Excuse me?"

"The *Dashing Resolve* is too well known. Imperial eyes see her, they'll know exactly who's on board. She needs a new transponder and a new name before we approach."

I clutched at my chest. "A new name? That's like telling a proud Corellian racehorse it's now called 'Glue Bucket.'"

K-2SO helpfully added, "Statistically speaking, changing her name will increase our survival odds by twenty-six percent."

"That's all very well for statistics, but ships are about spirit!" I protested.

Thea laid a hand on my arm. "Monty, it's for the mission."

I sighed theatrically, then turned to Reginald. "Fine. What's the alias?"

Reginald, who'd been leaning against the hull in his usual unimpressed way, flipped a switch on the console. "Done. She's now registered as the… *Modest Comet.*"

"Modest Comet?" I repeated, appalled. "That's not even accurate. There's nothing modest about her, or me."

"That's the point," Cassian said, already walking toward his ship. "Modesty keeps you alive."

I muttered under my breath as we made our way back aboard. "If this works, I'm repainting the hull in gold and telling everyone she's called the Magnificent Meteor."

By the time the *Dashing Resolve* had been stripped of her gleaming nameplates, repainted in a dreary "Imperial Acceptable Beige," and re-registered as the *Modest Comet*, I felt as though I'd attended my own funeral.

"She's a beauty," Reginald said, giving the hull a perfunctory slap.

"She's unrecognizable," I corrected, staring mournfully at the matte finish. "It's like putting a smock on a holopainting. No one will know it's me."

"That's the point," Cassian said flatly. "If they see you coming, we've already lost."

I muttered something about artistic crimes and followed the others into the cargo hold, which was now cleared for what Cassian called "operational rehearsal" and what I immediately recognized as a dress rehearsal. Luthen had sent one of his associates to act as a "suspicious Imperial dignitary," which in practice meant a woman with a stare sharp enough to strip paint faster than a sandstorm.

Cassian paced like a drill sergeant who'd misplaced his sense of humor. "You'll be in that exhibition hall for hours. No one there can suspect you're with the Rebellion."

"Of course not," I said, taking my seat. "I'll be too busy dazzling them with conversation and charm."

"That's the problem," K-2SO added in. "Your conversation could compromise the entire operation."

Thea slipped into her role instantly, gliding across the hold in her mock gown with the perfect balance of polite disinterest and subtle curiosity. Reginald loitered by the refreshments table, real food this time, muttering about wasted man-hours.

When my turn came, I strode forward with the kind of confidence that has launched fleets and doomed empires. "Good evening, Baroness," I said to the dignitary, "Montgomery Starfall… "

Cassian groaned. "Alias. Alias."

"Right, yes, of course," I said smoothly. "Count Aurelius Montague Starfall."

Cassian closed his eyes. "Just Count Aurelius. No middle names. No 'Starfall.'"

"I think you'll find a noble title needs a middle flourish," I replied. "Otherwise, it sounds cheap. Like a discount baron."

K-2SO's optical sensors dimmed slightly. "The only discount here is in your operational reliability."

The dignitary cleared her throat. "And what is your interest in the exhibition, Count Aurelius Montague Star…"

"Aurelius," Cassian snapped midway.

"Yes, yes, Count Aurelius," I amended. "My interest lies purely in the preservation of galactic heritage, the advancement of culture, and the careful selection of hors d'oeuvres… "

"No food," Cassian yelled before I could complete my sentence.

"Fine. And the preservation of moustaches as a galactic art form."

Thea smirked, clearly enjoying herself. Cassian buried his face in his hands. "We are doomed."

The next hour was a blur of mock inspections, faux introductions, and "how not to get arrested" drills. I flubbed the Imperial salute ("Oh, I thought you meant wave"), invented an elaborate family tree for Count Aurelius that involved a scandal with a Bothan opera singer, and was informed by K-2SO that I had a 37% chance of surviving if I spoke more than seven sentences in front of an actual Imperial officer.

By the time Cassian dismissed us, Thea was flawless, Reginald was muttering about the indignity of being labeled my valet, and I had mastered one crucial skill: how to make "Count Aurelius Montague Starfall" sound entirely natural, no matter how much Cassian shouted at me for it. But first, we had to make a side trip to Takodana.

Takodana's markets were not for the faint of heart, nor for anyone with a delicate sense of smell. Stalls crammed under tarpaulin awnings bulged with relics, gemstones, weapons, and the occasional "mystical talisman" that was almost certainly a repainted engine part. The air hummed with haggling, laughter, and the faint sizzle of something edible but unidentifiable.

"This is where we find it," Cassian said, steering me through the crowd. "Something expensive, something with perfect paperwork, and something we can use to smuggle what Luthen needs."

"I am excellent at finding expensive things," I assured him. "And paperwork? My dear Cassian, if the galaxy has an art form more refined than forged certificates of authenticity, I have yet to discover it."

Thea slipped her arm through mine, her voice warm in my ear. "Just remember, Monty, we're not here to buy the shiniest thing."

I frowned. "Why would we not buy the shiniest thing?"

"Because shiny things attract attention," Cassian snapped.

"Exactly!" I said brightly.

Reginald trudged behind us, scanning the stalls with a mechanic's eye. "They've got a Mark V hyperdrive coupler over there. I could use that."

"You're not here to shop for the Resolve," Cassian warned.

"The Modest Comet," K-2SO corrected, his voice dripping with synthetic disdain.

"She deserves dignity, even in disguise," I said, patting the ship's new registry papers tucked into my satchel.

We stopped before a stall draped in rich fabrics, its shelves laden with glittering artifacts. The dealer, a Zygerrian with teeth that could double as vibroblades, grinned as her gaze fell on me.

"Count Aurelius," she purred, bowing low.

I arched an eyebrow in curiosity. "You've… heard of me?"

"Of course. Word of your discerning tastes precedes you."

Cassian muttered under his breath, "Luthen's plants are worth every credit."

"Plants?" I asked.

"Nothing," he said quickly, diverting me toward the merchandise before I could ask more.

Thea's lips curved in a secretive smile. She knew something I didn't.

I, naturally, took it as further proof that my reputation had simply traveled faster than I had. "Well then, you'll know I'm a connoisseur of only the finest… "

Cassian interrupted me midway, "We're here for something Alderaanian, discreet, and well-documented."

The Zygerrian produced a crystal decanter, its facets catching the sun. "Last of its kind," she whispered. "From the royal table itself. Comes with provenance documents."

K-2SO scanned it. "It's hollow. Interior dimensions match the specifications Cassian gave us."

"Perfect," Cassian murmured.

I leaned in. "Naturally, it's worth more than you're asking. I'll give you twice the price."

Cassian's head whipped toward me. "What?"

"It's called building trust," I explained.

"It's called blowing our budget," he hissed.

Thea's hand slid over mine. "Monty, dear, let's negotiate like rebels, not like royalty."

In the end, we walked away with the decanter, its hidden compartment ready for Luthen's purposes and its provenance impeccable enough to fool an entire panel of Imperial curators. Reginald muttered about the hyperdrive coupler all the way back to the landing pad.

As we boarded the *Modest Comet*, Thea caught my eye, smiling that smile that made entire battlefields worth surviving. "You know," she said, "when you're not trying to bankrupt us, you make a pretty good spy."

I preened. "Darling, I make everything look good."

Cassian groaned. "Force help us at the exhibition." I was still basking in the afterglow of my flawless performance on Takodana. "Did you see the way she lit up when she recognized Count Aurelius?" I said, leaning back in the pilot's chair as if I'd just won a race through the Core Worlds.

Cassian didn't even look up from his datapad. "Luthen prepped her for that."

"Exactly," I said. "And yet, I elevated it."

Thea, seated across from me, smirked. "We'll see how elevated you feel in Hall Three."

"Hall Three?" I asked, already imagining a wing of the station dedicated to my glory.

Cassian finally looked at me. "That Alderaanian decanter you just bought? It's already logged in the exhibition's registry. Turns out, it was supposed to be on loan from a private collection. That means it's being publicly delivered, with us."

K-2SO chimed in from the corner, his voice as dry as Jakku sand. "Congratulations. You're a glorified courier with a moustache."

Cassian continued, ignoring the droid. "We hide Luthen's cargo inside the decanter before it's handed over to the curators. It goes straight into the display under security. Nobody searches it, because it's already been cleared."

I nodded approvingly. "So our mission is… to attend a glamorous social function under the guise of art enthusiasts, subtly protect a priceless artifact, and then quietly make off with the actual prize?"

"That's right," Thea said.

"Finally," I said, standing to adjust my cape, "a mission worthy of my skills."

Reginald grunted from the rear of the cabin without looking up from a panel he was repairing.

"What was that?" I asked.

"He said," K-2SO translated, "that you're going to trip over your own cover story before the appetizers are served."

The exhibition hall rose like a palace from the void, gleaming domes linked by golden-lit corridors. We docked under the watchful gaze of security droids and attendants, the decanter now nestled in a velvet-lined case that looked like it could double as a throne for a small monarch.

Cassian's plan was simple: blend in, stay quiet, watch for trouble.

Naturally, I ignored this.

The moment we stepped through the main entrance, I announced in a voice that could have reached the docking bay, "Count Aurelius, patron of the arts, liberator of oppressed artifacts, and collector of exquisite conversation!"

Cassian groaned. Thea hid a smile. K-2SO muttered something about "statistical proof that volume correlates with failure."

The hall was a cathedral of excess, towering crystal chandeliers, walls draped in Naboo silks, and floating holo-sculptures that shimmered as you passed, adjusting their forms to flatter your angles. A Bith string quartet played from a levitating stage, bowing out the sort of music that makes even the most suspicious guests feel cultured.

I, of course, already was.

Cassian strode ahead, eyes locked on his target, which was the display pedestal in Hall Three where our prize awaited: a crystal Alderaanian decanter, flawless to the casual eye, but known to us as a smuggler's masterpiece with a hidden compartment concealing vital intelligence.

Our job was simple in theory: I distract the room while Cassian and K-2SO liberate the intelligence from the and slip it into the hidden compartment in our decanter, leaving the original gleaming innocently in place. If done right, no one would suspect a thing.

Thea glided up beside me, her gloved hand brushing mine, the kind of touch that says I'm with you and don't you dare mess this up all at once. K-2SO trailed behind, towering above the crowd and looking about as inconspicuous as a bantha at a dinner party.

"You are drawing unnecessary attention," K-2SO announced in a voice that carried over the music. Several dignitaries turned to stare.

"That's called presence, my good droid," I replied smoothly, pausing to nod at a passing senator who may or may not have been nodding at me.

Cassian's voice hissed in my earpiece. "Monty, eyes forward. We're two minutes from the target."

"I am perfectly capable of blending subtlety with unforgettable charm," I whispered back.

"Unforgettable is the opposite of what we want," Cassian muttered.

We crossed the threshold into Hall Three, and I stopped dead.

Suspended above the room, cascading in layered arcs, was the hall's centrepiece: immense, translucent star maps, each sheer enough to see the constellations beyond it. Beams of light shifted through them, making you feel as if you were drifting through the galaxy itself.

The plaque at its base read: **Through the Starry Veils, An Alderaanian Masterwork.**

I nearly dropped my champagne. "Would you look at that? Art that captures the very essence of heroism."

Cassian didn't slow down. "It's fabric and light, Monty. Keep moving."

"Fabric and light?" I gasped. "Cassian, my dear fellow, that is a metaphor made manifest! Through the starry veils we venture, unseen yet radiant, risking all for beauty, for truth, for… "

"For the love of the Force, walk," Cassian growled. "You've got one job tonight: keep eyes on you, not on us."

Thea lingered beside me, her eyes reflecting the shimmering constellations. "It is beautiful," she said quietly.

"Not as beautiful as you," I murmured, and for a heartbeat the mission faded away, replaced by the warmth in her smile.

Cassian's voice cut in again. "Focus. The real decanter's under the primary light rig, two guards, one curator, three cameras. We'll handle it. You and Thea take the floor and make sure nobody's looking our way when we move."

I tore my eyes from the starry veils. "Very well," I sighed, straightening my cape. "Let us dazzle them until they forget why they even came."

K-2SO muttered something about statistical improbabilities as Cassian steered him toward the display. Thea looped her arm through mine, and together we stepped into the crowd, ready to make the most dangerous part of the plan look like the grandest party trick in the galaxy.

Thea and I mingled into the crowd like a comet into an asteroid belt, the kind of entrance that forces people to rearrange themselves in orbit. I offered nods to dignitaries, warm smiles to trade barons, and the occasional raised eyebrow to anyone who looked like they might be considering an Imperial donation.

Within moments, I had a half-circle of admirers, all leaning in as I launched into a dramatic retelling of the time I evaded three pirate skiffs by flying through the skeletal remains of a space leviathan. Was it technically true? Absolutely, give or take the Leviathan, the number of pirates, and the fact that it was actually an abandoned mining rig.

While the laughter and gasps grew, I spotted Reginald Starjammer on the far side of the hall, operating our "logistics station," a high-top table with a discreet commlink to the *Modest Comet*, as the *Dashing Resolve* was currently known for this mission.

Reggie, never one to seek the spotlight, was half-listening to the chatter around him while absently popping small, glossy orbs into his mouth from a crystal bowl on the table. They looked like candied nerfberries, rich, dark, and faintly glistening.

"Good, aren't they?" a passing guest said in a voice that suggested more amusement than politeness.

Reggie gave his trademark grunt of agreement and popped another in. "Bit moist," he mumbled under his breath, wiping his fingers on a napkin before reaching for a third.

Back in my corner, I could feel Thea squeezing my arm just enough to remind me we had a job to do. I gestured grandly toward the balcony, drawing my audience's attention upward to the glowing holofresco overhead. "Ladies, gentlemen, and assorted sentients, a reminder that the galaxy is not simply survived… it is lived!"

As the crowd's attention swung toward my theatrics, Cassian's voice murmured in my earpiece: "We're in position. Keep it going." His voice crackled again: "Almost at the target. Two guards, light patrol… K-2, wait…"

K-2SO's clipped tones came through crystal clear. "I am perfectly capable of eliminating a light patrol. I just prefer to do it with panache."

I smiled faintly, swirling my drink to seem completely composed while also buying them precious seconds. "And panache, my dear guests, is the only thing that separates the daring from the merely adequate!" I declared to my audience, punctuating it with a sweeping gesture that made a senator from Corellia spill her drink.

Across the hall, I observed Reggie popping another of the glossy seeds into his mouth and reaching for another.

A server approached, leaning down to murmur something to him. He froze mid-chew.

"Those aren't for guests, sir," the server explained. "They're festival seeds. The Eldrans enjoy sucking the sweet coating off before discarding them. Their saliva contains a natural preservative, quite safe for them, of course, but for most other species it has… digestive consequences.”

Reggie's chewing steadied. His eyes flicked to the half-empty bowl, then to the three or four he'd already eaten. His face went from its usual granite stillness to something approaching existential dread. Silently, he placed the half-eaten seed back onto the napkin, pulled a flask from his jacket, and began gargling brandy like a man who'd just accidentally swallowed a live mynock.

Thea caught sight of him over the rim of her glass and had to conceal her laugh with a cough. I, of course, remained the very picture of composure, though I made a mental note to check our refresher's plumbing before leaving the Modest Comet.

“Monty,” Cassian hissed in my ear, “We've got it. We're moving to extraction. Keep the floor distracted another thirty seconds.”

“Thirty seconds?” I repeated brightly for the benefit of my enthralled guests. “Then I shall tell you exactly how I escaped the Tibran Vortex in nothing but an escape pod and a firm belief in my own magnificence… ”

Somewhere in the distance, a small commotion began as Cassian and K-2SO slipped away. In the foreground, Reggie was still glaring at the crystal bowl like it had committed a personal insult, brandy in hand.

By the time I excused myself from my audience, the real prize was already safely off the floor and on its way to the *Modest Comet*. The mission was a success, though I suspect Reggie might remember the seeds far more vividly than the decanter.

I excused myself from my latest audience, a group of Core World dignitaries who were still chuckling over my anecdote about the time I “accidentally” landed in a royal reflecting pool, and made my way gracefully toward the meeting point. Across the hall, Cassian and K-2 had melted into the crowd with the decanter housing important intelligence, their path toward the service exit perfectly timed to my distraction.

Reggie, however, had abandoned his post at the edge of the room and was standing near the bar, brandy glass in hand. He took a gulp, grimaced, and took another. The barman gave him a wary look.

"What are you doing?" I asked as I swept past.

"Sterilizing," he muttered darkly. "Brandy kills everything."

I raised an eyebrow but decided not to pry. Reggie's idea of 'everything' often included me.

Thea appeared at my side then, her arm linking with mine as naturally as if we'd just been admiring the art. "Cassian and K-2 are clear," she murmured, her eyes scanning the crowd. "We just have to walk out, nice and easy."

"Nice and easy," I repeated, smiling as though we were about to step onto a sunlit promenade and not into the teeth of Imperial security.

We'd almost reached the archway leading to the main corridor when the air seemed to tighten. A voice, crisp and too precise, cut across the polished chatter:

"You. Stop right there."

The voice was sharp, trained, the kind that had ruined a great many evenings across the galaxy. I turned, keeping my most composed Count Aurelius smile in place, and found an Imperial Security Bureau agent blocking our path. Square jaw, slicked hair, posture like a parade drill, he practically radiated pretension.

"I know you," he said, narrowing his eyes at me. "That face. You're not Count Aurelius. I've seen you… somewhere." He tilted his head, as though sifting through a file in his mind. "Rebel watch list, perhaps?"

Before I could charm my way out of it, Thea stepped forward, shoulders squared, voice sharp enough to cut transparisteel.

"That's quite an accusation, Agent… " she trailed off, as though waiting for him to supply his name.

"Varrik," he said, puffing himself up. "ISB, Outer Rim branch. And you are?" His tone said nobody can outrank me.

Thea's lip curved in a cold half-smile. "ISB, Internal Affairs Division. Clearance Aurek-One-Seven-Dorn. Field Supervisor."

Varrik snorted… actually snorted. "Internal Affairs? This is a field op, not a desk audit. I'll decide… "

She didn't let him finish. In one smooth motion, she produced a small black datacard case from inside her cloak, flicked it open, and let him glimpse the gleaming ISB seal alongside a rank code so high it made my knees feel wobbly, and I knew it was fake.

Varrik's eyes widened just enough to betray him. "That clearance… that's… "

"Need-to-know," she cut in, voice dropping to a low, lethal murmur. "And you don't need to know. What you do need is to walk away before I have your assignment downgraded to cataloguing defective stormtrooper armor in a climate-controlled warehouse on Raxus Prime."

The agent's mouth opened, closed, then stayed shut.

"Understood?"

"Yes… ma'am."

"Good." She gave him a smile that seemed less of a smile and more of a victorious smirk. "Enjoy the rest of your evening."

He stepped aside, still watching us as we passed.

I leaned closer to her as we slipped into the next hall. "Darling… since when do you carry ISB credentials?"

"Since about ten seconds ago," she murmured without breaking stride. "Now walk faster before Varrik remembers he hates me."

We cleared the archway into Hall Three just in time to see Cassian and K-2SO emerge from a service corridor, both moving with that particular mix of casualness and absolute urgency that only professionals can pull off. Cassian had the decanter cradled in the crook of his arm, wrapped in a cloth like an expensive bottle of wine nobody was supposed to notice.

K-2SO, on the other hand, noticed everything. "There you are," the droid said flatly. "We were beginning to think you'd been detained."

"We were," I said, brushing a bit of lint from my cape. "But Thea here dissolved the problem with the kind of precision usually reserved for surgical strikes."

Thea didn't look at me, but I saw the faintest twitch at the corner of her lips. "Keep moving."

Cassian gave her a quick nod of respect, which, if you know Cassian, is like a standing ovation. "Exit's this way. I've got two more patrols moving through the east gallery in five minutes."

We started weaving through the exhibition crowd, keeping our pace brisk but never suspiciously so. My role in the plan was clear: be the distraction if anyone got too close. A skill, I might add, I was born to perfect.

"Don't make eye contact," Cassian murmured as we passed a group of uniformed officers.

"Too late," I said. "I believe I just sold them on my latest line of moustache wax."

K-2SO's head swiveled toward me. "I am ninety-two percent certain you are not joking, which is exactly why this mission will fail if you open your mouth again."

Before I could respond with a suitably devastating retort, we hit the main concourse, a grand space framed by towering transparisteel windows showing the twinkling cityscape beyond. Somewhere out there, the *Modest Comet* was docked under a false registry, waiting to spirit us away.

We were halfway to the lift when I caught sight of Varrik again at the far end of the hall, scanning the crowd with a predator's focus. His gaze swept over the mass of guests and then stopped on us.

"Thea," I murmured.

"I see him."

"Plan?" Cassian asked, tightening his grip on the decanter.

"Get to the ship," Thea said without missing a beat. "We'll handle this." Cassian and K2 disappeared in an instant. Thea and I kept weaving through the crowd.

We were almost to the grand atrium when I spotted him again, Varrik, weaving through the crowd like a man on a mission. My stomach tightened.

"He's gaining on us," I muttered under my breath. "I knew it. He's put two and two together and realized I'm not Count Aurelius, I'm Montgomery Starstalker, and we're kriffed."

"Just keep walking," Thea murmured, eyes forward.

Varrik reached us, a little out of breath, and stopped dead in our path. For a moment, he just stood there, gaze flicking between us like he was trying to decide which of us to shoot first. Then, to my utter shock, his expression softened.

"Director," he said to Thea, inclining his head, "Count. I owe you both an apology. My earlier… tone was inappropriate. I allowed personal suspicion to cloud my judgment."

Thea handled it flawlessly, giving him the kind of neutral smile you'd use for a dignitary you barely tolerate. "Apology noted."

"I insist," he continued, "on escorting you to your vessel. As a courtesy."

A courtesy. Right! My mind spun. Was this a trap? A stall tactic? A way to get our ship's registry on record?

"That's unnecessary," Thea said evenly. "We have our own arrangements."

"Please," he pressed, his voice almost too sincere, "It's the least I can do."

I spotted Cassian and K-2SO in the distance, already heading toward the side exit with the decanter. If this ISB sycophant decided to tag along all the way to the hangar, our cover would unravel before the *Modest Comet* even powered up.

Before I could voice my panic, Thea gave him the kind of look that could slice durasteel. "Agent Varrik, you've already done enough tonight. I'd hate for the after-action report to note that you abandoned your post to play chauffeur. Good evening."

It was masterful, polite enough to avoid offense, pointed enough to end the conversation. He faltered, then stepped aside with another stiff bow.

We walked past, my pulse still pounding. "For the record," I murmured to her, "I thought he was coming back with stormtroopers and possibly a small tank."

She didn't look at me. "For the record, so did I."

We cleared the crowd and slipped into one of the quieter service corridors leading to the hangar. The tension was finally starting to bleed off when I spotted Reggie leaning against a wall, brandy glass in hand.

He didn't look relieved after seeing us. He looked… pale.

"Reggie, what are you doing?" I hissed.

"Trying," he said with a grimace, "to get the taste out of my mouth."

That's when I noticed the half-empty glass of amber brandy on a crate beside him.

"Please tell me," I said slowly, "was there something wrong with those berries you were eating?"

"I assumed they were complimentary snacks. Bit damp, though. Thought it was the humidity." He stared at the brandy, then at me, then took the biggest gulp I've ever seen a man take without drowning.

Thea smirked as Reggie joined us. "At least you didn't have to distract a suspicious ISB officer."

"True," Reggie said, already scanning for the nearest bar. "But I'd take him over those berries any day."

Cassian and K-2SO joined us from a different corridor, Cassian carrying the decanter wrapped in an innocuous display cloth. K-2SO was muttering something about "inefficient security layouts" and "human error being vastly underestimated." We merged into the trickle of departing guests, heading toward the hangar where the *Modest Comet* awaited.

That's when the alarms began.

It started with a low, pulsing chime, the sort meant to get everyone's attention without causing panic. Then the heavy, mechanical clang of blast doors sliding shut echoed through the exhibition hall. Red security lights strobed along the ceiling, and a voice crackled over the comm:

"Attention guests: Please remain where you are. Security inspection in progress."

Cassian shot Thea a look that needed no translation. "They've flagged the decanter."

Montgomery Starstalker, ace pilot (and master of style), was not about to be cornered like a trapped womp rat. "Fear not," I declared, "I have an escape plan."

"No, you don't," Cassian said nonchalantly.

"Not yet," I conceded, "but I'm working on it."

That's when Thea stepped forward, all calm elegance, scanning the tightening ring of uniformed guards. "Follow my lead," she murmured.

Before anyone could question her, she strode toward the security checkpoint with the imperious confidence of someone used to giving orders, the crowd parting instinctively. She flagged down the ranking officer and, in a voice just loud enough for nearby guards to hear, said:

"This group is under my protection. I have urgent clearance to transfer them to secure holding off-site."

The officer's brows knit. "Ma'am, we have to detain… "

"Do you want responsibility for delaying the Chancellor's cultural envoy?" Thea snapped, producing a small, triangular dataplaque from her satchel. It was one of Luthen's special forgeries, so perfect it might as well have been real.

The officer paled slightly, the dataplaque's seal flickering under the emergency lights. "Of course, your eminence. My apologies."

"Good. Then open the hangar doors, and I'll forget you hesitated."

The guards stepped aside like she'd just cleared them with a lightsaber. We moved quickly, trying not to look like the most suspiciously smug group in the galaxy.

As soon as the hangar was in sight, Cassian muttered, "Remind me never to play sabacc with her."

"I already have," I replied, "it didn't end well."

We crossed the threshold into the hangar just as the doors sealed behind us. The *Modest Comet* waited, gleaming and innocent, our ticket out of trouble.

Cassian and K-2SO headed straight up the boarding ramp, Cassian disappearing inside with the decanter while K-2SO muttered something about "carbon-based overconfidence" and "the inevitability of failure." Reggie stomped up next, still cradling his brandy glass like it was the only thing keeping him alive.

I, of course, paused at the base of the ramp, turning back to the hangar like a holodrama hero surveying the battlefield one last time. "You know," I said to Thea, "when they tell this story, they'll talk about your composure… but they'll linger on my poise."

"They'll linger on how you almost blew the cover," she replied, brushing past me.

Inside the cockpit, I slid into the pilot's seat with the gravitas of a man about to perform a masterpiece. Reggie took his engineering station, still muttering, "Just… get us out."

"Fear not," I announced, flicking a row of switches with a flourish. "The Modest Comet was born for moments like this."

"It was born as the *Dashing Resolve*," Reggie corrected.

"Yes, but tonight she's an unassuming transport with no known ties to the most devastatingly handsome pilot in the galaxy."

The comm crackled. "Security lockdown still in effect. All departing craft must submit to inspection."

"Oh, they wish," I said, throwing the repulsorlifts to full and banking hard before the ground crew could even look our way. Thea braced herself against the bulkhead as the hangar's containment field flared past us, the sudden shift in gravity pressing us into our seats.

Two TIEs peeled off from their patrol vector, swinging to intercept. Cassian's voice came over the intercom from the rear: "Subtle. I thought you were going to keep this quiet."

"This is quiet," I insisted, diving into a corkscrew roll that spun us neatly between the two TIEs. "The galaxy's watching, Cassian, subtlety must still look good on the holos."

A burst of green cannon fire stitched the space where we'd been a second earlier. Thea's hand found my shoulder, steady, unflinching. "Three more on our six."

"Let them chase," I said, punching the throttles. "They'll never catch the Comet."

Reggie grunted behind me, "Monty… the hyperdrive's still in warm-up. We need thirty seconds."

"Thirty seconds? That's practically an eternity!" I said, diving toward the shadow of a nearby freighter. We skimmed so close, the nav alarms howled in protest.

"Ten seconds!" Reggie called.

The TIEs closed in, laser fire sparking off the freighter's hull just meters from our port side.

"Punch it!" I yelled.

The stars elongated into streaks, and with one last flick of my moustache, the *Modest Comet* leapt into hyperspace, leaving nothing behind but bewildered Imperial pilots and, I like to think, a deep sense of aesthetic envy.

The *Modest Comet* purred along in hyperspace, the blue-and-white tunnel of light wrapping the viewport like a silk scarf caught in the wind. I leaned back in the pilot's seat, stretching with the languid satisfaction of a man who had just saved the day in style.

Cassian, standing just behind me, did not share my sentiment. *"You call that quiet?"* he said flatly, which sounded like a taunt rather than a statement.

"My dear Cassian," I replied, swiveling around with the grace of a lounge singer at final bow, "if it were any quieter, the galaxy would have fallen asleep and missed the performance entirely."

K-2SO's photoreceptors flickered in disdain. "Performance. Yes. That's certainly one word for it. I personally prefer 'avoidable chaos' or 'premature celebrity suicide.'"

From the galley, Reggie groaned loudly. "Can we just acknowledge that I've been poisoned?"

Thea, who had perched herself on the edge of the copilot's seat, arched a brow. "You're not poisoned, Reggie. You just ate something that wasn't meant for... well... anyone."

"I told you," he muttered, rubbing his stomach. "I thought they were complementary."

Cassian frowned. "What did he eat?"

I cleared my throat diplomatically. "Let's simply say they were... pre-enjoyed berries."

K-2SO cocked his head. "Pre-enjoyed?"

"They'd had the... outer peel removed by a previous diner," I said.

Thea winced. "By 'pre-enjoyed,' he means another species' saliva."

Reggie buried his face in his hands. "I'm never going to be clean again."

Cassian shook his head, probably wondering why this was the crew Luthen had arranged for him. "The important thing is, we secured the intelligence." He nodded toward the small, heavily wrapped crate secured to the bulkhead.

"Indeed, we did," I said, rising from the pilot's chair and sweeping over to it like a stage magician about to reveal his final trick. "Ladies and gentlemen, this is a victory for the Rebellion, and yet another page in the legend of Montgomery Starstalker."

K-2SO's head swiveled toward Thea. "I'm beginning to understand why you keep him around. He's completely impervious to shame."

Thea smiled faintly, her gaze lingering on me. "No. He just believes the galaxy's a better place when he's in it."

Cassian gave a long, quiet exhale and, for the briefest moment, didn't argue.

Later, when the *Modest Comet* had safely tucked into the slipstream of hyperspace, I found Thea by the forward viewport. She was leaning on the rail, her eyes fixed on the swirling blue of the jump, the same way she'd looked at that art piece back in Hall Three.

"Still thinking about it?" I asked, stepping up beside her.

Her lips curved. "The Starry Veils? Yes. There was something about it… like you could lose yourself in it and still feel completely safe."

I glanced at her profile, the glow of the hyperspace tunnel painting her in shades of that same exhibit light. "I suppose that's why it's famous. People see what they want to see in it. Some see freedom, some see home… when I look through the starry veils… " I let my gaze linger on her. "I see you."

That earned me a sideways glance, the kind that says you're impossible but also don't stop talking.

She shook her head with a small laugh. "You and your lines, Monty."

"They're not lines," I said, feigning injury. "They're statements of record, filed in the official archives of brilliance."

We stayed like that, watching the endless blue, until the hum of the engines seemed to fade into the stillness between us. Thea's hand brushed mine on the railing, whether by accident or design, I didn't ask.

And in that quiet, I realized something I'd never say aloud: I didn't need the Starry Veils hanging on my wall. I already had her standing beside me.

6
THE MOUSTACHE

L et us pause, dear reader, to appreciate one of the galaxy's greatest assets: the moustache.

Or rather, my moustache.

A resplendent marvel, its curls sweep like the S-foils of a starfighter in perfect attack position, defying both gravity and common sense. Many pilots boast of blaster accuracy, death-defying maneuvers, or, Force forbid, luck. I, Montgomery Starstalker: ace pilot, diplomat, and intergalactic legend, know the truth. Victory begins at the upper lip.

The Moustache in Combat

There's psychology in it. When you're dogfighting in the black, TIEs screaming toward you, what do you think your opponent sees as you flash past their viewport? They see power. They see authority. They see the magnificent twirl of my moustache, projected flawlessly in their targeting HUD, reminding them of their own insignificance in the vastness of the galaxy.

A properly maintained moustache conveys unshakable confidence, and confidence makes an enemy hesitate. That hesitation is all I need to line up my shot and turn their cockpit into fireworks over some unfortunate moon.

I once had a TIE "Ace", Dastar-Lee on my tail. His targeting lock was solid until he caught sight of my moustache's perfect curve in his scope.

He missed. Repeatedly. Moments later, he became a cautionary tale in the Imperial flight academy.

And there's practicality, too. In the atmosphere, the moustache serves as an impromptu wind gauge, every curl twitch telling me about crosswinds and thermal shifts before my sensors can. A whiskered co-pilot, always in tune.

The Moustache in Diplomacy

Combat is only half the story. Imagine a tense negotiation with a warlord from the Zeron Cluster, jagged teeth bared, delegates whispering doom behind their star charts. Then I enter, moustache gleaming like a beacon of trustworthiness and masculine allure.

The trick is knowing how to use it

- Stroke it slowly when weighing a proposal.

- Twirl it lightly to suggest cunning.

- At the moment of decisive declaration, adjust the curl with both hands, so your words thunder like an X-wing squadron on the attack.

I once turned a moustache-skeptical Grand ambassador into a staunch facial-hair convert by the end of a single session. Secured a fleet of cruisers for the Rebellion and a recruit for my growing "Moustache of Integrity" movement.

The Commercial Empire

Naturally, I couldn't keep the secret to myself. Thus was born Montgomery's Magnificent Moustache Wax™, crafted with a hint of rebellion, a dash of flamboyance, and the scent of cinema flowers.

Developed in the cockpit of my T-65 while dodging an Imperial blockade, no less. The marketing wrote itself:

Defy tyranny. Defy gravity. Defy mediocrity.

It became an instant sensation. Pilots across the fleet tried to emulate my look. A few even claimed measurable tactical improvements, though most simply enjoyed looking as heroic as possible while ordering caf. Rumor has it a Rebel strategist once used my "Black Ops Edition" for deep-cover shine in covert missions.

A Moment with Thea

It's not just the pilots who noticed. During the planning of a pivotal mission, I caught Thea, Blue-4U herself, stealing a glance. She denied it, but I know admiration when I see it. For just a heartbeat, her hand hovered, as if she might reach out and touch greatness. I'll leave that for historians to decide, but between us, dear reader, I rather wish she had.

The Legacy

The moustache has stood through hyperspace jumps, fighter explosions, and the unblinking gaze of Imperial propaganda. It has seen the galaxy at its worst and its best. Like me, it remains defiant, unbowed, and magnificent.

So the next time you see someone wearing a moustache and feel a twinge of inspiration, or envy, remember: they're not just wearing facial hair. They're wearing the spirit of rebellion. Starstalker style.

And if they're not using Montgomery's Magnificent Moustache Wax™? Well, friend… they're missing out on the galaxy's most essential grooming tool.

Empires may rise and fall. Stars may burn and fade. Democracies may wax and wane.

But a grand moustache?

A grand moustache is eternal.

You're welcome.

7
THE ART OF DIPLOMACY

No one denies the importance of strategy, cunning, and courage in the fight for galactic freedom. But let me tell you, dear reader, the true battlefield of the Rebellion wasn't always fought in starships or on war-torn planets. No, some of the fiercest campaigns unfolded under glittering chandeliers, between rounds of Devaronian fizz, and in whispered negotiations over a plate of Alderaanian canapés.

Victory is born not only in star charts but in social circles. There is no party too grand, no negotiation too tense, that Montgomery Starstalker cannot turn into a masterpiece of diplomacy and revelry. Whether it's a clandestine soirée on Corellia or a lavish gala on Naboo, my mere arrival doesn't just light up the room; it galvanizes the galaxy.

Hosting, you see, is a delicate dance, a balancing act of charisma, charm, and the unshakable ability to make every guest feel like the most important being in the galaxy… second only, of course, to me. A true host can bring together ambassadors and admirals, smugglers and spies, rebels and royalty, weaving alliances with the ease of a maestro conducting a symphony in hyperspace.

But it's not just my diplomacy that makes me unforgettable. It's my entrance. When I walk into a gathering, heads turn, conversations pause, and the air itself takes on an electric charge. My arrival is a performance of confidence and intrigue.

Take the time I made my grand debut at a diplomatic gala on Alderaan. Most arrived in dignified shuttles. I came in on a swoop bike, through the garden terrace, dismounting with a perfect half-spin and a bow. The host called it unconventional. I called it magnificent. And so did everyone else once the applause started.

It's not uncommon, at these affairs, to see seasoned admirals fumbling their words or to overhear guests whispering in awe, unsure whether they're more stunned by my presence or by a moustache so flawlessly groomed it could hold its own in a parade review.

A Mon Calamari diplomat once confessed that my attire, a silver-threaded cape, crimson boots, and a sash boldly embroidered with Victory Is Inevitable, was so dazzling she completely forgot her opening arguments.

But perhaps my most surprising admirer, though he would never admit it, of course, was none other than the Empire's most brilliant tactician: Grand Admiral Thrawn. Yes, that Thrawn. The cold, calculating mastermind whose piercing red eyes can make even the most seasoned hero think twice.

Now, somebody might say that Grand Admiral Thrawn's genius was born of his culture, his rigorous study of art, and his unmatched strategic brilliance. But I must share the truth. He learned from me.

The story begins at a diplomatic gathering on Coruscant, an event so lavish that Imperial officers and Rebel sympathizers mingled under the polite fiction of neutrality. Naturally, I was the guest of honor… though my invitation was discreet. The Empire could hardly advertise the presence of the galaxy's most dashing and decorated Rebel hero.

I attended incognito, wearing a brilliant white suit, a cape embroidered with subtle gold stars, and my moustache temporarily sporting a gold rinse dusted with glitter so understated no one could possibly identify me.

Enter Thrawn, towering, enigmatic, and immediately drawn to me as if by gravitational pull. He found me holding court near the banquet table, regaling a semicircle of senators with the tale of how I once escaped an Imperial blockade using nothing but charm, cunning, an emergency tin of Montgomery's Magnificent Moustache Wax, two small combs, and three strands of Wookiee hair.

"I find your ability to influence others… intriguing," Thrawn remarked, his voice as cool as a vacuum. "Diplomacy and manipulation are not so different from warfare, after all."

"Admiral," I replied, flashing my most disarming smile, "the battlefield of diplomacy requires a softer touch. Strategy isn't just brute force; it's finesse, style, and knowing how to leave a lasting impression."

I proved my point with a single toast. One glass raised, one perfectly chosen phrase, and two ambassadors who'd been squabbling for months were suddenly laughing like old friends, convinced the fate of the galaxy depended on their cooperation. Moments later, I orchestrated a "chance" encounter between an Imperial governor and a Rebel operative, planting the first seeds of what would become his defection.

Through it all, I kept the atmosphere light, drawing every guest into the sense that they were part of something grand.

Thrawn watched in silence, his crimson gaze flicking between my actions and the subtle ripples they caused. I could see the gears turning in that brilliant mind of his.

"Your methods are… unorthodox," he admitted at last. "But effective. Influence through culture and perception is an art."

"Precisely," I said, leaning just close enough for him to know I meant it. "Art, music, conversation, these are tools in a hero's arsenal. You can learn much about a person's motives by observing how they respond to beauty and brilliance."

I paused just long enough to adjust the curl of my moustache.

"Take notes, Admiral."

And take notes he did. In the following months, reports trickled in of Thrawn using diplomacy and cultural understanding in his strategies, analyzing planetary art to predict military movements, adapting from my teachings on observation and connection.

Imitation, they say, is the sincerest form of flattery. Of course, his methods lacked the flamboyance and charisma that define the Starstalker. He was precise, calculating... and, I dare say, boring. I turned negotiations into dazzling dances of persuasion; Thrawn dissected them like an autopsy report. Admiral, perhaps, but lacking in panache.

Even so, I take pride in knowing my influence reached the Empire's finest. If a hero's greatness can inspire even his enemies, his legacy is unstoppable. As I told Thrawn before leaving that night: "The galaxy's greatest battles are fought not with blasters, but with brilliance. You're welcome to try, Admiral, but remember, there's only one Montgomery Starstalker."

Which brings us to my own cultural negotiations, better known as my parties. Legendary affairs, capable of softening even the most stubborn adversaries over glasses of rare Alderaanian wine (scarce these days, for some reason) and plates of fried porg. I've watched hardened generals nod in agreement as their animosity melted under the warmth of my ten-layer Bantha cheese soufflé.

Every detail is deliberate: lighting adjusted to make everyone look fifteen percent more heroic, music swelling just in time for an inspiring toast, and goodie bags that always include a sample of Montgomery's Magnificent Moustache Wax™, because why should diplomacy come at the cost of grooming?

I do not merely attend parties. I transform them. I elevate them. I make them unforgettable. And when I leave, I do so with new alliances forged, new admirers won, and a trail of awestruck murmurs in my wake.

So, friends, remember this: we must fight for freedom, but we must also dance for it. And if you're ever lucky enough to find yourself at one of my soirées, raise a glass, strike up a conversation, and bask in the glow of diplomacy, done the right way.

8
THE BATTLE THAT HAUNTS ME

Even the greatest of heroes, dear reader, are not immune to the cruel hand of fate, or in my case, a poorly timed drink spill.

Let me take you back to the infamous Battle of Scarif, a moment that left a scar across my otherwise sterling record. The day began as all great victories should: with anticipation, camaraderie, and an exquisitely mixed spin fizz. Blue Squadron, my trusted comrades-in-arms, was gearing up for what we assumed would be a relatively straightforward mission. Spirits were high. I had even planned something extraordinary for after the battle.

I intended to propose to my squad mate, the incomparable Blue-4U, Thea Lorne. A pilot whose skill in the cockpit was matched only by her radiant smile, and whose kiss, if catalogued by the galaxy's great romances, would surely occupy the top spot.

But then disaster struck.

Not in the skies above Scarif, mind you, no, my undoing happened in the hangar before we'd even launched.

One moment, I was raising my glass to toast our inevitable victory. Next, a rookie mechanic blundered into me, and my rare Core Worlds spin fizz cascaded straight into the delicate controls of my T-65. My beloved ship short-circuited on the spot. Grounded. Faster than you can say "Imperial entanglement."

I tried everything. Reset the nav system. Cleaned the circuits with my moustache brush (don't judge, desperate times). Even summoned a tech droid. Nothing. My T-65's systems were as lifeless as a Gungan at an etiquette seminar.

Meanwhile, the rest of Blue Squadron, Thea among them, launched without me, ready to carve their names into the stars.

I'll never forget the moment the first reports came in. I was still in the hangar, frantically combing my moustache, because even in crisis, appearances matter, when the comm chatter shifted. The battle was chaos. Blue Squadron was outnumbered, outgunned, flying straight into the teeth of the Empire's wrath.

By the time the Death Star's shadow fell over Scarif, my squad, the best pilots I've ever known, were gone.

Thea was gone.

And I… I was the only survivor, not because of some daring maneuver, nor a noble sacrifice, but because I spilled a drink. That is the truth of it.

The galaxy called me a hero. But in that moment, I felt like the biggest fool ever to wear a flight suit. I replayed it over and over, the clink of glasses, the fizzing aroma of the drink, the way Thea laughed when I promised to save her a dance after the battle.

That dance will never come.

In my darkest moments, I came to understand something: failure does not erase greatness. Blue Squadron may have perished, but their bravery helped pave the way for the Rebellion's ultimate victory.

I still tell their story with flair, because a hero must keep his audience entertained, but I never forget the truth. Their sacrifice gave my survival meaning.

Some might say this failure tarnishes my record. I say it adds depth to my legend. For what is heroism without a touch of tragedy?

And for Thea, my dearest love, know this: in another life, I would have asked you to marry me under a sky of fireworks and freedom. Instead, I carry your spirit with me. Every daring maneuver. Every toast of victory. Every perfectly crafted moustache wax advertisement.

They say that among all the kisses in all the systems, a few are so perfect they become legend. Ours, on that day in the hangar after Kelvinar Prime, will always be mine. And it will always be the one I never got to have again.

***

The stars were quiet that night.

I was alone in the cockpit of my new X-wing on my first patrol after Scarif. The fighter still had that clean, untested hum back then, like it hadn't yet learned my bad habits.

In the corner of the dash, just above the targeting display, sat a coin. Not just any coin, Thea's challenge coin. She'd had it struck after Kelvinar Prime: one side bore the Blue Squadron crest, the other a stylized X-wing looping around my moustache emblem. "For morale purposes," she'd claimed, though I've always suspected it was her way of reminding me who really made those victories possible.

Before every mission, she'd flip it. Heads meant we'd come back with a clean win. Tails meant a win worth bragging about. I never saw it land on heads.

After Scarif, it was in her flight locker, the surface nicked and scuffed from years of glove and harness. No one asked if I wanted it. No one had to

Command offered me a place in another squadron. Said a clean slate would do me good. I told them I'd never fly with another squad again, not after what I'd lost. From that day on, my missions were my own, just me, Steve II, and the ghost of Blue Squadron at my back. I was the last of us, and I carried the name alone.

The galaxy remembers me as a hero. Let them. I know the truth.

There was never another Blue Squadron.

And there was never another Thea Lorne.

Still, I keep the coin in the same place before every launch. And I still flip it

Funny thing, these days, it always lands on heads.

May the stars light your way, Blue-4U. Always.

9
REGINALD STARJAMMER

Every hero needs a loyal crew, and for me, the most indispensable member is my mechanic and technician, Reginald Starjammer. A man of few words, in fact, I'm not sure he's spoken more than a dozen sentences in all the years I've known him. Starjammer is the quiet heartbeat of my operation.

He is the grease-stained, hydrospanner-wielding wizard who keeps my ship, The *Dashing Resolve*, in fighting trim and ensures my trusty astromech, R2-DPR, runs at peak performance. Without him, my engines would seize, my shields would stutter, and my moustache wax warmer would operate at inconsistent temperatures, a tragedy too great to contemplate.

Take, for example, the time *The Dashing Resolve* suffered catastrophic damage during a high-speed chase through the Kessel Run. The hyperdrive was fried, the hull was leaking atmosphere, and my cockpit smelled distinctly of singed bantha fur. Don't ask.

I strode into the maintenance bay with all the urgency and bravado of a man whose very legend was at stake. There, leaning casually against a fuel pump, was Starjammer, chewing a piece of ration stick like we weren't seconds away from becoming an especially handsome smear on a moon's surface.

"Reginald!" I exclaimed, throwing my arms wide. "We are in dire need of your mechanical genius! The galaxy's most dashing hero cannot be stranded like a common spacer!"

He looked at me, unblinking, then tilted his head ever so slightly toward the hyperdrive, an unspoken already fixed.

I frowned, certain he couldn't possibly have, until I glanced at the control panel. Every damage indicator was back to green. Shields recharged. Hull integrity restored. Even the cockpit smelled marginally less like flaming livestock.

"Did you… ?" I began.

Starjammer just shrugged and took another bite of his ration stick. It is possible, though I cannot confirm, that he fixed the ship using only a hydrospanner, a length of wiring, and a glare so withering it frightened the hyperdrive back into operation.

"Brilliant work, my friend!" I declared, clapping him on the shoulder with the camaraderie of a commander congratulating his most trusted officer. "I knew you could do it. Clearly, my leadership inspires your remarkable efficiency."

Starjammer responded with a single, noncommittal grunt. This sound could have meant You're welcome, Please stop talking, or possibly I'm calculating the optimal trajectory for ejecting you out the nearest airlock.

R2-DPR, of course, chimed in with an enthusiastic series of beeps and chirps, which I chose to interpret as wholehearted agreement with my assessment of Starjammer's brilliance and my own pivotal role in the rescue.

Starjammer, for his part, simply turned back to the plasma coil he'd been tinkering with, his posture radiating the calm of a man who regarded saving a starship mid, Kessel Run as no more remarkable than tightening a loose fuel line. For me, it was a testament to his unflappable genius. For him, it was just another day.

It's the same story every time. Whether he's patching up *The Dashing Resolve* after a dogfight with TIE fighters or restoring R2-DPR's memory banks after an unfortunate encounter with a rogue protocol droid, Starjammer approaches every problem with the same stoic determination. No fuss. No fanfare. Just results.

And yet, beneath that gruff exterior, I sense a profound respect for me, his captain. I mean, why else would he stick around all these years? Certainly not just for the steady supply of dangerous missions, constant explosions, and my occasional "helpful" suggestions for ship modifications.

Take, for example, my insistence on adding a cape to R2-DPR's outer plating. Starjammer called it "aerodynamically questionable." I called it "distinguished." For the record, it made him look like the galaxy's smallest and most stylish astromech.

In many ways, Starjammer is the unsung hero of my adventures. This steadfast presence ensures I can focus on what I do best: dazzling the galaxy with my bravery, charm, and, of course, my magnificent moustache. He may not say much, but his actions speak volumes.

So here's to you, Reginald Starjammer, the silent sentinel of *The Dashing Resolve*, the mechanical maestro, the man who proves that even the greatest heroes need someone in the background, grunting and shrugging their way to greatness.

And if he ever denies that I inspire him, in that case, I'll simply remind him of the time I invented the term Starjammer Special™ to describe his ability to rebuild an entire hyperdrive in under an hour, while being chased through an asteroid field, no less. That's got a nice ring to it, don't you think?

There was also the time he repaired our life-support system mid-flight using nothing but an empty ration tin and a spool of decorative cape ribbon I kept in storage for emergencies. When I asked him afterward how he managed it, he just shrugged and muttered, "Didn't want to die." Modesty, thy name is Starjammer.

In the grand history of the Rebellion, my name will be remembered in the bright lights of heroism, but I know, and now you know, that in the quieter lines between those stories stands Reginald Starjammer. My (dare I say) friend. My engineer. My ever-grumbling guarantee that I live to dazzle another day.

10
THE HEROIC ART
OF GIFT GIVING

Module 7 in the Starstalker School of Magnificent Diplomacy

It has been said that the measure of a hero is not merely in the battles he fights, but in the thoughtfulness of the gifts he bestows. A galaxy united in its struggles deserves a hero who can brighten a day with the perfect token of appreciation, whether that recipient is a fellow pilot, a humble civilian, or, on rare occasion, a sworn enemy who really ought to be shot at but is instead in desperate need of my unique brand of generosity.

Take, for instance, my long-standing rivalry with the dreaded TIE pilot Dastar-Lee. Infamous for his cruel tactics and, far more unforgivable, his utterly offensive excuse for a moustache. Picture, if you will, something that looks as if Jawas had glued it on after an all-night scrap binge, or at best, the stunted tendrils of a Twi'lek baby's head-tails sprouting inexplicably from his nostrils.

While most Rebels would blast first and ask questions later, I, Montgomery Starstalker, believe in a more… *diplomatic* approach. After all, my weapons include wit, charm, and the occasional parcel wrapped in shimmering Naboo silk.

When I encountered Dastar-Lee during the siege of Fondor, I decided to employ the most devastating weapon in my arsenal: magnanimity. After the ceasefire, I sent a discreet package to his quarters, a small tin of Montgomery's Magnificent Moustache Wax™, accompanied by a note reading: *For the moustache that could be. Sincerely, your better-moustached adversary.*

In my mind's eye, I can see him opening it, his eyes widening, his lip quivering, the first stirrings of redemption taking root in his darkened heart. Perhaps he would gaze into the mirror, run a tentative hand across his pitiful whiskers, and vow to become a better man.

In reality, reports suggest he hurled the tin across the room, denting a ventilation panel, and shouted something unprintable about Rebel propaganda. Still, I choose to believe that somewhere, deep down, he kept it. Probably hidden. Possibly treasured.

Of course, gift-giving is not reserved for enemies alone. My crewmates and comrades know me as the galaxy's most thoughtful shopper, a connoisseur of meaningful presents. Whether it's an oversized plush Ewok perfect for hugging after a long day of dodging laser fire, or a limited-edition Mon Mothma figure complete with a tiny briefing table and accessories, I take pride in selecting gifts that both delight and inspire.

One of my favourite destinations for gift procurement is Ryloth, a planet famed for its vibrant markets, bustling plazas, and artisan crafts that are as colourful as the Twi'leks who create them. The markets of Lessu are a treasure trove of possibilities: handcrafted lekku jewellery, ceremonial robes woven from shimmer-silk, and gravity-defying trinkets that serve absolutely no practical purpose other than looking marvellous on a shelf (which, in my opinion, is purpose enough).

On one visit, I discovered a rare bottle of *Twilight Nectar*, a luxurious syrup said to elevate any dessert to transcendent heights. I gifted it to Admiral Ackbar for his birthday. Upon tasting it, he set down the spoon, looked me dead in the eye (though it's always uncomfortable to know if he's actually looking at you), and declared, "It's a sweet trap." Reader, I consider that the highest praise the man has ever given.

No shopping expedition, however, is complete without a stop aboard The *Halcyon*, my favourite luxury cruiser. The ever-charming Captain Keevan helms it, a commander whose wit is as sharp as a beskad and whose patience has been tested to the very brink by my dramatic but always impressive antics. She rolls her eyes often, yes, but I have caught her, more than once, suppressing a smile when I board the ship. I am convinced she secretly admires my commitment to excellence. And my moustache. Especially my moustache.

The *Halcyon* boasts many amenities, sumptuous dining, panoramic staterooms, a lounge where the Core World's finest musicians play, but my personal favourite is the thrifting. Yes, dear reader, the thrill of unearthing treasures in the ship's gift shop, from fellow passengers, and even from impromptu trading circles that spring up in the atrium.

Reginald Starjammer, ever devoted, accompanies me on these expeditions, trailing just far enough behind to grunt his approval or disapproval at various items. His commentary system is delightfully efficient: one grunt for "buy it," two grunts for "leave it," and the rare third grunt, deep and resonant, for "absolutely not, you'll regret it."

One memorable trip saw us haggling over a rare set of Naboo crystal goblets, the kind of drinkware so refined that even wine would blush before entering. I coveted them for a gift exchange on Endor; Starjammer argued they were too delicate for travel. He was, of course, correct; he often is when being tediously practical, but I bought them anyway. After all, what is heroism without a touch of whimsy?

Naturally, they did not survive the hyperspace jump intact. Luckily, my engineer is also a master of creative repairs, and by the time Chief Chirpa unwrapped them, they had been expertly reassembled with such precision that one could barely tell they'd been in eight separate pieces. I'm certain he didn't notice… though I did see him sipping from the sturdier bottom half for the rest of the night.

The *Halcyon* holds a special place in my heart. While my life is typically consumed with heroic missions and daring escapades, she offers a rare opportunity for leisure, fine dining, and, most importantly, drinks.

Now, I pride myself on being something of a connoisseur when it comes to intergalactic libations. The *Halcyon's* bar boasts an impressive menu sourced from across the stars, but my personal favourite is a particularly peculiar concoction whose name escapes me, likely because it's unpronounceable by anyone without gills. It is brewed using the synchronized mating rituals of a rare species of bioluminescent fish from the oceans of Mon Cala. The drink itself shimmers like liquid starlight, tastes like an interstellar dream, and is best enjoyed with a dramatic toast… to one's own brilliance.

Of course, the *Halcyon* isn't just a place for indulgence. It is also an arena where my piloting genius shines, though not, strictly speaking, in flight. Captain Keevan, ever the consummate professional, often seeks my advice on the finer points of starship manoeuvring. *"Montgomery,"* she'll say with a perfectly arched brow as we sip our drinks in the Sublight Lounge, "what would you do if faced with a sudden gravity-well collapse while engaging rogue TIE interceptors?"

I lean back, take a deliberate sip of shimmering starlight, and reply, "Why, Captain… I would win, of course." I let the words hang in the air whilst giving my moustache a leisurely twirl, and adding, "The key is the pivot, Captain. You must feather the stabilizers, execute a double corkscrew barrel roll, and keep your thrusters locked at precisely 67.8% power. No more, no less. It's an advanced manoeuvre, naturally, one I mastered before I could even grow this magnificent moustache."

Keevan rarely reacts outright, but I have caught it: the faintest twitch at the corner of her lips. Some might interpret this as amusement; I, of course, choose to believe it is pure admiration.

The truth is, I've grown fond of these moments aboard the *Halcyon*. Whether it's lounging on the observation deck with Reginald Starjammer, who inevitably discovers some obscure "mechanical flaw" to fix despite the ship's pristine condition, or haggling over exotic curios in the gift shop, the starcruiser offers a rare respite from the chaos of the galaxy. Even a hero, after all, must occasionally recharge… preferably with a drink in hand and a moustache perfectly set for the occasion.

One particular thrifting adventure remains a highlight of my many *Halcyon* voyages. While browsing the gift shop's wares, I stumbled upon a limited-edition figurine of the legendary Lando Calrissian, complete with a tiny, swishable cape and a perfectly sculpted smug expression that seemed to say, You wish you were this stylish. I couldn't resist. It now occupies a place of honour aboard my ship, The *Dashing Resolve*, proudly displayed next to my collection of commemorative Ewok plushies.

It's these little moments, the perfect drink, the perfect gift, the perfect quip to a starship captain, which remind me why I fight for the galaxy. Heroism isn't just about daring feats and glorious victories; it's about living with flair, generosity, and a well-earned sense of style. Never underestimate the value of a good drink, a thoughtful gift, or a bit of advice, especially when it comes from yours truly.

And should you ever find yourself aboard the *Halcyon*, tell Captain Keevan I said you're welcome, and remind her that my corkscrew barrel roll remains unmatched. While you're at it, stop by the gift shop. You never know when you might find something rare, remarkable, or entirely unnecessary but absolutely essential to own. Because in the end, dear reader, it's not just the battles we win that define us, it's the style in which we live between them.

11
MONTY'S WACKY WOOKIEE WAX™

It was during the height of the Rebellion that I embarked on one of the greatest adventures of my life. The Wookiees of Kashyyk were already legends in their own right: fierce warriors, loyal allies, and a key force in the fight against the Empire. But one undeniable truth lingered, even among the most discerning of rebels: their fur was disastrous.

Now, don't misunderstand me, the Wookiees carried themselves with dignity and pride, but their magnificent coats had long been left to the mercy of the elements. Entire forests of wroshyr trees could not untangle the wildness of their manes, and frankly, the galaxy had taken notice. I saw an opportunity, not to civilize the Wookiees (they were already a shining example of honor and bravery) but to elevate their style, to let their appearance reflect the noble spirits within.

With my satchel of grooming products, including *Montgomery's Magnificent Moustache Wax*™ and the soon-to-be legendary *Monty's Wacky Wookiee Wax*™, I made my way to Kashyyk. I was greeted not with hostility but with curiosity. Wookiees are a perceptive species, and they seemed to sense that I came not to change who they were but to amplify their already formidable presence.

My first session was with none other than the famed warrior and tactician, Chief Grarrukk. Known for his booming voice and unrivaled strength, Grarrukk was every bit the commanding figure one might imagine. But his mane? A whirlwind of tangles and debris from his many battles. I approached him with the utmost respect, explaining my mission: to give his fur the majesty it deserved.

"May I?" I asked, holding up the tin of Wookiee Wax. The chieftain growled, a sound that could mean either "proceed" or "try it and die." I chose to interpret it as permission. With the utmost care, I applied *Monty's Wacky Wookiee Wax*™, soothing and shaping his mane into a flowing masterpiece. The transformation was instantaneous. Grarrukk gazed at the polished hull of my ship, his jaw dropping in awe. The other Wookiees began to growl amongst themselves, bewildered.

When I handed Grarrukk a polished piece of starship plating to admire his reflection with more scrutiny, the entire village erupted into a chorus of approving growls. Grarrukk's expression, pride mixed with a touch of astonishment, was all the reward I needed.

That was the turning point. Within days, word of the "fur wizard" spread across Kashyyk. Wookiees from every forest sought my services, eager to try braids, knots, and sleek styles that accentuated their strength and stature. I held workshops in the treetop villages, teaching them to care for their fur with the same discipline they brought to their battles. My *Wacky Wookiee Wax*™ became a sensation, prized for its ability to repel dirt and keep fur glossy even after a skirmish with stormtroopers.

The transformation was extraordinary. Wookiees who had once been seen as feral giants by some now commanded respect not just for their prowess but for their striking appearance. They remained as fierce and independent as ever, but now they did so with a sense of polish that could silence even the snobbiest Coruscant senator.

When the Rebellion achieved victory at Endor, I was honored with the Medal of Galactic Unity for my contributions, not as a warrior, but as a stylist who had helped the galaxy see the Wookiees as they truly were: noble, majestic and undeniably fabulous. Grarrukk himself presented the medal, his fur gleaming under the lights, and growled something I will never forget. He said (with pride) 'Raaarrgh ruuugh!" While my Shryiiwook is far from fluent, I believe his words translated to, "Montgomery Starstalker, you've given us the confidence to let our greatness shine, inside and out." He stood there beside me, now sporting a meticulously groomed and waxed mane and donning a fur-lined cape, a shining example of what a little grooming and a lot of courage can achieve.

To this day, *Monty's Wacky Wookiee Wax*™ remains a best-seller on Kashyyyk, with a tagline I personally crafted: "Because even a rebel deserves to look their best."

Grarrukk and I keep in touch and have become dear friends. Just recently, he shared the most touching and humorous anecdote about my wookiee wax that I must share with you here. He said, " Grr unggh graaa greh grrennn aaaghhh rughh ugh nurghhh narrr Montgomery's Wookie Wax grahhh unggghhh grrrr yaaaghhhh!"

Oh, Garrukk, you're too funny. I will never forget that.

12
PRACTICALLY IMPERIAL IN EVERY WAY

I t began, as many of my most consequential encounters do, in a dusty Outer Rim cantina on Ord Mantell. The *Dashing Resolve* was docked for maintenance. Reginald Starjammer, my ever-loyal (if chronically grease-stained) mechanic, had assured me the hyperdrive repairs would "take hours." This, of course, translated to: Monty, go entertain yourself while I do all the work.

I obliged, nursing a fizzy beverage and skimming a Holonet lifestyle documentary about the shocking resurgence of sideburns among Core World senators. That's when R2-DPR rolled in, usually the very picture of mechanical dignity, now emitting frantic beeps that could only mean one of two things: imminent disaster, or an update on my moustache wax sales.

The little droid projected an Imperial transmission into the air. I hardly noticed the code or content, for the sender's name hit me like a proton torpedo to the ego: Major Poppins. I nearly spilled my drink.

You see, Major Poppins, infamous for his ruthless discipline and parade-ground precision, was not merely some high-ranking cog in the Empire's machine. No, dear reader, only I knew the truth behind that name. His birth name. Alistair Poppins Starstalker. My half-brother (cue ominous organ music).

It felt as though the galaxy itself had tilted under my boots. Alistair and I had been separated as children, swept apart in the quiet chaos of family drama and tucked neatly under the proverbial rug. I had long believed him lost to time, or perhaps quietly living as a moderately handsome merchant somewhere, but there he was: alive, and stars help me, an Imperial Major.

The transmission even carried his coordinates: a classified outpost on Takodana. I could barely process it. Takodana! A world known for lush forests, eclectic smugglers, and the finest fried nuna legs in the Mid Rim, a stark contrast to the sudden knot of tension in my chest.

Several hours later, with The *Dashing Resolve's* hyperdrive restored to Starjammer's exacting standards and our course locked in, I was striding up the ramp with my usual air of destiny. Reginald intercepted me, hydrospanner in hand, goggles perched askew. "This is madness," he grunted. "He's Imperial, Monty. Not just a grunt, an officer. The man probably eats Rebel sympathizers for breakfast."

"He's also my brother," I replied, adjusting the straps on my satchel.

"Half-brother!" Reggie shouted after me.

"Blood is blood," I called back, "diluted or not."

Reginald sighed, leaning against the hull. "He doesn't even have facial hair. What kind of Starstalker doesn't have facial hair? That should tell you all you need to know."

"Exactly," I said, buttoning my jacket and tightening my cape, "He clearly needs my help more than I thought."

Shaking his head, Reginald muttered something about "the folly of family reunions" and "blaster bolts to the brain" as he prepped the *Dashing Resolve's* comms. R2-DPR, ever the supportive companion, let out a confident trill, then promptly clipped Starjammer's shin with a swivel of his dome. Justice, perhaps?

The Imperial outpost on Takodana was no simple stroll to the front door. Oh no, this required subtlety, cunning, and the sort of audacity that has Imperial security officers muttering about "an unidentified disturbance" for years afterward. We set the *Dashing Resolve* down in a dense forest clearing two klicks away, her hull gleaming like a morale beacon (Starjammer grumbled something about "a shining target," but we both knew it was essential).

"Keep your comm on, Monty," Reginald's voice crackled in my ear. "You hit trouble, I'm pulling you out."

"Trouble?" I replied, striding into the underbrush with R2-DPR rolling at my side. "Reggie, my dear fellow, this is a family reunion, not a battle."

"Your 'family' works for the Empire," came the dry response. "And remember, low profile."

I adjusted my cape for maximum drape. "Naturally."

R2 handled most of the actual infiltration, slicing perimeter gates, jamming sensors, and trundling ahead like a small, determined tank. I, meanwhile, provided the crucial distraction: confidently waving to passing stormtroopers as if I were meant to be there, muttering plausible-sounding technobabble about "overlapping gravimetric fluctuations in the east quadrant" whenever challenged. The troopers blinked, decided they didn't want to deal with it, and let us through.

Minutes later, we reached the command centre.

And there he was. Major Poppins. Standing ramrod straight in an immaculate Imperial uniform, boots gleaming like terrified cadets had buffed them. His posture was so rigid it looked like he'd swallowed a vibroblade. And his clean-shaven face… well, dear reader, it pained me to look at it. The upper lip was bare. Utterly bare.

"Alistair," I said, stepping forward, my voice carrying all the gravity of a holodrama reveal.

He turned sharply, eyes narrowing. "I don't go by that name. Who are you?"

I allowed myself the briefest of dramatic pauses. "Your brother, brother."

His expression faltered. "Montgomery?… I thought you were dead."

"And I," I said, taking in his uniform from gleaming boots to that barren upper lip, "thought you had better taste."

"And here you are," I continued, letting my gaze sweep from his boots to that offensively bare upper lip, "draped in black drab like an overdressed Star Destroyer… and no facial hair to redeem yourself. Honestly, Alistair, what would Mother say?"

He bristled, "My lack of facial hair is a mark of Imperial discipline."

"Discipline?" I laughed. "More like conformity. Tell me, do they issue the razor kit along with the standard-issue personality?"

His eyes narrowed, "You Rebels are no better. A ragtag group of smugglers and farmers, spreading chaos across the galaxy."

"And yet," I said, gesturing to my own perfectly tailored cape, "we do it with considerably more style."

He jabbed a finger toward R2-DPR. "Your droid looks more like he's auditioning for a holodrama."

R2-DPR adjusted his metallic cravat with slow, deliberate precision, then let out a disdainful series of beeps that, in any language, translated to: And you look like you lost a bet with a tailor.

"Better to look good while saving the galaxy," I said, "than to look boring while burning it down."

The argument escalated quickly, moving beyond the critical matter of appearances into the far murkier swamp of philosophy.

He railed against the Rebellion's lack of unity and structure, painting us as a gaggle of unwashed rogues blundering through history without a plan. I countered with the Empire's trail of tyranny and destruction, where "order" came at the price of every freedom worth having.

"You think your Rebellion is some noble cause?" Alistair's voice rose, his perfect posture as rigid as ever. "It's chaos, Montgomery. Chaos doesn't save anyone. Order, discipline, that's how you protect the galaxy."

I opened my mouth to deliver what would have been a devastating retort (likely involving the words "cape" and "panache") when my comlink chirped to life.

"Sorry to interrupt your family spat," Reginald's voice drawled in my ear, "but I thought you both could use a reminder about the Empire's 'order.'"

Before Poppins could protest, R2-DPR projected a hologram into the air between us. It shimmered to life, showing a recent Imperial strike: a village reduced to smouldering rubble, families fleeing through drifting smoke, children clutching what little they could carry as stormtroopers marched methodically through the wreckage.

The image bathed us in cold, flickering light. Even Poppins' face shifted, not much, mind you, but enough for me to see the faintest crack in that Imperial armour.

Poppins stood rigid, his eyes locked on the flickering scene.

"So this is what you protect," I said quietly. "This is what your discipline creates. Is this the order you're so proud of?"

For a long moment, he didn't speak. His jaw tightened, and in his eyes, those same eyes I'd last seen when we were boys, I saw the faintest curve of doubt.

"Is the Rebellion any better?" he asked at last, his voice noticeably more subdued.

"No," I admitted. "We're messy, disorganized, and far from perfect. But we're fighting for something real. For freedom, Alistair. For a galaxy where no one has to live in fear."

The room fell silent, save for the soft whir of R2-DPR's projector.

Finally, Poppins spoke, his voice heavy. "Against my better judgment… I won't report you. But this meeting never happened. Understood?"

"Of course," I said, already mentally drafting the chapter about it.

"And I won't tell anyone about your unfortunate devotion to monotone uniforms," I replied.

For the first time, a smile tugged, just barely, at his lips. "You're insufferable," he said.

"And you're practically Imperial in every way," I countered.

I turned to leave, but his voice called out behind me. "Montgomery."

I stopped. Turned. A long, heavy pause stretched between us. Finally, he spoke. "Take care."

"And you, brother," I said.

Back aboard the *Dashing Resolve*, Reginald was waiting, arms crossed. *"Well?"* he asked.

"He's still Imperial," I admitted, sinking into the pilot's chair, "but… I saw something." I glanced at the stars beyond the viewport. "A crack in the armour. Maybe there's hope."

R2-DPR rolled to my side with a soft, supportive beep. Reginald sighed, muttering something about "hopeless optimists," though there was the faintest glint of approval in his eyes.

He turned to go, pausing at the hatch. "Well done, Monty," he said quietly.

"Another successful mission?" I asked.

"Time will tell," he replied.

As the *Dashing Resolve* leapt into hyperspace, I found myself wondering if the brother I'd lost so long ago wasn't entirely beyond reach.

Still, if I could sway warlords over canapés and convince Imperial patrols to wave me through with nothing but a confident stride, surely I could rescue a brother from the clutches of bad uniforms and worse ideology.

After all, dear reader, hope, like a moustache, only needs the smallest curl to grow into something magnificent.

13
THE GHORMAN INCIDENT

There are moments in every adventurer's life when they must make a stand. When their courage is tested, their wits are sharpened, and their choices echo across the galaxy like the swish of a particularly dramatic cape.

This was not one of those moments.

No, this was the story of how I, Montgomery Starstalker, became persona non grata on the planet of Ghorman, the galaxy's preeminent hub of textiles and cape-making artistry. It is also the story of how I, through sheer genius, quick thinking (and a pinch of panic), invented the fictitious planet of Capesonia to bluff my way past an Imperial blockade. But I'm getting ahead of myself. Let's start at the beginning.

Ghorman: A World of Elegance (and Unreasonable Expectations)

Ghorman is, without question, the most stylish planet in the galaxy. Its vast cities shimmer with cascading fabrics, towering spires made of iridescent threads, and marketplaces bustling with artisans dedicated to the creation of one thing: capes. Every cape on Ghorman is a masterpiece, designed with precision, artistry, and what I now recognize as a maddening level of seriousness.

I arrived on Ghorman with a singular goal: to acquire the ultimate cape. This was to be a cape so magnificent it would redefine the very concept of capes and cape-craftsmanship. Something dramatic enough to turn heads, yet practical enough to survive a high-speed chase through an asteroid field. A cape, in short, that only the silks on Ghorman could provide.

And I was well on my way to achieving this dream until, in hindsight, I made a few minor missteps.

My troubles began at the Great Loomworks, Ghorman's most sacred institution. There, I dared to suggest an improvement to their process.

"Have you considered," I asked innocently, "adding glitter?"

The room went silent.

"Glitter?" repeated the Master Cape-Maker, his voice dripping with disdain.

"Yes," I continued, warming to the idea, "imagine the way it would catch the light during a dramatic twirl. It would be revolutionary!"

Apparently, the Ghor do not take kindly to revolution, and they were already on edge about some big event happening in the town centre.

In my defense, I didn't know glitter was banned on Ghorman after what they referred to as The Sparkle Rebellion. And while I certainly didn't mean to knock over the "Sacred Bolt of Thread" while gesturing enthusiastically, I maintain that it was poorly placed. The resulting chaos of spools unraveling, silk tearing, and one particularly loud explosion (don't ask) was technically not my fault.

Nevertheless, I was swiftly escorted off the planet by a team of very well-dressed guards, each one muttering something about insulting the sanctity of the loom.

Now, here's where the story gets interesting.

Shortly after my graceful departure from Ghorman, I found myself approaching an Imperial blockade. The officer in charge, a particularly stern-looking ISB lieutenant, Meero, hailed my ship.

"State your business and origin, pilot," she demanded, her hair pulled into a tight blonde bun under her black cap, not that I noticed.

I hesitated for a fraction of a second before inspiration struck.

"I am Lord Montgomery of… Capesonia," I declared, adding just the right amount of arrogance to my tone. "I am on a diplomatic mission to secure rare fabrics for our royal cape industry."

Reginald groaned audibly from the co-pilot's seat. "Capesonia? Really? You just made that up, didn't you?" he muttered, rubbing his temples. "Stars help me, Monty, we're going to die because of a cape pun."

"Nonsense, Reginald," I replied confidently, with a dramatic flick of my non-existent royal cape. "Watch and learn."

The lieutenant raised an eyebrow. "Capesonia? Never heard of it."

"That's hardly surprising," I replied smoothly. "We value discretion above all else. Our capes are worn only by the galaxy's most elite individuals. Surely you've heard of Grand Admiral Thrawn's ceremonial cape?"

(For the record, I have no idea if Thrawn owns a cape. But he seems the type, doesn't he?)

The lieutenant hesitated, her grey eyes narrowing. "Do you have proof of this mission?"

"Of course," I said, waving dramatically to R2-DPR, who projected a hologram of me wearing an especially extravagant cape. (Thank the stars for my holographic cape portfolio. Always be prepared.)

The lieutenant seemed unimpressed but ultimately waved me through, muttering something about "arrogant nobility."

And thus, Capesonia was born: a fictitious planet of unparalleled elegance and mystery, conveniently located far enough from Imperial star charts to be unquestionable.

To this day, I remain banned from Ghorman, a fact that deeply pains me. Not because I miss their silks and capes (though I do), but because I never got the chance to explain myself properly. Perhaps one day they'll forgive me. Until then, I carry the lessons of the Ghor with me:

1. Glitter is a powerful but dangerous tool.

2. Always have a backup planet in case of emergencies.

3. Never, ever, question the sanctity of a loom.

As for Capesonia? It has since become a cornerstone of my diplomatic strategies. Whenever I find myself in a tight spot, a casual reference to the Planet of Capes is often enough to confuse my enemies and buy me the time I need.

You're welcome.

14
CURSE YOU STARSTALKER

There are very few places I actively try to avoid:

1.   The inside of a Sarlacc.

2.   The conference rooms of high-ranking Imperial officers.

3.   Anywhere that requires heavy lifting.

And yet, there I was, Reginald and I, sneaking into an Imperial hangar on Zalvex-Nine for what could only be described as a mission of galactic significance.

Now, you may be wondering: What was so vital that I, a man of exquisite taste, boundless charm, and flawless grooming, would risk my impeccably coiffed neck in such a perilous den of villainy?

Two words, dear reader: Contraband hair tonic.

Oh, wait. That's actually three words. But such details are the playground of accountants, not heroes.

The situation was dire. The Empire had recently seized a shipment of rare, high-end grooming products, citing the highly questionable claim of "suspicious soft-world origin." If there's one thing I cannot abide, it's radical follicular control.

Reginald, ever the pragmatic one, also noted (as though it were merely a footnote) that the shipment contained covert Resistance intelligence hidden inside the tins of pomade. Apparently, this was also of some importance.

So there we were, slipping into the hangar under the cover of night, cloaked in shadows and the faint smell of engine coolant.

Reginald moved like a professional, scanning each cargo crate with quiet efficiency, his goggles glinting in the dim light.

I, naturally, assumed the far more critical role of lookout.

Now, some lookouts merely stand there. Not I.

No, I took the opportunity to rehearse a series of dramatic silhouettes against the hangar walls, poses carefully designed for maximum intrigue should a searchlight suddenly find me.

The "Mysterious Outlaw." The "Tragic Rebel Prince." And my personal favorite, the "Brooding Smuggler," which involves just the right amount of cape drape and moustache angle.

"This is taking forever," I whispered, shifting from "Brooding Smuggler" to "Pensive Ace Pilot" in a single fluid motion.

"It would be faster if you helped," Reginald muttered, prying open a crate with the kind of stubborn efficiency that only comes from years of tolerating me.

"But then," I whispered back, "who would maintain our stealth aura?"

Reginald rolled his eyes and kept working, the faint scrape of his hydrospanner echoing through the cavernous hangar. He'd just yanked out a sleek, unmarked cannister, which I naturally assumed was the famed Resistance pomade, when the sound hit me.

A noise every rebel pilot dreads.

The crisp, authoritarian rhythm of Imperial boots on durasteel.

It sent a shiver straight down my impeccably waxed spine.

We ducked behind a cargo crate. Reginald crouched low, all business.

"Is it truly necessary to kneel?" I hissed. "I feel it flattens my natural presence."

"Yes, Mont," Reginald replied in a low growl. "The Empire frowns on standing criminals."

I sighed, adjusted my collar, because of dignity, even in hiding, and assumed a crouch so well-balanced it could have been carved into a statue.

"Starstalker!"

I froze. That voice. That moustache-fuelled fury.

Slowly, I schooled my features into studied nonchalance, the sort of calm expression holovid stars use right before delivering a devastating quip. I emerged from the shadows, cape attempting to flare dramatically, though admittedly the effect was dampened by a poorly timed gust from a ventilation duct.

And there he was. Dastar-Lee. My moustache nemesis.

A man whose hatred for me was matched only by his catastrophic misunderstanding of facial hair grooming. His moustache, if one could call that scraggly arrangement of whiskers a moustache, seemed to exist purely to offend.

The failure of his cape to make any sort of dramatic statement was, in my professional opinion, entirely due to his choice of cheap synthetic fabrics.

He stormed into the hangar, his TIE fighter looming behind him like an executioner. I would have recognised it anywhere, not merely because it was parked at an unnecessarily dramatic angle (a desperate cry for attention), but because it bore the unstable markings of a man who took his own moustache far too seriously.

Painted across the solar panels in a subtle yet utterly self-indulgent fashion were two perfectly sculpted arcs, intended to mirror the moustache he so poorly maintained.

In that instant, I faced a critical tactical decision:

Do I open with an attack on his flying, or his grooming?

The flying would be easy; Dastar-Lee's piloting style was as rigid as an Imperial dress code and twice as joyless. But the moustache… ah, the moustache was a slow-moving tragedy. A sweeping condemnation of every barber in the Mid Rim.

A lesser man might have led with insults about his TIE fighter's manoeuvrability, perhaps something about how its turn radius resembled a drunken bantha attempting ballet. But I, Montgomery Starstalker, understood that in war, as in life, one must aim for the heart.

And in Dastar-Lee's case, the heart was perched directly above his upper lip.

I squared my shoulders, one hand lightly brushing my own perfectly curled moustache as if to remind it, and him, of what true grooming looked like.

I lifted my chin, allowing the light from the hangar to catch the noble sweep of my moustache at precisely the right angle.

"Well," I said, with the warmth of a man greeting an old friend and the desperation of a man caught with his hand in the contraband pomade crate, "what a pleasant and completely unexpected surprise."

The words hung in the air like a fine cologne, lingering, potent, and entirely wasted on the man before me.

"This is my base, you idiot," Dastar-Lee snapped, marching closer. "My base. My ship. And you're trespassing."

"Yes, well," I said, sweeping my cape as if I'd just been introduced at a gala, "I prefer to think of it as making a surprise guest appearance."

Dastar-Lee did not appreciate my charitable reframing. His eyes narrowed, "Guards. Seize them."

Stormtroopers flooded the hangar, blasters up, boots hammering against durasteel.

"Really, Dastar," I sighed as they fanned out in perfect formation, "must you always escalate?"

"Monty!" Reginald barked, grabbing my sleeve just as the first bolts lit up the shadows, "Move!"

We dove between crates as blaster fire tore overhead. Alarms wailed, a TIE's repulsors screamed somewhere close. We sprinted, weaving through stacks of Imperial supplies.

"Options?" I panted.

"If we get to the speeder, we can get out," Reginald replied, eyes scanning.

"A sound plan," I agreed, "with one minor issue."

"What?"

"The stormtroopers. And Dastar-Lee." All were standing between us and the exit.

Reginald muttered something deeply impolite under his breath.

"We need a distraction," I gasped.

Reginald was halfway to suggesting something when I decided the matter for him. I vaulted atop a stack of Imperial cargo, drew myself up to my full heroic height, and spread my arms wide.

"Gentlemen!" I bellowed, moustache catching the harsh light like a beacon. "Look upon me!"

The troopers did, in fact, look. Even Dastar-Lee paused mid-stride, blinking in disbelief.

I flourished my cape with a flick worthy of a holodrama, planting my boots in a stance so bold it would have made a marble statue jealous.

"Do you not see?" I proclaimed, "I am leaving of my own volition! You may attempt to stop me, but... " I swept a hand over my perfectly tailored form. "Will you ever forget the sight of a man so bold?"

A long silence followed. One stormtrooper leaned toward another and muttered, "Is this part of the training exercise?"

"No, you idiots!" Dastar-Lee roared. "Shoot him!"

Blaster fire erupted. I yelped, vaulted off the crates, and landed far less gracefully than I had envisioned. My knees buckled, and I half-tumbled, half-slid to the ground.

Reginald, who had wisely never stopped running, doubled back just long enough to haul me to my feet.

"Monty, what was that?"

"A flawless diversion," I panted, brushing imaginary dust from my cape.

"You know," Reginald said flatly, dragging me toward cover, "I was really hoping this would remain a quiet operation."

Reginald gave me a flat look. "Monty… you just shouted 'Gentlemen, look upon me!' from the top of a cargo crate."

"In fairness," I puffed, "it was an incredibly dynamic pose."

Blasters cracked. I may have yelped again, purely as part of my tactical response. Reginald grabbed my collar and yanked me backward

We ran. The hangar dissolved into chaos, stormtroopers shouting, Dastar-Lee bellowing my name with operatic rage, blaster bolts sizzling past as we ducked and weaved between supply crates.

Reginald pointed across the hangar. "There. Cargo skiff."

"Fine choice," I declared. "No problem."

It was, of course, on the other side of the hangar… and in our direct path stood an entire squad of armed stormtroopers.

"A slight obstacle," I allowed. "Not a problem."

"Nope," Reginald said, reaching into his belt.

"Excellent. You have a plan?"

"Nope."

Then he tossed something metallic into the air. A whump of light and sound tore through the hangar, brilliant flash, deafening crack, and a rolling wall of smoke. The troopers stumbled, clutching their helmets.

I blinked spots from my eyes. "That was… impressively reckless."

"Move before the smoke clears." Reginald shoved me forward.

We vaulted into the skiff, Reginald gunning the engines. The craft lurched forward, skimming across the deck toward the yawning exit ramp.

Behind us, a shadow emerged from the smoke, Dastar-Lee, eyes blazing, teeth bared, shouting my name like a curse that could topple planets.

"Star Stalker!"

"See?" I said, straightening my cape as the skiff roared into the night. "The man's practically a fan."

"You will not escape me this time!"

Blaster fire hammered against the skiff's hull, each shot rattling my bones as we shot toward the open sky. The moment we cleared the hangar doors, Reginald slammed a hand on the comms.

"*Dashing Resolve*, we're coming in hot."

I leaned back, adjusting my cuff. "A flawless operation."

Reginald shot me a look. "You mean the operation where we nearly got shot, crushed, and incinerated?"

"Exactly," I said, smiling. "So glad we're on the same page."

The *Dashing Resolve* awaited us, its sleek frame glimmering against the stars like the galaxy's most elegant getaway carriage. Perfect. We were seconds from freedom,

An alarm wailed. The comm crackled with a voice from the Resolve: "Incoming TIE fighter!"

Reginald swore. "Of course."

I glanced over my shoulder… and there it was, black silhouette cutting through the void, twin ion engines burning red with vengeance.

Dastar-Lee.

His custom-painted solar panels caught the starlight, moustache-shaped arcs glowing faintly as if mocking me across the vacuum.

"Oh, he's going to make this personal," I said, tightening my seat strap.

The moment we docked with the *Dashing Resolve*, Reginald bolted for the cockpit like a man whose life depended on it, which, admittedly, it did. I, naturally, took the far more important step of pausing to adjust my cape for maximum dramatic flow before striding after him.

The Resolve roared to life, lifting off just as Dastar-Lee's TIE fighter locked onto us.

"Star Stalker!" his voice crackled over comms, dripping with moustache-fueled rage.

"Persistent as ever," I mused, sliding into the co-pilot's seat.

"He's locked weapons!" Reginald barked, fingers flying over the controls.

"No, no," I said, watching the TIE close in, "let him get just a little bit closer."

Reginald's head whipped toward me, "Monty, are you insane?"

"Possibly," I admitted.

Outside, Dastar-Lee's fighter lined up for the kill, cannons glowing. I flicked on our comms.

"Dastar-Lee, my dear boy, before you obliterate us,"

"Die, Stalker!" he roared.

"Well, that's rude," I replied.

His cannons powered up… then sputtered with an unpleasant whine. A flicker of red lights danced across his console before the TIE shuddered violently, yawing out of control.

"What's happening?!" Dastar-Lee's voice cracked with panic.

"Oh dear," I said sweetly, "has something gone wrong?"

From the pocket of my cape, I produced a small coupler, the very one I'd liberated from his TIE during the chaos in the hangar, and set it gently on the console before me.

Reginald glanced at it, then, with a grunt, dropped a handful of TIE fighter components beside it: wires, circuits, and what looked suspiciously like an ion regulator.

We locked eyes and smiled in mutual appreciation.

"Reginald," I said, "what possessed you to do that?"

He leaned back, arms crossed. "Great minds think alike."

"Now," I said with a smug nod, "let's not get too ahead of ourselves, Reggie. This only means I won first."

"Curse you, Star Stalker!"

I turned back to the viewport just in time to see Dastar-Lee's TIE lurch sideways, sputter like an asthmatic bantha, and then, gloriously, power down completely.

His voice, now far more panicked, screeched over the comms.

"You! Star Stalker!"

The fighter drifted helplessly into the void, a pathetic, moustache-shaped silhouette shrinking against the stars.

I let out a slow, satisfied breath and brushed a few imaginary flecks of dust from my lapel. "Well," I said, "that went beautifully."

Reginald's expression was unreadable. After a long pause, he muttered, "Congratulations, Monty. Another successful mission."

I grinned. "Yes, yes, it was."

With that, I leaned back in my seat as the *Dashing Resolve* jumped into hyperspace, leaving one very humiliated moustachioed pilot to bob helplessly in the cold dark. A fine evening's work, capped by the galaxy's finest moustache.

15
GRIDLUCK AND THE GASTRONOMIC TRIAL OF TARGOS MINOR

The assignment came directly from Mon Mothma herself, which should have been my first clue that something was off.

We met in her private briefing chamber aboard the diplomatic cruiser *Auralis*. The room was elegant and understated, much like the Chancellor herself, with smooth lighting, star charts lining the walls, and the faint scent of polished wood and dried tea leaves.

She gestured for me to sit. "I need someone tactful for a small mission to Targos Minor."

"Targos Minor," I repeated. "Outer Rim, agricultural zone, largely neutral in the current conflict. Known for community cohesion, fermented beverages, and frequent civic holidays."

"Exactly," she said with a slight smile. "You've read the brief."

"Why not send Andor?" I asked. "He's excellent at these quiet outreach assignments."

Mothma's smile did not waver, but something was flickering behind her eyes, a private joke, perhaps, or the ghost of a memory. "Cassian lacks the… stomach for this particular mission. And patience. And, frankly, the cultural elasticity."

"Elasticity?"

"You'll see."

I hesitated. "Is there something I should be aware of?"

"There is a community event the locals are quite proud of. Your attendance would be seen as a meaningful gesture."

"What sort of event?"

"Oh, nothing dangerous," she said, looking back to her datapad with carefully arranged neutrality. "Just… immersive. They're very proud of their traditions."

I narrowed my eyes. "I notice you've used the word 'proud' twice now."

"Three times, actually," she said absently.

There was a pause.

"Will Reginald be joining you?" she asked.

"Of course. He's eager to stretch his legs. Or, at least, he didn't say no in time."

Mothma stood. "You'll do well, Montgomery. You're adaptable. Observant. You don't panic under stress. Just remember: diplomacy isn't always a matter of high politics. Sometimes, it's simply about showing up. And staying seated."

That line haunted me more than it should have.

The community center on Targos Minor was, in a word, humble. The walls were constructed from recycled freighter panels, the serial numbers still half-visible beneath uneven coats of blue paint. The seating was a mismatched collection of plastoid fold-outs, the air rich with the scent of overboiled kelp broth and whatever had died in the ventilation system years ago.

On a low stage, an Ithorian announcer hunched over a malfunctioning vocal amplifier, wheezing into the mic like a deflating kloo horn.

"Wzzzz, grid number seven. That'sss seven on the upper spiral. Sssso noted."

The crowd of local civilians responded with a collective hiss, as if the announcement were sacred and mildly disappointing.

We were seated halfway down the center aisle, flanked by creatures of varying appendage counts, all riveted to glowing hexagonal game boards in front of them. The game was called Gridluck, an ancient Targan pastime with rules no offworlder truly understood. It involved a board of luminous tiles, some kind of spiraling numerical logic, and sudden outbursts of noise when someone thought they'd won

Reginald squinted at his board. "Do we... mark something?"

"No," I said. "The tiles mark themselves. It's psychically attuned to the caller's tonal emissions."

"You just made that up."

"I absolutely did."

Another number was called. A chime rippled through the hall. One of my hexagons flickered green.

Reginald leaned in. "I think I'm winning."

"You can't win until someone screams 'Flush the moons.'"

"What does that mean?"

"I haven't the slightest idea."

We might have continued like that, quietly baffled, respectfully bored, had it not been for the creature across from us.

It was a plump, gelatinous being with swollen features and damp, sagging skin that pulsed faintly with every breath. It had spent most of the evening half-conscious, its gill flaps fluttering out of sync, its eyelids halfway closed. But as the rounds progressed and the hall grew warmer, it began to stir.

It began with a wet, chesty rumble, like soup boiling in a metal pipe. The creature sat upright, gurgled, and then, without warning, unleashed a violent sneeze so forceful it sent a sheet of greenish phlegm exploding across the table.

The sound it made was less like a sneeze and more like someone stepping on a sack of eels.

A high-velocity blast of mucus sprayed across its own Gridluck card, the table, and parts of the unfortunate individuals seated on either side. The volume of fluid defied logic. It clung to surfaces like glue and dripped in viscous strings, shimmering under the overhead lights. Bits of half-digested food, or possibly teeth, were suspended in the slime.

I recoiled. Reginald let out a strangled gasp. "Oh, oh stars. Monty. It hit my boot."

"Don't move," I said. "If you don't move, it can't see you."

"It's not alive, wait, it's moving!"

"It's dripping, Reginald. Dripping is not movement. Dripping is gravity's mercy."

Another sneeze rocked the table. This one louder. Wetter. A glob of mucus landed on the card with a splatter so heavy it sent a nearby drink wobbling. The creature's eyes rolled back. It slumped in its hover-chair, head tilted, mouth ajar, phlegm slowly oozing from both nostrils like lava from a doomed volcano.

A young Besalisk in a janitor's vest approached, took one look at the situation, and, without a word, slapped a biohazard sticker on the creature's forehead and began wheeling it away. Behind it, a slime trail glistened   mournfully.
Reginald's hand trembled. "It touched the edge of my cup. Monty. I was drinking that."

"You weren't drinking that. You were drinking something next to that. Technically different liquids."

"My soul is unclean."

But the worst was yet to come.

From the back of the room, an elderly alien shuffled toward the table. Species unclear. She had knobby limbs, translucent skin like wet parchment, and a dozen blinking eyes arranged in a gentle spiral across her forehead.

Without hesitation, and without so much as a "pardon me," she picked up the slime-covered Gridluck card with her bare, bony hands, the mucus stretching in long strands between her fingers.

Reginald made a noise I can only describe as a dry scream. I tried not to breathe.

The old woman squinted at the glowing, dripping card. Then, in what felt like slow motion, she began wiping the surface off with her palms, spreading the phlegm around in wide, patient circles. She rubbed her hands together thoughtfully. A large green glob dangled from her pinky, then snapped and landed on her sleeve.

She did not react.

"I think I blacked out for a second," Reginald whispered. "Did she just massage the card clean with her flesh?"

"She did."

"She's not stopping."

"No, she's… she's doubling down."

The woman nestled into the now-abandoned mucus seat, smoothed the card down, and clicked her tongue in satisfaction. Just then, a tile lit up on her grid.

She raised one shriveled hand and rasped, "Flush the moons."

The room exploded in applause.

Confetti rained from a trapdoor above. Someone handed her a gift basket filled with pickled meat tubes and a holographic voucher for ten free Gridluck games. The Ithorian announcer made a wet honking noise of congratulations.

Reginald was trembling. "I'm going to throw up. I swear to every celestial alignment in the Mid-Rim, I'm going to absolutely,"

"Control yourself," I hissed. "We're diplomats."

"I'm about to diplomatically projectile vomit. Onto your boots. Hold still so I can aim."

We sat in stunned silence.

The woman continued playing, her hands still damp, her expression serene. Gridluck resumed.

I turned to Reginald. "Let's never speak of this again."

He nodded, pale as lunar chalk. "I need to burn this memory out of my head with a laser scalpel."

"You can go first."

"I think I inhaled a particle. I feel it… in my throat. It's there. Living. Breeding."

But we didn't leave because our diplomatic shuttle was still locked. And also because the pilot was seated three tables over and had just shouted, "Flush the moons, baby!"

Targos Minor would haunt our dreams.

We met with Ambassador Cleet outside the community hall, beneath a corrugated awning that flapped in the planet's dry breeze. He was a tall, angular being with shimmering opal skin and a slow, ceremonial blink. His robes were crusted with celebratory confetti and what I hoped was broth.

Reginald stood beside me, listing slightly. His face had the pallor of wet flour. One hand clutched a foil-lined illness bag, the other was wrapped in a damp cloth he'd soaked in antiseptic spray and pressed to his upper lip for the last twenty minutes.

"Ambassador," I said with a polite incline of the head, "on behalf of the delegation, thank you for hosting us at your… vibrant civic gathering."

Cleet beamed. "It was our deepest honor to welcome offworld participants. Few visitors are bold enough to join in Gridluck. Even fewer stay through a full-cycle round. You are now, officially, part of Targan cultural memory."

Reginald made a soft moaning sound. I elbowed him.

The ambassador continued, gesturing toward the hall. "You stood your ground during what we refer to locally as a Great Purge Moment. A rare phenomenon. Celebrated. It's the omen of renewal."

"Ah," I said carefully. "Yes, we… felt the spiritual cleansing."

Reginald whispered, "I think I have spiritual bacteria in my bloodstream."

"We have already submitted your names to the next volume of Civic Champions. You'll each receive a commemorative plaque," Cleet added proudly. "One engraved, one embossed. They will arrive in fourteen to sixteen planetary weeks."

"That's… extremely generous," I said, through clenched teeth.

Reginald leaned closer. "Monty, if that plaque smells even faintly like mucus, I'm launching it into a star."

Cleet turned to Reginald, his smile wide and unblinking. "You, sir, displayed remarkable intestinal fortitude."

"Not… not really," Reginald croaked. "I think I ruptured mine."

"You did not flee. Many have fled. Some have fainted. One once self-immolated in the hallway."

"That… feels relatable."

A brief pause. Somewhere behind us, someone sneezed. Reginald flinched like he'd been shot.

Cleet clasped our hands, phlegm still visibly clinging to one of his cuffs. "Thank you, honored guests. May your next visit be blessed with equally fertile fluids."

"We'll… pencil it in," I said.

As we boarded the shuttle and the hatch sealed behind us, Reginald collapsed into his seat and immediately began rubbing disinfectant onto his temples.

"I swear to every star in the sector," he muttered, "if even one droplet made it inside me… "

"It didn't."

"I can feel it fermenting in my soul."

"You're being dramatic."

"I've seen things, Monty. It blinked. The mucus blinked."

I stared out the viewport as the engines warmed. The community hall below shrank with distance.

"I'm never playing gridluck again," I said

Reginald groaned. "I'm never eating again."

We left Targos Minor in silence. Some victories are quiet. Some are sticky.

This one was both.

16
CSL'S JEWEL: THE HALCYON

When one has saved the galaxy a handful of times and done so with impeccable style, it is only natural, dear reader, to treat oneself. For me, Montgomery Starstalker, dashing adventurer, enterprising gentleman, and groomer of galactic proportions, no humble shore leave would do. My taste demands the extraordinary, the elegant, the unapologetically luxurious. And so, when the stars aligned, I booked passage aboard the legendary *Halcyon*, pride of Chandrila Star Lines, jewel of the Core Worlds, and the only vessel in the galaxy whose guest manifest can rival my own in terms of prestige.

From the moment the *Dashing Resolve* eased into the docking bay of the Chandrila Star Line terminal, I knew this would be no ordinary journey. Beyond the bustle of the spaceport, the jewel of our destination awaited, the legendary *Halcyon*, pride of Chandrila Star Lines, gleaming high above the planet's atmosphere like a floating palace.

Reginald Starjammer, my ever-faithful mechanic and occasional voice of reason, eyed the departure concourse with his usual blend of suspicion and disdain.

"Ship's a ship, Monty," he muttered, hoisting his travel pack as if it contained his disapproval along with his tools.

I placed a hand on his shoulder, speaking with the gravitas of a man delivering a profound truth.

"A ship, dear Reginald, is never just a ship when it comes with Alderaanian brandy older than most moons, a holo-spa that can make even a Rodian look presentable, and the sort of company that might mistake us for legitimate aristocracy. This… " I declared, gesturing toward the shimmering passenger shuttle that would ferry us upward, "is not mere transport, it is the opening act to a performance in which I am, naturally, the star."

We boarded the shuttle, its interior a plush blend of velvet seating and panoramic viewports that framed the planet shrinking below. As the repulsors hummed and we rose through the cloud layers, the *Halcyon* emerged in full, an elegant colossus adrift among the stars. Even I, Montgomery Starstalker, momentarily abandoned my practiced nonchalance.

Reginald, however, merely grunted.

"Looks expensive."

"Luxury always does," I replied, straightening my cape for the grand docking. "Now, do try not to look like you're here to fix the plumbing."

The shuttle aligned with the *Halcyon's* docking collar, the doors sliding open to reveal the ship's gilded arrival hall, the beginning of a voyage that, I already suspected, the galaxy would be talking about for years.

Reginald muttered something under his breath about me needing a vacation from myself, which I chose to interpret as agreement, while R2-DPR, our ever-dapper astromech, rolled along behind us whistling what I could have sworn was the jaunty opening of a Corellian waltz.

The *Halcyon's* atrium was nothing short of breathtaking. Towering ceilings arched high above us, inlaid with intricate designs that shimmered like constellations caught mid-dance. Holo-light fixtures mimicked the gentle twinkle of far-off starfields, while the air was alive with the mingled voices of passengers from every corner of the galaxy. Service droids glided between the throngs, bearing trays of glittering, champagne-like flutes filled with beverages that promised sophistication, or at least something with bubbles.

And then, the voice.

"Starstalker."

Rich, melodic, and unmistakable.

I turned, grinning broadly, to find myself face-to-face with Captain Keevan herself. Her uniform was crisp enough to deflect a blaster bolt, her posture radiating command, and yet there was that faint spark in her eyes, the sort that suggested she had already calculated exactly how much trouble I would cause on this voyage, and was bracing for impact.

"Captain Keevan!" I exclaimed, spreading my arms as if to embrace not just her, but the entire atrium. "It's been far too long."

She arched an elegant brow.

"Montgomery… I'd say it's a pleasure to see you, but your reputation usually precedes you. Should I be preparing for trouble?"

I gave her my most innocent smile, the kind that, historically, has led to the evacuation of at least three starports.

"Captain, I'm here purely for leisure. The only kind of trouble you'll find from me will be the delightful sort."

Behind me, Reginald coughed into his hand in a way that sounded suspiciously like "Lies."

Keevan gave me that practiced captain's smile, the kind that says I am both polite and faintly exasperated, before adding, "Try to stay out of trouble, Starstalker. This is a peaceful cruise. It's the 275th anniversary of the Chandrila Star Line."

"Captain, you wound me," I replied, placing a hand over my heart as if she'd fired a blaster bolt straight through it. "Trouble follows me, not the other way around."

Our quarters aboard the *Halcyon* were nothing short of magnificent, with plush furnishings, a simulated hyperspace view drifting lazily past the windows, and a welcome basket that featured artisanal Wookiee chocolates alongside a bottle of Chandrilan Reserve that shimmered with the promise of regrettable decisions. Reginald eyed the bottle with the weary suspicion of a man who knew exactly where the evening might end, while R2-DPR chirped with delight at a small tin of complementary gear oil tucked among the treats.

As I unpacked my bespoke travel wardrobe, silks, capes, and at least one pair of boots that could double as a diplomatic incident, Reginald flipped through the itinerary.

"Gaya's performing tonight," he said, raising an eyebrow. "Apparently it's… a big deal."

"A big deal?" I gasped theatrically. "Reginald, Gaya is a galactic icon! Her voice has inspired rebellions, healed ancient feuds, and once, once! , reconciled two Hutts over an unpaid sabacc debt. She is nothing short of a legend."

"And you," Reginald muttered, "are nothing short of dramatically impaired."

"Precisely why this crew suits me so well," I replied with a grin.

As evening fell, the *Halcyon's* corridors shimmered with warm gold light, guiding us toward the grand dining hall. Tonight was the night, the much-anticipated performance by Gaya herself, and somehow, through a mix of charm, luck, and sheer inevitability, I found myself seated at the Captain's Table.

Captain Keevan sat at my right, ever-composed, her uniform crisp enough to cut transparisteel. Reginald sat to my left, radiating the stiff discomfort of a man who considered luxury dining to be a dangerous distraction from mechanical readiness. R2-DPR occupied the discreet corner near the wine service droid, whistling a tune suspiciously close to "The Blue Bantha Waltz."

When Gaya entered, the room shifted. Her gown caught the light like ripples over a Mon Calamari sunset, and her presence commanded silence before she sang a note. Then her voice soared, rich, liquid, and impossibly precise, weaving tales of unity, of distant worlds, of love found and lost. Here and there, her lyrics curved into something more daring: subtle nods that those in the know could read as rebellion. Keevan's eyes flicked sideways at me once, a silent question. I responded with the smallest smirk.

I may or may not have wiped a tear from my eye during her ballad "Stars Over Chandrila." If I did, Reginald was merciful enough not to comment, though I caught the tiniest upward twitch at the corner of his mouth. By the time she closed her set with her infamous hit "Coaxium," the hall was alive with applause, the air thrumming with collective joy. For a moment, the galaxy seemed to hold its breath.

Then the mood shifted. The applause faltered as Lieutenant Croy entered the hall. His uniform was immaculate, but the man wore his authority like an over-tightened collar; you could practically hear it creak. He scanned the room with a mixture of suspicion and self-importance, his gaze lingering uncomfortably on the Captain's Table. I straightened my posture and tilted my head just enough to let the light catch my moustache's most distinguished curl. If he was looking for trouble, I'd give him refinement.

Keevan's fork hovered halfway to her mouth. "Stay in your seat, Monty," she murmured without looking at me.

"Of course," I whispered back. "I always follow orders… unless they're inconvenient."

Croy's boots clicked across the floor, each step a precise percussion, until he stopped directly behind me.

Then he addressed the entire hall.

"Ladies and gentlemen," Croy sneered, his voice dripping with authority. "As a representative of the First Order, I must remind you all that any support for insurgent activities is a crime punishable by,"

His speech was cut short by a perfectly aimed spray of sparkling wine, courtesy of R2-DPR. The droid chirped with feigned innocence, its dome spinning in mock confusion as the glittering beverage rained down upon the Lieutenant's polished uniform.

The dining hall erupted in laughter. Croy, dripping with bubbly and seething like a faulty blaster coil, locked eyes with me.

"Montgomery Starstalker," he growled. "I should have known."

I raised my own glass in a leisurely toast, moustache impeccable under the golden light. "Always a pleasure, Lieutenant. Droids these days have a mind of their own. Sorry, old boy, welcome to the party."

A ripple of chuckles followed, but Keevan's eyes told me I'd just signed my name on the evening's trouble ledger. And she wasn't wrong.

It was only the beginning.

What had started as a refined holiday would soon unravel into an adventure unlike any other. Because even amidst the chandeliers and champagne of the *Halcyon*, whispers of danger and intrigue lurked in every shadow.

And if the galaxy needed a hero… well, who better than Montgomery Starstalker?

17
A SECRET STONE

Dinner had concluded in a swirl of decadent dishes and even more decadent gossip. Now, dessert was arriving beneath the soft, golden glow of the *Halcyon's* chandeliers, a procession of sugar sculptures and glowing pastries so elaborate they might have been stolen from a Naboo opera set. One confection resembled the twin moons of Vandor balanced on spun-sugar comet tails. Another pulsed gently with edible starlight.

Even Lieutenant Croy, still nursing his wounded pride and a distinctly damp uniform, had thawed enough to nibble a delicate fruit tart, but he did so while continuing to send me the kind of glances that said, I am definitely plotting your arrest, but this crème pâtissière is exquisite.

Reginald Starjammer sipped his after-dinner caf like a man suspicious of both the drink and the entire notion of dessert. "Monty," he said, eyeing the sugar-sculpture centerpiece as if it might explode, "if you'd told me we'd be dining on Chandrilan soufflé, hot-spice chocolate, and in this level of pomp, I would've stayed on the *Dashing Resolve* to change the oil filters."

"Reggie," I said, taking in the glittering hall and the hum of a hundred conversations, "you can't polish an oil filter to reflect the soul. This… " I gestured to the chandeliers, the music, the faint scent of caramelized victory in the air, "… this is how the galaxy should be saved, in style."

I smirked. "Nonsense, Reggie. Life's too short to skip dessert. Besides, you've earned a treat after surviving the Gridluck fiasco."

Reginald froze mid-sip of his caf, his face tightening as though the very word had a stench. "That wasn't a fiasco, Monty. That was biohazard trauma."

I waved a hand. "Semantics. A few airborne… particles never killed anyone."

He set his cup down with a pointed clink. "It sneezed in my drink."

"And yet here you are," I said cheerfully, taking another bite of soufflé.

Before he could hurl back whatever scathing remark was forming, the energy of the room shifted. Conversations slowed, heads turned, and the air took on that subtle hum that precedes the arrival of someone extraordinary.

Gaya, the Twi'lek icon herself, glided into the dining hall, her lekku adorned with delicate silver chains that caught the chandelier light like threads of starlight. Her gown shimmered with iridescent blues and purples, each movement sending ripples of color down its flowing fabric. She carried herself with the kind of grace that wasn't learned, it was born, shaped by a lifetime of commanding rooms without raising her voice.

Beside her was Raithe Kole, her manager, who looked like he could talk his way into or out of anything, with the roguish smirk of someone who probably had.

They crossed the floor without hesitation and slipped into the two empty chairs at our table as though they'd been expected.

"Mind if we join you?" Raithe asked, his tone smooth, his grin calculated. "I hear this is the most… entertaining table in the hall."

I set down my fork with a practiced flourish. "In that case, you've chosen extremely wisely."

Maya's eyes found mine, and I'll admit, for a fraction of a second, I forgot my next line. Her gaze had that rare quality of making you feel both seen and measured, like she already knew what you were going to say.

Raithe spoke in a lower tone, his words wrapped in the kind of charm that made you lean in without thinking. "We have business to discuss, and this table looks the sweetest in more ways than one."

I gestured expansively. "Be my guest. There's always room for friends. And by the look in your eye, Raithe… trouble."

He flashed a sly grin. "Guilty as charged."

Gaya leaned forward, her voice soft enough to disappear beneath the clink of dessert forks around us. "Montgomery. Reginald. We're in need of your… particular brand of expertise."

"You mean," I said, straightening in my chair, "impeccable style and dashing heroics?" I speared a candied blossom from my plate and popped it in my mouth.

"Precisely," Raithe said, smirking. "Half of it, at least."

"It's about the Hayananeya."

Reginald nearly spat out his caf. "The Hayananeya? As in the legendary artifact said to hold more secrets than the Jedi Archives?"

Gaya's nod was slow, deliberate. "We've confirmed it's here, hidden aboard the *Halcyon* itself. Inside the ship's hyperspace compass. It's currently on display in the atrium, behind reinforced transparisteel, and protected by a very high-tech alarm system."

Gaya's eyes softened, the playful gleam giving way to something older and heavier. "The Hayananeya is more than an artifact," she said. "For my people, it's a starstone, carved from the heart of Ryloth's twin moons and passed from clan to clan for centuries. It's said to hold the navigational memories of a hundred Twi'lek caravans, the songs of our migrations, and the names of those we lost to slavery. To others in the galaxy, it's simply a priceless relic. To us… " She rested a hand lightly on the table. "It's a piece of who we are."

Raithe leaned in, voice low enough to be swallowed by the hum of dessert chatter. "We have reason to believe the stone was… let's say acquired under circumstances not entirely aligned with galactic law. It's being paraded here as a glittering showpiece for this anniversary cruise to Batuu." He shot a glance at Gaya. "She and I intend to liberate it and see it returned to her people before certain unsavoury forces, imperial collectors, private syndicates, decide to claim it for themselves."

I turned to Reginald, who had set his cup of caf down with the deliberate care of a man who suspected the conversation had just become his problem. "And how exactly," I asked, "do you plan to pull off the galaxy's most stylish heist?"

Raithe's grin widened, all teeth and trouble. "We've found a flaw in the compass's security matrix, a quirk in the alarm system's calibration. It has keys to weight, electromagnetic signature, and internal temperature. If we insert a decoy matching those parameters exactly, we can swap the real Hayananeya without setting off so much as a polite beep."

"That," Gaya said, fixing me with a gaze as rich and sharp as her singing voice, "is where you come in. Word around the ship is you have a particularly resourceful astromech and a mechanic who can make miracles from scrap. We could use both. And," she added with a slow smile, "you do have a reputation for causing… memorable distractions."

Reginald drummed his fingers on the table, wearing the sort of face that tried to say reluctant but instead whispered intrigued. "A decoy stone, huh? Where do we get one of those?"

"We have a contact on Batuu," Raithe explained. "Her name is Zabaka, a Toydarian toymaker with an eye for flawless replicas. She can craft something convincing enough to fool the compass's sensors, but we can't exactly meet her while Captain Keevan is keeping tabs on all her guests."

Gaya leaned closer, her voice dropping to a hush that barely reached over the clink of dessert spoons. "The plan is simple. When the *Halcyon* docks at Black Spire Outpost tomorrow, Zabaka will board briefly under the guise of official business and slip us the decoy. Then, during my performance in the atrium, I'll create a suitably dramatic distraction. The crowd's eyes will be on me, Raithe, and Monty will make the swap."

Reginald arched a brow. "And if something goes wrong?"

I offered a breezy shrug, though I could already feel my pulse quickening at the thought of the risk. "Then we improvise," I said. "Wouldn't be the first time I've had to improvise in the face of Imperial entanglement... in front of an audience."

Gaya's lips curved into a determined smile.

"All we need is your help, Monty. We trust you."

I made a show of stroking my moustache, as though I were weighing the moral implications, when in truth my mind was already spinning with possibilities.

"How," I said at last, "could I possibly say no to the galaxy's greatest singer... and its suavest scoundrel?"

Raithe gave an exaggerated bow from his seat. "You flatter me."

"Have your people contact Zabaka," I instructed Reggie. "Once she's on board, I'll need you to handle any last-minute modifications. Make sure the decoy stone's readings match the real Hayananeya's exactly. R2–DPPR can manage the mapping of the atrium's security grid."

Reggie sighed in that way he does when he wants me to believe he's annoyed, but the spark in his eyes betrayed him.

A hush fell over our table. The hum of conversation and the clink of utensils drifted around us, punctuated by Lieutenant Croy's loud complaint that someone had "mysteriously" pilfered his dessert fork, almost certainly courtesy of one of Raithe's discreet little distractions.

"Tomorrow night," Raithe said at last, leaning back with that rogue's grin. "Halfway through Gaya's encore."

"Perfect," Gaya whispered, reaching for a delicate pastry. "Just don't miss your cue."

The four of us exchanged a conspiratorial look as I raised my glass in a silent toast. The stage was set. By this time tomorrow, the Hayananeya would be free of its transparisteel prison, and no one, especially Lieutenant Croy, would be the wiser.

As dessert drew to a close, we parted with careful nonchalance. My heart was thrumming with the familiar pulse of danger and intrigue. After all, nothing says "holiday" quite like an impossible heist on a luxury starcruiser.

18

A DRINK ON THE WRONG SIDE

It was still the same starry evening aboard the *Halcyon* when Reginald and I decided to pay a visit to the famed Sublight Lounge. After all, plotting a high-stakes heist was thirsty work, and I had heard rumors of a beverage garnished with genuine Felucian glow-leaves. How could any man of taste resist?

We made our way through the atrium, the hum of conversation blending with the soft, ever-present thrum of the ship's engines. My eyes, however, drifted, inevitably, to the hyperspace compass on display. Its transparisteel casing shimmered under soft, reverent lighting, casting faint glints across the polished floor. A thrill of anticipation slid down my spine at the thought of our upcoming liberation of the Hayananeya.

But that thrill was quickly tempered by the sight of a First Order uniform stationed near the entrance to the Sublight Lounge.

If it isn't, ah, oh dear, you'll have to remind me of your name, I said, tilting my head with exaggerated innocence.

Lieutenant Croy turned on his polished heel, boots squeaking on the immaculate deck. His expression wavered between irritation and forced politeness.

"It's Croy," he said with clipped precision.

"Lieutenant Troy," I replied warmly, ignoring the correction, "right, of course! Such a memorable name. Forgive me, I've had a rather busy day."

Reginald cleared his throat, leaning in and murmuring, "Monty, you know it's,"

I waved him off conspiratorially. "Let the man speak, Reggie. I'm sure Lieutenant Troy has something important on his mind."

Croy's eye twitched. "It's Croy. With a C."

"Decoy, you say? Fascinating," I said, snapping my fingers as though finally catching the correct pronunciation. "Apologies, my dear Lieutenant, it's been an awfully eventful evening. Please, carry on."

Reginald pursed his lips, trying and failing to suppress a grin. "Yes, do carry on, Lieutenant Joy."

Croy cleared his throat, gripping his hat as though it might anchor his patience. "Captain Starstalker, I've been observing your… presence on this voyage. You and your companions are quite," He paused, searching for the right word. "… spirited."

"The First Order values individuals with… shall we say… influence."

I rested one elbow on the plush bannister overlooking the atrium, leaning into the word as though it were the opening note of an aria. "Influence, you say? Why, I'm flattered." I turned to Reginald with mock solemnity. "You heard that, old friend, the good Lieutenant Ploy thinks we have influence."

Reginald snorted. "Influence, style, same thing, right?"

Lieutenant Croy forced a tight smile. "We in the First Order are prepared to reward those who pledge their loyalty. Imagine, front-row status in the new order. A galaxy free from the chaos of rebels and smugglers. You could be part of something greater."

I tapped my chin, giving an exaggerated display of contemplation. "Something greater, you say? That would be appealing… if I didn't find your colour scheme so tragically dreary. Honestly, Lieutenant Coy, tell me, do you ever wake up yearning for a pop of colour in your wardrobe?"

His cheeks flushed the faintest shade of pink. "Our uniforms reflect discipline and unity," he said stiffly. "We don't need… flare to enforce order."

"Discipline, a noble concept," I conceded with a gracious nod, "but I do prefer a galaxy where one can choose their own style. Don't you think a splash of crimson on those trousers would really bring out your cheekbones?"

Reginald muttered, "Here we go," into his calf, while Croy's lips pressed so thin they could have been a single line of Imperial regulation text.

Lieutenant Croy drew himself up taller, clutching his datapad as though it were a lifeline. "If you were truly to embrace the First Order, Captain Starstalker," he pressed on, "you could wield influence over others… enjoy a certain leniency in your travels. I'm sure a man of your… resourcefulness would benefit from fewer Imperial entanglements."

I pretended to mull it over, stroking my waxed moustache. "Leniency is lovely," I admitted, "but I have a personal policy about freedom of movement, and the aesthetic wonders of the galaxy. I'd hate to be restricted to the black-and-white palette of your brig should I ever… borrow something interesting."

Croy's eyebrow arched sharply. "Borrow something interesting?"

"Hypothetically, of course, Lieutenant Hoy." I winked. "I'm simply saying, if I stumbled across a priceless artefact that might be used for the greater good, I'd rather not be bogged down filling out Imperial paperwork about it."

Reginald muttered, "And there it is," under his breath, while R2-DPR gave an approving chirp. He gave me a pointed look, and I decided, magnanimously, to change the subject. I bowed slightly, one hand to my chest.

"I do appreciate the offer, truly, Lieutenant, but I'm afraid my loyalty lies elsewhere… somewhere closer to the quaint notion of, oh, what's the word? Ah, yes, actual freedom."

Croy's mouth tightened into a thin white line. "You'll regret turning your back on the First Order," he said, voice low and dangerous. "But for now, I'll keep your… disloyalty off the record."

"What a dear you are, Lieutenant Roy," I replied, letting my voice drip with mock sincerity. "Your benevolence knows no bounds. Come along, Reginald, time to wet our whistles in the Sublight Lounge."

As we swept past him, I caught the faint sound of Croy muttering through clenched teeth, "It's CROY. With a C."

Reginald finally let out the chuckle he'd been suppressing.

"Well done, Monty. Now we have the Imperials watching our every move."

I gave a light shrug. "Better to have them watch us here than snooping around behind our backs. Besides, if anyone can handle a spotlight, it's me."

He shook his head. "You're lucky you're charming, or you'd already be in detention."

"Charming is my middle name," I said smugly, pushing, well, attempting to push open a door that didn't exist. I quickly recovered with a smooth step into the curved archway. "Now," I declared, "let's see what sort of delightful cocktails they have on offer. Something tall, colorful, and potent enough to make me forget our little brush with, ah, yes, fascism."

∗∗∗

The Sublight Lounge welcomed us like a scene from one of the more decadent chapters of my life. The lighting was a soft interplay of blues and golds, casting a warm sheen over glassware and the polished bar. A trio of Bith musicians played a languid, hypnotic melody from the corner, their long fingers dancing over instruments as if coaxing secrets from the air.

Passengers lounged in deep chairs, some lost in murmured conversation, others studying the shimmering drinks in their hands as though divining the future from the bubbles. We claimed a small table with a view of the bar, strategically, of course.

A server droid glided over, its polished chrome chassis gleaming in the ambient light. Moments later, two glasses were placed before us: mine, the famed Felucian Glowleaf Fizz, the rare leaves casting a soft green radiance across my gloves; Reginald's, a no-nonsense Corellian brandy, served in a heavy glass with no garnish, no frills.

"See, Reggie," I said, raising my drink, "this is the kind of refinement a hero deserves after a day's work, or in our case, a day's preparation for a night's work."

He narrowed his eyes slightly. "You mean the job tomorrow?"

"My dear Reginald," I smiled over the rim of my glass, "you make it sound so… criminal. I prefer to think of it as liberation. With panache."

19
OF CAPTAINS AND FANS

The Felucian Glowleaf Fizz shimmered in the dim light, the leaves in its garnish releasing faint motes of gold with each swirl. Somewhere behind us, the smooth pulse of jizz shifted into a slower, more sultry number, the kind of tune that coaxed conversation down to conspiratorial murmurs. A gentle warmth settled over the Sublight Lounge, not from the drink, though that certainly didn't hurt, but from the heady blend of perfume, polished brass, and the soft whir of the droid bartender sliding from table to table.

Reginald nursed his brandy with the air of a man pretending he wasn't enjoying himself. "Well," he muttered, "at least this place doesn't smell like coolant and singed wiring."

I leaned back in the booth, taking in the scene, the star-skate paneling shimmering like ripples of moonlight, the easy laughter of passengers still glowing from dinner, the occasional appreciative glance toward my moustache, which tonight was nothing short of a galactic landmark. Somewhere near the back, a Rodian was losing badly at sabacc to a Trandoshan who clearly had more cards than the deck allowed. All in all, it was the perfect picture of leisure… the kind that never lasts for me.

Right on cue, the music swelled, a subtle signal that the room's attention was about to be drawn elsewhere. And then she appeared. Captain Keevan stepped through the lounge's arched entry, tall and sharp as a vibroblade, her Pantoran features calm but carrying an undercurrent of urgency. Even through the crowd, I caught the exact moment her gaze locked on me.

"Montgomery," she said, her voice warm but underpinned with quiet urgency as she slid into the booth across from us.

"Captain," Reginald greeted, tipping an imaginary hat with exaggerated politeness.

I had been preparing to regale her with the full and glorious account of my verbal fencing match with Lieutenant Croy, but the measured look in her eyes told me this was not a casual social call. I leaned forward slightly, smoothing my moustache into its most diplomatic arc.

"To what," I asked, "do I owe the pleasure?"

For the briefest moment, her gaze lingered on the glass of Shayne Reserve in my hand, perhaps imagining it for herself, before she set her shoulders. "I need your help."

That earned her my full attention. Captain Keevan's expression was as composed as ever, but the edge in her voice betrayed a flicker of unease. "The First Order's presence on this voyage has me… uneasy. Croy's security detail is small, but they're already testing boundaries. This cruise is meant to be a celebration, Montgomery. I will not have it turned into a parade of intimidation."

Reginald, arms folded, gave a slow nod. "And you're worried Croy will turn it into exactly that."

"Exactly," Keevan said. "You're a decorated pilot. Rumor has it you've flown more missions for the resistance than most people have flown commercial. You have a particular… aptitude for unpredictable situations. I could use that on my side."

I couldn't help the grin tugging at my lips. "Captain, flattery will get you everywhere. Though I must warn you, some say it's my moustache that does most of the heavy lifting."

Her mouth curved ever so slightly. "I've noticed it does seem to have a morale-boosting effect. From what I've observed, the passengers can't stop talking about 'the gallant man with the impeccable moustache.'"

"It's the wax," I said with a wink. "Montgomery's Magnificent, available soon in select systems. But enough about my facial hair. You're asking me… to keep an eye on the First Order?"

"I'm asking you to be ready," she replied, her tone sharpening. "If they push too far, I want someone who can respond quickly and creatively. And I suspect you excel in both."

"Well," I said, swirling the last sip of my Glowleaf Fizz, "creativity is my middle name. Right after 'Charming.'"

Reginald muttered, "And just before 'Trouble.'"

I ignored him entirely. "Consider your request accepted, Captain. The moustache and I are at your service."

Keevan's eyes softened, just a fraction. "Then let's hope we won't need you, Montgomery. But if we do… " She left the sentence unfinished, her meaning hanging in the air between us before she rose. Keevan held my gaze a moment longer, then gave the faintest of nods. "Thank you, Montgomery. I won't forget this. Just remember, we're here to ensure the safety of everyone on board."

"Understood, Captain," I said, tapping my glass gently against hers. "Consider it done."

Her eyes lingered for half a beat more before she straightened, her tall frame cutting a striking figure as she moved toward the lounge exit.

Reginald leaned in just enough to mutter, "Now she's gone and encouraged you."

I opened my mouth to deliver a witheringly charming retort when a young man practically bounded up to our booth, an eager grin spread across his face. His curls bounced as he stopped short, as if he'd just stumbled into the holoreel version of his dreams.

"Excuse me, Captain Starstalker?" he blurted, his voice tripping over itself with excitement.

I leaned back, modestly adjusting my moustache. "The one and only, my good man."

"I'm," he took a quick breath, "I'm Sandro Alamander."

Recognition flickered; the rising musician who'd been warming up the crowd with melodic preludes before Gaya's set. His starry-eyed gaze could have lit the room without the help of the lounge's ambient glow panels.

"I've heard so many stories about you," Sandro continued, hands gesturing wildly. "Your adventures. Your heroism!"

Reginald raised an eyebrow in my direction. "You mean all the tall tales Monty likes to spit about himself."

Sandro shook his head emphatic. "No, I did research! It's all in the Holonet archives, the Battle of Atera, the Skirmish at Kessel's Edge…" He leaned forward, almost reverent. "You're a legend."

I turned a slow, triumphant smile toward Reginald. "Hear that, old friend? A legend."

Clearing my throat to disguise just how flattered I truly felt, I gestured for Sandro to join us. He slid into the booth like an overeager cadet reporting for duty, practically vibrating with excitement.

"Captain Starstalker," he said, leaning in, his voice hushed as if sharing classified intel, "I want to write a song about you, a grand ballad, something that captures the spirit of your bravery. Maybe… maybe I could even perform it tomorrow night in the atrium!"

I swirled my drink thoughtfully, as though I had entire fleets to consider. "Well, I'm certainly honored," I replied, "but I shall be quite occupied tomorrow evening." I tapped my chin, letting my expression grow distant, as though I were weighing matters of galactic import. "Though… a tune praising my gallantry could be a welcome distraction for certain… parties."

Out of the corner of my eye, I caught Reginald's quick glance, sharp, suspicious, but tinged with interest. My mind flicked to the plan with Gaya and Raithe to swap the Hayananeya from its glass prison.

"So, you're willing to let me do it?" Sandro's eyes were wide, hopeful, and entirely oblivious to the wheels turning behind my moustache.

I exchanged a conspiratorial look with Reginald, who gave a resigned shrug. "Monty, if this is what I think it is," he muttered, "you might be onto something."

Turning back to Sandro, I gave him the calm, approving smile of a man accustomed to inspiring entire movements. "Let's just say," I said, lowering my voice, "that if you were to regale the entire ship with a rousing tribute to yours truly tomorrow night, I wouldn't object. You might even find me in the front row… offering creative input."

Sandro practically glowed. "I've got to go write this down, thank you, Captain Starstalker! This is a dream come true!"

I raised my glass in mock solemnity. "For both of us, my boy. For both of us."

As the young musician dashed off, I downed the last of my drink, the gentle fizz and glow-leaf garnish leaving a pleasant warmth in its wake. Tomorrow would be far more than a day of sightseeing on Batuu; we had an artefact to liberate, an Imperial officer to outwit, and now a full-blown musical spectacle in my honour.

"So," Reginald said dryly, "are we done collecting side quests for the evening, or should we invite more chaos to our table?"

I clapped him on the shoulder. "My dear Reginald, chaos finds me whether I invite it or not. Let's just hope a touch of heroics and a well-timed song will be enough to keep the First Order off our backs."

We rose from our booth, the soft clink of glasses and the low hum of conversation following us into the corridor. I caught my own reflection in the polished metal wall, cape draped perfectly, moustache immaculate, and allowed myself a small, knowing smile. Tomorrow was the day of the big heist, and if all went according to plan, no one… not even Lieutenant What's-His-Name… would be the wiser.

20
DROID TALES

The corridor leading to our cabin was hushed, the lights dimmed to a pleasant twilight glow. Even aboard the *Halcyon*, the crew simulated night to encourage rest, though the stars beyond our viewport showed no such hour. R2-DPR rolled ahead, his dome lights pulsing like a discreet invitation for Reginald and me to catch up. The faint hum of the ship's engines was almost hypnotic after the evening's whirl of music, conversation, and subtle sparring with the First Order.

By the time we reached our door, the day's excitement had begun to settle into a drowsy, satisfied warmth. Reginald keyed the panel, and the door slid open with a soft hiss, revealing our quarters, only for both of us to pause at the sight waiting inside.

A lavish gift basket sat atop the table by the viewport, positioned so the starlight spilled across it in a dramatic glow. Even from the doorway, I could see the ornate labeling: Montgomery's Magnificent Moustache Wax™, in a variety of exotic scents, alongside an array of other premium grooming products. Every item bore the elegant crest of the Chandrila Star Line.

Reginald stepped forward and plucked the small card resting against a tin of pomade, reading aloud with one eyebrow arched:

"Compliments of Captain Keevan. Thank you for your support in maintaining the ship's safety."

"Looks like you made an impression, Monty," he said dryly.

"I certainly hope so," I replied, already crossing the room to inspect my bounty. I tipped my head toward the mirror on the wall, admiring how the low light caught the curve of my moustache. "I usually do."

The basket was nothing short of a feast for the face: classic pomades in five distinguished scents, the sandalwood from Scarif smelled positively heroic, alongside beard oils, precision combs, and even a limited-edition *Halcyon* hull polish, allegedly intended for metal surfaces. Naturally, I intended to test it on my boots.

Reginald dropped into the corner chair with a tired groan, stretching his legs toward the viewport. "Well, at least the captain knows how to butter you up."

I grinned. "She understands the importance of morale."

 "That's quite a stash for your 'stache," Reginald quipped, taking stock of the haul.

R2-DPR gave an inquisitive whistle at the array of tins and bottles, tilting his dome as though seriously considering whether any could be repurposed for droid polishing.

"Let's not forget," I said, plucking a small tub of glimmering wax, "there are two of us here who can actually grow facial hair. Though I suppose this means I'll wake up tomorrow looking even more dashing, if that's possible."

Reginald picked up a jar of moustache cream labelled Voscsillian Citrus Delight, inspecting it as though it might be booby-trapped. "I think I'll do a thorough test in the morning. But for now? I'm beat."

He headed for the sleeping alcove, where a cosy bunk was tucked away behind a sleek sliding panel. "Dibs on the bunk," he announced.

R2-DPR warbled a sharp protest, swivelling his head toward the same space.

"There's a charge port right next to it, R2," I reassured, patting the droid's dome. "It'll keep you topped up all night."

The little astromech gave a satisfied beep and trundled into place, plugging in with a soft click. The gentle hum of recharging filled the cabin, a soothing undertone against the quiet.

"I'll take the big bed," I said, stretching luxuriantly and already imagining the dreams of triumph and perfect moustache symmetry that awaited me.

A discreet chime at the cabin door interrupted my reverie. Reginald groaned from his bunk. "If that's Croy, tell him I've defected to the spa."

I slid the door open to find a member of the *Halcyon's* blue crew standing there, their deep blue jacket crisply pressed above tailored grey trousers, posture the very model of efficiency. In gloved hands, the crewman held a small silver tray upon which rested a folded slip of parchment, sealed with deep crimson wax.

"For you, sir," they said with a polite bow, then slipped away down the corridor without another word.

The seal cracked with a satisfying snap, and I unfolded the paper. Raithe Kole's familiar, flowing script covered just a few short lines:

The fireworks at the fountain will be delayed. The petals will not arrive in the garden. We'll tend them ourselves when we walk under the spire. Keep your gloves ready.

—R

I read it twice, then a third time. Outwardly harmless, almost poetic, yet every phrase was laden with meaning. "Fireworks" was the distraction.

"Petals" meant the delivery. "Garden" was the *Halcyon*. And "under the spire"… well, that needed no explanation.

Reginald sat up, hair sticking out like a startled Tooka cat. "That look on your face is never a good sign. What now?"

"Let's just say," I murmured, folding the note and slipping it into my jacket, "our little gardening project just went off-ship."

R2-DPR gave a low, suspicious beep from his charging port. He'd clearly learned by now that my metaphors were never about actual horticulture.

I tucked the folded note from Raithe into my jacket, but the coded words refused to leave my mind. The excitement of the day had me wired, even though my body ached for rest. Reginald was already half-asleep, sprawled on his bunk like a man who'd fought a krayt dragon in his dreams.

Sighing, I wandered over to the small console by the bed and brushed my fingers over one of the glowing controls. Overhead, the built-in screen flickered to life, and the cheerful, stylized face of D3–09, the *Halcyon's* ever-helpful guest relations droid, blinked into view.

"Good evening, honoured guest," D3–09 said in a voice so warm it could butter toast. "Would you like a bedtime story tonight?"

I blinked. "A bedtime story?"

From the bunk, Reginald rolled over, muffling a laugh into his pillow. "Why not, Monty? Seems like your kind of thing."

R2–DPR let out a short beep that I could only interpret as, Do it.

I shrugged. "All right, bedtime story it is."

"Wonderful!" D3–09 chirped, its pixelated smile widening. "This story is brought to you courtesy of the *Halcyon's* Soothing Space Slumbers program." A short jingle played, something between a lullaby and a cruise line commercial, and the screen dissolved into a pastel tableau of cartoonish starships drifting among pink and violet planets.

The droid's voice softened into a singsong narration.

"Once upon a time, there was a brave adventurer named Montgomery Starstalker. He was very heroic. So heroic, in fact, that his moustache sparkled with courage."

I tilted my head at the screen. "Sparkled with courage?" I mouthed to Reginald.

He grinned back at me. "They've done their research."

"One day," D3–09 continued, "Montgomery boarded the grand starcruiser named the *Halcyon*. There he met the noble Captain Keevan, a wise and kind captain who guided the ship through the starry skies. But oh no!"

The screen shifted to an animation of a cartoon Keevan trapped in a narrow corridor, a ludicrously round "space beastie" with googly eyes and too many teeth snarling in her path.

"One evening, Captain Keevan fell into terrible danger, cornered by a fearsome stowaway… "

From his bunk, Reginald smothered another laugh. "If it ends with you defeating it by waxing your moustache into a weapon, I'm leaving."

Montgomery, with his shining moustache and quick thinking, dashed to her rescue, at least, according to D3–09. "He wrestled the snarling space beastie with all his might, determined to save the day!" the droid declared. "And then… he used his trusty grooming comb to tickle the monster into submission. Tickle, tickle, tickle!"

I snorted, biting back a laugh as the cartoon version of me valiantly flourished a moustache comb, subduing a purple blob-like creature that promptly collapsed in a fit of giggles.

"And so," D3–09 continued grandly, "Captain Keevan was saved. She thanked Montgomery with the finest moustache wax in all the galaxy, ensuring his heroic whiskers would forever be remembered among the stars."

On screen, cartoon Keevan and cartoon me posed under a shower of confetti, my animated moustache glowing like a neon halo.

"And from that day on," the droid concluded softly, "the *Halcyon* and Captain Keevan were safe, thanks to the bravery of Montgomery Starstalker… and his magical, wonderful moustache. The end."

The screen faded back to D3–09's friendly face. "Sleep well, travellers. May your dreams be filled with cosmic wonders." Then the panel went dark, leaving the room in the soft amber glow of the cabin lights.

For a moment, there was silence. Then Reginald broke into a fit of laughter. "I didn't know your moustache had magical properties, Monty. Tickling monster space beasties, new technique for the fight books?"

"You know what they say," I replied, stifling a yawn. "A moustache is only as magical as the man who wears it."

Still, it was a rather flattering portrayal. R2–DPR let out a sleepy beep that seemed to translate as, You're both ridiculous, before shutting down for the night

Yawning, I sank deeper into the plush bedding, letting the day's plans tumble out of my mind. Tomorrow would be a test of skill and cunning, collecting Zabaka's decoy stone, orchestrating Gaya's performance, and keeping Lieutenant Croy blissfully ignorant of our true intentions.

If a childlike bedtime story was anything to go by, I had faith I'd find a way to prevail, preferably with a flourish.

"Good night, Reg," I murmured.

"Good night, Monty," came his drowsy reply.

And with that, lulled by the hush of the *Halcyon* and the comforting knowledge that my moustache had never looked better, I closed my eyes, and I drifted off into dreams of cosmic wonders, heroic moments, and tomorrow, brimming with adventure.

21
THE REQUEST

Morning aboard the *Halcyon* arrived not with blaring alarms or the jolt of re-entry, but with a quiet, deliberate elegance. The cabin's lighting shifted from soft twilight to a warm golden glow, imitating the rise of a sun that wasn't really there. It was almost enough to make a man forget there was a heist on the horizon.

I woke from a sleep unusually deep for me, no doubt aided by the bedtime story from D3-09, which still lingered in my mind like a particularly flattering holo-reel. Reginald Starjammer was already at the cabin's small table, hunched over a gleaming component from the *Dashing Resolve's* sublight thrusters. He didn't even look up as he muttered, "Morning, Monty. Hope you're ready for a busy day."

R2-DPR chirped a cheerful greeting from his charging port, his dome rotating just enough to make it clear he'd already been awake and monitoring ship chatter for hours.

I rose, took one look in the mirror, and felt a surge of entirely justifiable pride. My moustache, still holding the perfect sweep I'd cultivated last night, was now enhanced with a subtle sheen thanks to the Captain's gifted Sandalwood of Scarif wax. Truly, an inspiration to moustaches everywhere.

"Breakfast," I declared, stretching like a man about to accept a medal. "We've got a priceless artifact to liberate, a possible run-in with stormtroopers, and a freshly waxed moustache to introduce to the galaxy. Priorities, gentlemen."

The dining hall was alive with the hum of morning excitement, a low but vibrant thrum beneath the crystal glow of chandeliers shaped like swirling starbursts. Beyond the broad viewports, space stretched endlessly, black velvet scattered with diamond-sharp stars, the steady drift of distant nebulae adding faint washes of color to the darkness.

Long buffet counters shimmered under the glow panels, where steaming platters of Banel egg frittatas nestled alongside crystal bowls brimming with the sun-bright fruits of Felucia. Beside them sat towers of delicate spiced Vasha cakes, their sugary edges crisp and curling like the petals of some rare bloom. Servers in crisp Chandrila Star Line uniforms swept between tables with practiced grace, balancing trays of caf, Muja berry juice, and delicacies whose names alone could buy a man's silence in certain ports.

The air was rich with scents, spiced citrus, slow-baked nerf sausage, and the warm vanilla-like aroma of sweetened rootleaf bread. Guests laughed over shared plates, the day's excursion to Batuu already the main topic of eager chatter.

Reginald steered us to a table near one of the largest viewports, where the shifting panorama of the galaxy made even a humble breakfast feel grand. I had barely sat down with my plate of steaming Vasha cakes, perfectly arranged, of course, when a quiet, robed figure seemed to materialize at the edge of our table.

It was one of the Saja: one of those mysterious, Force-sensitive guides who sometimes traveled aboard the *Halcyon*, sharing their knowledge of ancient lore with the curious and the worthy. Their presence seemed to still the air around them, like the moment before a great secret is spoken.

She wore simple, flowing robes, the kind that whispered with each step, and carried herself with an aura that made me instinctively sit up straighter. Her gaze lingered for a curious moment on my moustache, an occupational hazard when one's grooming is this distinguished, before she inclined her head in a respectful bow.

"Montgomery Starstalker," she said in a gentle, measured tone. "Word of your many journeys precedes you."

I managed a friendly smile, careful not to scatter Vasha cake crumbs across my perfectly pressed tunic. "I do get around," I admitted.

"I am Saja Telin," she continued, her voice low and even. "I sense… something aboard this vessel. A convergence of destinies." Her expression was serene, but there was a weight beneath her words. "Captain Keeven has spoken highly of your resourcefulness. There is something I would ask of you."

From across the table, Reginald, who'd been eyeing a suspiciously vibrant Muja fruit, looked up with the familiar wariness of a man about to be volunteered for danger. "What sort of something?"

The Saja pressed her palms together. "There is an artifact aboard this ship, one I believe may hold a deep connection to the Force. If it is what I suspect, its presence here is… dangerous. Such an object should be safeguarded before it draws unwanted attention."

My stomach gave a small, knowing twist. That description sounded very much like the Hayananeya. My eyes flicked to Reginald's, and I saw the same thought mirrored there.

"I see," I said slowly, forcing a measured calm into my voice. "And you'd like us to keep an eye out for it?"

She nodded, her expression serene, but her voice carrying quiet urgency. "Gather what information you can. If it aligns with my suspicions, I would ask you to return with your findings. The Force calls some of us to be guardians… even in small ways."

I placed a hand over my heart, letting just enough gravity slip into my tone to match hers. "Saja Telin, I am honoured you trust me with this. Consider it done."

She bowed slightly and drifted away, her robes whispering against the polished floor. A moment later, she was gone, swallowed into the gentle bustle of the dining hall as though she'd been no more than a breeze stirring the room.

Reginald exhaled slowly, watching her vanish. "That's more than just a random request. She knows something's up."

"Likely," I said, spearing the last bite of my Vasha cake and polishing off the plate with unhurried satisfaction. "And the fact she approached me means it's about to get interesting."

Rising from the table, I straightened my jacket and smoothed the perfect sweep of my moustache. "Come on, old friend. We've got a shuttle to catch, and a few very delicate errands to run before we're back aboard."

The shuttle from the *Halcyon* to Batuu was a sleek, streamlined craft, its curved walls lined with softly glowing strips of light that gave the impression of slipping through a dream. Rows of cushioned seats faced wide panoramic windows, framing the endless black of space that gradually yielded to the mottled greens and browns of the planet below.

Gaya and Raithe Kole had departed earlier on a discreet errand, meeting their contact, the Toydarian artisan Zabaka, to finalize the crafting of the Hayananeya's decoy. That left Reginald, R2-DPR, and me to join a mix of eager families, weathered adventurers, and a few off-duty crew members who had the look of people with "business" in the port below.

As the shuttle broke through the atmosphere, the first spires of Black Spire Outpost emerged from the haze, jagged towers of ancient black rock, their tips catching the morning light. They rose like petrified sentinels above the sprawling forest canopy, their shadows stretching far over the treetops. This was a place steeped in stories, some whispered in hushed tones, some shouted over a pint in the cantina, and the air seemed to hum with equal parts promise and danger.

"Remember the plan," I murmured to Reginald as R2-DPR trilled beside us, his dome swiveling with barely contained impatience. "We meet Gaya at Oga's Cantina, confirm the decoy is ready, and see what other intel we can shake loose."

Reginald gave a curt nod. "And if the First Order's poking around… ?"

I allowed myself a roguish grin. "We do what we do best: improvise… and dazzle them with charm."

Black Spire Outpost pulsed with life. Voices in a dozen languages mingled with the low hum of idling starship engines. The air carried the scent of spiced meats sizzling on open braziers and the sharper tang of exotic fuels. Merchants hawked their wares from colorful stalls, hand-carved trinkets, weathered scrap that might once have belonged to a Jedi's ship, and suspiciously fresh Ronto wraps that dared you to question their origin.

We threaded our way through the crowd toward Oga's Cantina. Its heavy blast doors slid open with a hiss, and the pulse of alien music washed over us, deep bass thumps and syncopated percussion that set the walls humming. Neon light bounced off rows of jewel-toned bottles stacked high behind the bar, each filled with something that promised either delight or regret.

The air inside was thick with the sweet, spicy aroma of Batuu brews and the metallic tang of machinery. Oga herself loomed behind the bar, her keen eyes scanning the crowd like a security droid with a personal grudge. She didn't smile. She never smiled.

Gaya and Raithe were nowhere to be seen. Likely they were tucked away in one of the cantina's shadowed back booths, the kind with just enough privacy to conduct delicate business with a Toydarian artisan. Zabaka wasn't the sort of being you called to the center of a room; if she was here, she'd be somewhere the light couldn't quite reach.

A short, heated exchange at the far end of the bar snagged my attention. A local farmer, broad-shouldered, sunburnt, and wearing the kind of patched clothes that had seen more seasons than most droids, was in a tense standoff with a surly Devaronian. The farmer's voice was low but urgent, the kind of tone a man uses when every credit matters.

"… those crates were for my people," he said, fists clenched. "Families are waiting."

The Devaronian smirked, his horns catching the neon light. "Should've kept a better eye on them, friend. Docking fees aren't cheap."

Reginald, already halfway through his Batuu Brew, glanced at me and groaned. "You can't help yourself, can you?"

I tipped my glass toward him in mock salute. "I have a reputation to maintain."

Moments later, I'd insinuated myself between the two, all polite smiles and disarming charm. It didn't take long, just a few well-placed questions and a casual reference to knowing exactly which warehouse bosses owed me favors to learn the truth. A pack of small-time thugs had "relocated" the farmer's crates to Docking Bay Nine, intending to sell the goods on the quiet.

We slipped out of the cantina, R2-DPR rolling behind us with a distinctly eager trill. The bay wasn't heavily guarded, just two thugs nursing cheap liquor and worse judgment. One of them made the mistake of drawing a blaster.

The shot sizzled past my ear, but before I could even flinch, R2 snapped his shock arm forward, deflecting the bolt into a conveniently placed fuel drum. It burst in a harmless but impressive shower of sparks, and the two would-be toughs bolted like womp rats.

With the coast clear, we retrieved the crate, a battered thing, stamped with the markings of the farming settlement outside the outpost, and wheeled it back through the winding streets to its rightful owner. The farmer's relief was so genuine, it made me feel taller than I already am.

"Let me buy you a round," he insisted, reaching for his credit chip.

I gave him my most gallant bow. "Another time, perhaps. Tonight, we've got our own mischief to attend to."

And with that, Reginald, R2, and I slipped back toward Oga's, the brief detour already fading into the hum of the outpost, just another problem solved in passing, as one does.

22
A CLOSE
CALL

Back in Oga's, we finally spotted Gaya and Raithe tucked into a dimly lit corner booth with a small Toydarian female whose wings thrummed with quiet excitement. Her broad grin suggested she already knew she'd impressed us.

"Zabaka," Raithe said, waving us over. "Artist, genius, and occasional menace to marketplace security."

Zabaka puffed up, holding out a cloth-wrapped bundle with the pride of a jeweler presenting a crown.

"It's perfect," Gaya murmured as we joined them, shifting to make space

Raithe loosened the wrapping just enough for me to catch a glimpse. The decoy stone was exquisite. Same shimmer, same heft, same air of "touch me and a Jedi might appear."

"She's matched the weight and the energy signature exactly," Raithe said in a low voice. "The *Halcyon's* sensors won't know the difference."

Zabaka gave her battered toolbox a fond pat. "My best work yet. I even polished the edges so it looks like it's been handled over time, not fresh from my bench."

"Impeccable," I said, sliding her a discreet container of credits. "It's almost a pity you can't be aboard to see your masterpiece fool the First Order."

That earned me a sharp shake of her head. "Not possible. That officer, Croy, put a stop to any non-passenger boarding while you're docked. No crew guests, no vendors, nothing. He even turned away a merchant with a captain's letter. Whatever you're planning, you'll have to do it without me."

Raithe leaned in, lowering his voice further. "Which means we're changing the swap team. Originally, Monty and I would have handled the stone during Gaya's distraction. Now… it'll be me and Reginald. Monty, you'll still be in play, but your job will be to make sure Croy is glued to your every move."

I set my glass down with a look of tragic acceptance. "So I become bait."

"Not just bait," Gaya said, eyes glittering. "A star attraction. Make him believe you're up to something else entirely."

I smirked. "Darling, misleading a man while looking magnificent is practically my native language."

Zabaka chuckled and slid the bundle toward Raithe. "Then I'll leave you to it. Just don't drop it, moustache-man, or I'll have to charge you double."

"Perish the thought," I said, giving her a parting flourish of my hand. "Your decoy is safe with us, and your name will be sung in legend… possibly to a jizz-wail backing track."

Zabaka's grin widened as she nudged the cloth-wrapped decoy toward me. "There. Straight into the hands of the hero."

I reached for it with an appropriately solemn nod, but before my fingers even grazed the bundle, Reginald's arm shot across the table like a striking viper.

"I'll take that," he said, voice flat but eyes brimming with unspoken accusation.

I pulled back, affronted. "You wound me, old friend. I can be trusted with priceless artefacts."

"You left an actual priceless artefact in a refresher stall on Ord Mantell," Reginald replied without blinking. "And the bartender had to return it to you with tongs."

"That was one time," I said with a huff. "And I was distracted by a very complex drink order."

"Which you also forgot," Reginald added, sliding the decoy carefully into his satchel and tightening the straps as if securing the crown jewels. "Better it stays with someone who doesn't mistake artefacts for drink coasters."

"I have never,"

"You have. Twice," Raithe cut in, smirking.

Gaya hid a smile behind her glass. "Boys, if you're finished, we have a timetable to keep."

Reginald patted the satchel like a doting parent. "Safe and sound."

I leaned back, giving him my most magnanimous wave. "Fine. But when history tells this tale, I expect the part where I heroically agreed to let you carry it to be heavily dramatized."

Reginald lowered his voice as he slipped the decoy into his satchel with the care of a man sealing away a bomb.

"Right. Now we just need to get this back to the *Halcyon* without drawing attention."

I nodded. "And," I added, tapping the side of my nose conspiratorially, "I have a side mission from a certain Saja. We need more intel on the stone's origins, just in case it really does tie into Force-sensitive relics."

Gaya arched an eyebrow. "Intriguing… "

Raithe tilted his head. "Sounds like something you'd normally take three weeks to embellish into a personal epic."

"Normally, yes," I said, "but sadly, we're on a timetable."

Gaya leaned in. "Then we should head out before any troopers take an… "

She didn't get to finish. The cantina doors slid open with a pneumatic hiss, and a squad of First Order stormtroopers strode in, visors sweeping the crowd. They moved with the same rigid authority as Lieutenant Croy, but blessedly, the man himself was not among them.

"Uh-oh," Reginald muttered.

Zabaka reacted instantly, darting behind a hulking Ithorian at the bar, her wings folding tight to vanish into the alien's shadow. Gaya and Raithe exchanged a glance, subtle tension rippling between them.

I kept my smile casual, leaning back as if the sudden arrival of heavily armed soldiers was simply a charming addition to the décor. "No need to panic, friends. We simply make for the side exit, quietly, gracefully,"

"Quickly," Reginald cut in.

"Yes, yes," I conceded, rising smoothly. "Quietly, gracefully, and quickly."

We slipped away through the crowd, weaving between patrons who were doing their best to look uninteresting. The side door was half-hidden behind a row of neon-lit bottles, and with a last casual glance toward the troopers, I gestured the others through.

It wasn't until the cool Batuu air hit my face that I let my grin slip into something sharper. "Well. That was invigorating. Who's ready for a shuttle ride?"

Outside in the shaded alley behind Oga's, the cantina's bass thrum gave way to the low murmur of the market.

Reginald adjusted his satchel, keeping one hand over the decoy. "So, this mysterious side errand, care to explain why we're not heading straight for the shuttle?"

"Saja Telin asked me to locate something while we're here," I said, lowering my voice. "An old carving hidden somewhere in Black Spire. She wants a holo-scan of it."

"That's it?"

"That's it," I said with a shrug. "No questions asked. She seemed to think it's important."

Five minutes later, stretched to ten thanks to a detour around a pair of stormtroopers, we found it: a faint engraving on an ancient arch near the old water tower, its lines delicate and oddly precise, almost like a map frozen in stone.

I scanned it with my wrist comm, the display briefly highlighting a strange cluster of points before I closed the file and sent it to Saja's secure channel.

"There. Mission complete," I said. "Now let's get to the shuttle before Croy's bucketheads get curious."

That's when a voice rang out behind us, sharp, mechanical, and far too close.

"Stop right there."

We turned to find a stormtrooper stepping from behind a stack of weathered shipping crates, blaster leveled at chest height. His white armor gleamed in the afternoon light, a cruel contrast to the dingy alley.

The rest of his squad emerged in a flanking spread, boots crunching on the dusty permacrete, cutting off both ends of the street.

Gaya's inhale was sharp, like the first note before a scream. Raith's hand hovered near the butt of his concealed blaster. R2–DPR gave a low, warning beep, dome swiveling as if calculating angles.

And me? My heart was hammering against my ribs like it wanted to make its own daring escape.

The lead trooper's modulated voice crackled: "No sudden moves."

The words hung in the air, as heavy as a blast door.

We had the decoy stone. We had the scan for Saja Telin. And we had… absolutely no plausible alibi that wouldn't invite further questions.

I stepped forward slowly, palms raised, moustache twitching with what I told myself was confidence and not nerves. "Gentlemen," I began, "I can explain everything… "

"Captain Starstalker!" the trooper blurted, voice cracking through the modulator. His blaster dipped, then lowered entirely. "Montgomery Starstalker, sir, I'm a huge fan!"

I blinked. So did everyone else. Reginald's jaw actually dropped. R2–DPR let out a confused bloop, and Zabaka stifled a snicker behind her wings.

"Yes! It's really you!" the trooper went on, almost tripping over his own words. "Your exploits are legendary! I read all about the skirmish at

Castle's Edge, and that business on Corellia with the green freighters, it's… it's such an honor, sir!"

He holstered his blaster and snapped into a salute so sharp it nearly took his own helmet off. "Would it be, well, too much trouble… could I get an autograph?"

The tension that had been throttling the air a moment ago dissolved like mist under a twin sun. My lips curled into my trademark grin. "Well, I never turn down a loyal supporter," I said warmly, throwing Reginald a wink. He, of course, rolled his eyes and mouthed, you're impossible.

The trooper fumbled in a belt pouch, eventually pulling out a stylus. Then, after a moment of uncertainty, he extended his armored forearm toward me. "Right here, sir, if you don't mind."

I hesitated only briefly. After all, how often does one get to deface First Order property with style? Then, with a grand flourish, I scrawled:

Montgomery Starstalker

(accompanied by a dashing little moustache doodle).

"There you go, my good man," I said, handing back the stylus. "Wear it with pride, and perhaps a little more… color next time?"

He gave a sheepish chuckle, muttered his thanks, and waved us on.

The trooper made a sound that might've been a giggle. "Thank you, sir, really, you've made my entire rotation. I'd better not hold you up. 'Till the Spires, Captain."

He saluted again, autograph and all gleaming on his armor, before jogging off to rejoin his squad.

Reginald exhaled sharply, the kind of breath you let out when you've just avoided a detention cell. Gaya let out a relieved laugh. Raithe smirked, shaking his head. R2–DPR warbled in disbelief, the tone halfway between what just happened? and you've got to be kidding me.

"Well," Raithe said dryly, "that was unexpected. Are all your fans that devoted, Monty?"

I clapped him on the shoulder, grinning. "Devotion has a way of crossing boundaries, my friend. Even bureaucratic, militaristic ones."

Zabaka fluttered her wings, visibly relieved. "Let's not press our luck. Time to see you off to that shuttle, before autograph boy realizes he forgot to arrest you."

We slipped through the winding alleys of Black Spire, steering clear of any more white armor, the buzz of the marketplace slowly fading behind us. The shuttle platform rose ahead, gleaming in the sun. A crew attendant in the crisp uniform of the Chandrila Star Line waved us forward.

"Passengers returning to the *Halcyon*, this way."

Gaya and Raithe exchanged quick farewells with Zabaka; hers was a discreet nod to Reginald as she passed off one last tool in case the decoy needed a tweak. I gave her a gallant bow, which earned me an amused snort from her.

Then it was up the boarding ramp, through the climate-sealed hatch, and into the soft hum of the shuttle cabin. As we lifted off, Batuu's jagged spires receded beneath us, replaced by the glittering stars, and looming ahead was the *Halcyon's* majestic profile.

"Back to the floating palace," Reginald murmured.

"Back to the stage," I corrected, leaning back in my seat with a grin. "Our heist awaits."

23
BACK
ON BOARD

Between Gaya's untouchable stage persona and my newly discovered stormtrooper fan club privileges, we reached the shuttle with surprisingly little fuss, a minor miracle, considering how the day had begun. Once aboard, the return to the *Halcyon* was smooth, almost suspiciously so. The shuttle's gentle hum and the soft hiss of the cabin seals closing were a far cry from the bustle of Black Spire. Through the wide viewport, the Starcruiser's gleaming hull grew larger with each passing moment, suspended like a jewel in the black velvet of space.

Reginald sat opposite me, one hand resting, perhaps a touch too protectively, on the satchel that now cradled the decoy stone. Gaya and Raithe leaned close together, their murmured conversation barely audible over the shuttle's engines, but I caught fragments: timing… distractions… atrium sightlines. The swap wasn't tomorrow's concern anymore. It was tonight's.

Zabaka had peeled off back at the spaceport, her part of the mission done, and, judging by the satisfied flutter of her wings, handsomely paid for. That left the rest of us hurtling toward the gleaming doors of the *Halcyon*, the clock ticking down to a very dangerous evening. I adjusted my cuffs and offered the group my most confident smile. "Well," I said lightly, "no time like the present to make history… or headlines."

The shuttle doors hissed open, and we stepped once more into the *Halcyon's* resplendent atrium. The air here always seemed subtly perfumed, carrying the mingled scents of polished wood, warm fabrics, and the faintest trace of expensive Core World teas. Passengers bustled about, their voices overlapping in a lively chorus of Batuu tales, daring market bargains, questionable street food choices, and one very excited child waving a stuffed Tooka like a war trophy.

From her post near the control panel, Captain Keevan surveyed the atrium. Her sharp eyes found mine, and though her face kept its practiced calm, there was the tiniest quirk of a brow that clearly translated to: No trouble, I hope. I gave her my most innocent smile and a subtle thumbs-up, which in my case could mean anything from mission accomplished to brace yourself.

The others melted away into the flow of passengers, Gaya and Raithe drifting toward their own preparations for tonight's spectacle, Reginald keeping his satchel close enough to guard with his life. My path led elsewhere. The Saja, Telin, was waiting.

I found her in one of the *Halcyon's* quieter alcoves, a small meditation nook set apart from the glitter and chatter of the atrium. Soft light spilled down over pale stone benches, and the gentle hum of the ship's engines seemed muted here, as if sound itself knew to tread lightly. Telin stood motionless, palms together, eyes closed, not asleep, but listening in some deeper way, her presence like a calm tide rolling beneath the noise of the ship.

"Montgomery… " she greeted both Montgomery and Reginald softly, eyes opening with the kind of quiet focus that could make even the most battle-hardened pilot rethink his posture. "And Reginald. You've returned safely."

"And with news," I said, lowering my voice and glancing over my shoulder. The bustle of the atrium was distant enough, but old habits die hard. "We've confirmed that the artifact, sometimes called the Hayananeya, is indeed aboard. For now, it seems to be in… safer hands than most."

Telin's gaze sharpened slightly, a subtle tell that I had her full attention.

"It's rumored," I continued, "to have ties to the Jedi's past, though I can't personally vouch for that." I reached into my jacket and produced the small holoscan puck we'd acquired on Batuu. "However… this might be more your territory."

The device activated with a soft hum, projecting a faintly glowing 3D image above my palm, a smooth fragment of carved stone, etched with faint, curling lines. The pattern looked almost random, like a child's scribble… until I noticed how Telin's eyes narrowed ever so slightly, her breath stilling.

"A detail you might appreciate," I said lightly, "since I'm told it could be the sort of thing that unlocks more than just a display case."

She didn't speak at first. Instead, her hand hovered just over the projection, not touching, as if the image itself carried weight. Then her gaze lifted to mine, the calm tide of her voice carrying something heavier now.

"This is… important. I will study it further. You've done well, Captain Starstalker."

Telin's fingers curled back to her palms, as though she'd just touched the edge of a memory she had never expected to find.

"This pattern… " she began slowly, her voice dipping into that faraway tone that people use when speaking more to themselves than anyone else, "is older than the High Republic. Perhaps older than any chart in the New Republic archives. I've only ever seen its likeness once, in a place not easily found."

"Well," I said, flashing my most rakish grin, "now you've seen it twice. You're welcome."

Her lips curved faintly, though it wasn't quite a smile. "You don't realize the weight of what you've brought me, Captain."

"I'm sensing it's heavier than my moustache wax collection," I quipped, because someone had to lighten the mood.

"Infinitely heavier," she replied without hesitation. "If my suspicions are correct, this could lead to something… long hidden. But it must remain between us until I am certain." Her eyes swept over me and Reginald in a way that suggested she was measuring more than just trust. "The fewer who know, the better. There are those aboard who would stop at nothing to possess it."

I tipped my head in mock solemnity. "My lips are sealed. Not even Lieutenant Croy's unrelenting charm could loosen them."

She dipped her head in acknowledgment, but her focus didn't waver from me. It was as if she were watching something invisible hover in my orbit.

"There is an aura about you, Montgomery. A sense of connection that goes beyond chance. Have you ever felt something… guiding you?"

I shifted under her gaze, feeling an odd warmth creep into my face. "Well, I tend to trust my instincts, if that's what you mean. They've saved my hide more than once."

Her eyes drifted, of all things, to my moustache. "Your presence in the Force is… unusual. Subtle, yet undeniable. It is as though… " She hesitated, then allowed the barest hint of a smile. "Let us simply say the Force can manifest in any form it chooses... even through a well-groomed moustache."

I arched a brow. "So you're saying my moustache might be Force-sensitive?"

Reginald groaned. "Don't encourage him."

Reginald snorted. "Wait... are you saying his moustache is Force-sensitive?"

A moment of stunned silence hung between us. My jaw dropped. I genuinely couldn't decide whether to be baffled, flattered, or immediately demand a title like Master of the Upper Lip.

R2-DPR let out a surprised chirp, swiveling his dome between us as if to confirm he'd heard correctly.

Saja Telin didn't confirm it outright... but she didn't deny it either. "The Force works in mysterious ways," she murmured, her tone as serene as the soft hum of the meditation nook. "Perhaps, in time, you might even learn to harness it, moustache and all."

I straightened, smoothing the very subject of our discussion. "Well... I'm open-minded. But that's quite a revelation."

Sh gave a slow, assuring nod and stepped aside as a family of curious passengers entered the nook. "Thank you for the update on the artefact. Please, be cautious. The First Order is persistent... and even a small ripple in the Force can draw unwanted attention."

Her gaze lingered on me for just a second longer before she turned away, as if she could already see the currents of chaos swirling around me.

Telin inclined her head. "May the Force guide your next steps. You will need more than luck tonight."

She regarded me for a long moment, her gaze thoughtful, as though she were listening for something I couldn't hear.

"Sometimes," she said quietly, "the Force calls from unexpected places. One does not need to wield the light to feel its resonance."

And with that, she turned and slipped back into the quiet flow of the ship's life, leaving me staring after her, the holoscan's faint glow still humming in my palm before I powered it down.

Reginald and I left the nook, our footsteps echoing softly along the polished corridor. He made it a full ten paces before bursting into laughter, shaking his head. "Force-sensitive moustache. That's a new one, even for us."

I couldn't help but grin, though a sliver of wonder curled in my chest. "What can I say? I've always suspected my facial hair was... extra extraordinary."

R2-DPR beeped in playful agreement, his dome tilting toward me like he was already calculating its midichlorian count.

"So," Reginald said, smirking, "when we orchestrate the swap for the Hayananeya tonight... might want to brush up on your Force moustache twirls."

I gave a mock flourish, twisting the tips of my moustache with great ceremony. "Joke all you want, Reg. If this moustache truly resonates with the Force... well, it might just come in handy."

We both chuckled, but the levity only masked the charge in the air. Tonight was the night, the decoy was ready, Gaya's distraction was set, and the first order would be prowling the ship like carrion birds.

Between Croy's scrutiny, the precision the swap demanded, and the fact that my moustache had just been promoted to potential cosmic conduit, the stakes had never been higher.

I cast one more glance at the swirling starlines through the atrium windows, then straightened my collar. "Right, Reg. Let's get to it."

24
A GRAND PERFORMANCE

The narrow service corridor behind the *Halcyon's* grand dining hall practically hummed with anticipation. Raithe Kole paced in tight, restless loops, muttering the plan under his breath like an incantation. Reginald Starjammer, by contrast, leaned against the wall with mechanical calm, methodically checking the contents of his toolkit as if we weren't about to attempt one of the boldest heists in the cruise line's history. Ouannii, Gaya's Rodian accompanist, stood off to the side, spinning her flute in nimble fingers, her bulbous eyes flicking between us and the chronometer.

And then, of course, there was me.

I stepped into the little huddle like a leading man striding onto his mark, my latest cape billowing just enough to announce itself without actually hitting anyone in the face. Tonight's ensemble was nothing short of operatic, a deep emerald cascade with gold trim that caught the corridor's light and scattered it across the walls like a portable disco. The high collar framed my face in shadow and mystery, perfect for the sort of daring maneuver that might be painted onto the side of a star freighter one day. I tilted my chin just so, letting the gold gleam dazzle them.

"Monty," Reginald said, squinting at me as though trying to solve a puzzle, "what in the galaxy are you wearing?"

"This... " I replied, spreading the cape with a flourish worthy of an opera finale, "is the Starfire Cascade. Custom-made on Naboo by the finest cape artisan in the galaxy."

Ouannii tilted her head, her large Rodian eyes glinting as she took in the emerald-and-gold spectacle. "Honestly... it's kind of amazing."

"It's ridiculous," Raithe muttered without even looking up from pacing. "You'll light up like a beacon if Croy so much as glances your way."

"Nonsense... " I said, sweeping the fabric dramatically around my shoulders, "capes are the pinnacle of sophistication. Besides, it's a conversation starter."

"A conversation starter for Croy to arrest you," Reginald muttered, deadpan.

Ouannii gave a shrug and a faint smile. "I like it. He looks like a walking chandelier, but... it works for him."

"Thank you, Ouannii," I said, bowing my head with mock solemnity. "At least someone here understands the power of style."

"Focus," Raithe snapped. "We don't have time for cape critiques."

Everyone knew he was partly right, but I was entirely right about the cape.

With that, we broke apart, each heading to our posts. The *Starfire Cascade* swirled behind me like a comet's tail as I strode toward the dining hall, earning a quiet snicker from Reginald. Let them laugh. They'd see, this cape would earn its keep.

Inside, the atmosphere was electric. Guests clustered in glittering knots, the hum of conversation buzzing under the soft music. Stage lights swept the polished floor in slow arcs, catching the sequins of my cape so they burst like miniature supernovas. I eased into my seat, arranging the fabric just so, tilted, angled, and ready to weaponize every stray beam of light.

A few passing guests whispered, clearly dazzled by my impeccable fashion sense. Did they know it was all part of the act? Of course not.

Across the room, Lieutenant Croy stood in his immaculate dark gray officer's uniform, posture ramrod straight, eyes like a hawk searching for prey. His gloved hands were clasped behind his back, the crisp lines of his jacket so severe they might cut transparisteel. He prowled the room with slow, deliberate turns of the head, scanning for trouble.

I smiled faintly. He wouldn't find it, at least not where he expected it to be.

The lights dimmed, and a hush rolled over the dining hall like the soft fold of a velvet curtain. The first lingering notes of Poverty of Love drifted through the air, Gaya's voice at once achingly tender and impossibly strong. It wove a story of the quiet price of stardom, the hidden ache beneath the roar of applause, and the way adoration could feel like both a crown and a cage.

The audience leaned forward as one. Couples clasped hands. Strangers shared small, wordless glances. Even Lieutenant Croy, the perpetual sentinel in his pressed charcoal officer's coat, appeared momentarily disarmed, his sharp eyes softening, his shoulders losing that ever-present parade rest stiffness.

At her side, Ouannii's flute curled around the melody like silver smoke, each note delicate enough to float away but sure enough to hold the crowd in its spell. The stage lights shimmered across Gaya's gown, painting the air with shifting hues of rose and gold.

But this was more than a performance.

Out on the observation deck, beyond the glow of the dining hall, the real work had begun. Raithe and Reginald were crouched in the shadow of the hyperspace compass display, their silhouettes bent over the reinforced transparent-steel housing. Reg's toolkit lay open, every tool in perfect order despite the quick pace of their mission.

Click.

The first latch yielded with a soft metallic sigh, the faintest vibration passing through the frame as the seal disengaged. A muted glow spilled forth from within, bathing their faces in the ethereal purple-blue light of the Hayananeya.

It was even more mesmerizing up close, the facets catching the light like tiny frozen waves, a depth to it that felt almost alive. Its glow cast long shadows along the deck plating, illuminating the tight concentration on Reginald's brow and the quick, deliberate movements of Raithe's hands.

Inside, Gaya's voice soared toward the first emotional peak of the song, and I, seated just where the lights would catch the glint of my cape, shifted slightly in my chair. This was the moment where a simple turn of the head, a flash of gold sequins, and the right expression could be the difference between success and an evening in the brig.

Gaya's voice shifted into her second number, the melody darker now, more deliberate. This was no love ballad; it was a haunting hymn to the Hayananeya itself. She sang of its beauty, its promise, and the ruin it brought to any fool who thought they could own it.

The irony wasn't lost on me. Out on the observation deck, Raithe and Reginald were elbows-deep in making that exact theft a reality.

From my place in the dining hall, I let my gaze slide toward Lieutenant Croy. His composure was slipping; there was a stiffness to his jaw, a slight twitch of his gloved fingers. He could feel something was afoot, and if I didn't keep him busy, he might just stumble across it.

I rose smoothly from my chair, letting the cape flare behind me in a cascade of golden light, as if the spotlight itself had been waiting for the cue. The movement turned more than a few heads, which was precisely the point.

"Lieutenant!" I called warmly, closing the distance and clapping him on the shoulder before he could sidestep. "Marvelous performance tonight, don't you think?"

He turned, brow furrowing. "Starstalker," he said, his voice clipped, "what are you doing here?"

"Enjoying the finer things in life, of course," I replied, gesturing toward the stage with the flourish of a born raconteur. "Gaya, singing about a stone! Brilliant. Truly inspired."

Croy's eyes sharpened, suspicion darkening them. "What do you know about the *stone*?"

Only that it's the stuff of legend," I said, spreading my arms wide as if to embrace the very concept of mystery, my cape shimmering like a restless starfield. "Why, if I had a credit for every myth about it, I'd be wealthier than a Hutt."

Parlor tricks don't impress me," Croy growled.

"Really?" I lifted a brow, feigning surprise. "Because your menacing scowl is quite compelling."

Out on the observation deck, Ouannii slipped in just as Reginald bypassed the final lock. The case clicked open, and the Hayananeya's glow spilled into the dim space, cool purple-blue light washing over their faces like the heart of a frozen star.

"Wow," Ouannii breathed, eyes wide. "It's even more beautiful than I expected."

"Focus," Raithe said sharply, sliding the real stone into his satchel while Reginald lowered the decoy into its cradle.

The swap was seamless. Reginald's fingers danced over the controls, rearming the security system with only seconds to spare, just enough time for the glass to seal and the glow to return to its 'untouched' state.

Then, boots. Heavy, synchronized, and getting closer.

They froze.

Ouannii's hand twitched toward her lumosynth, her eyes narrowing. "I'll handle that," she murmured, already preparing a distracting melody. "Go."

Raithe nodded, urging Reginald toward the opposite corridor. They were only steps away from disappearing when the intercom crackled to life.

"Attention all guests," Captain Keevan's voice rang out, calm but edged with urgency. "For your safety, please remain where you are. First Order personnel are conducting a security sweep."

In the dining hall, the shift in atmosphere was immediate. Croy's eyes locked on mine, suspicion sparking like a live wire.

The music cut mid-note. Gaya's voice faltered, her final lyric dissolving into stunned silence as Lieutenant Croy stepped forward, his dark officer's coat rippling like a shadow. His voice rang out, commanding attention.

"Attention, passengers!"

Every head in the hall turned. Crew froze mid-step, trays hovering in the air.

"By authority of the First Order," Croy declared, his tone swelling with smug satisfaction, "this vessel is now under our control. You will remain exactly where you are until further notice."

A ripple of alarm swept the room. Somewhere behind me, a wine glass shattered against the floor. Captain Keevan stiffened near the edge of the stage, her hands clenched at her sides, but she said nothing yet.

Croy's gaze found mine like a targeting reticle. His lips curled into that insufferable smirk. "Well, Captain Starstalker," he drawled, his voice dripping with the kind of mockery only a man who thinks he's already won can muster, "it seems your evening just became… considerably more complicated."

I tugged the *Starfire Cascade* tighter around my shoulders, the golden trim catching the light like a defiant flare. My mind raced, the stone was secure, the team scattered, and the *Halcyon* had just turned into a very luxurious prison.

I offered him my most insufferable grin. "Complicated, Lieutenant? I do my best work complicated."

But then Croy turned sharply toward the atrium, his boots striking the polished floor with military precision. He raised a gloved hand, and stormtroopers began pouring in from both entrances, their blasters held high as they fanned out to secure the crowd.

"Lock it down!" he barked, his voice reverberating off the vaulted ceiling. "No one in, no one out!"

This wasn't a battle I could win alone. Not here. Not with half the First Order standing between me and the exit. My mind flashed through the possibilities, most of them ending with me in a detention cell wearing a very unflattering jumpsuit.

No, there was only one person aboard the *Halcyon* with the authority and the will to match Lieutenant Croy in a contest of wits: Captain Keevan.

I scanned the hall, spotting her at the far end, her posture steel-straight, her eyes locked on Croy like two captains sizing each other up across an invisible battlefield. If anyone could keep the First Order from sinking their claws into this ship, it was her.

25
CROY vs KEEVAN

Croy cut a path straight through the atrium, his long strides forcing clusters of uneasy passengers to part like water before a prow. The chatter that had filled the space minutes earlier had thinned to a hushed, uneasy murmur. Every step of his polished boots rang sharp against the deck, each one a signal that control was shifting. I drifted a few paces behind, keeping my movements casual but my eyes locked on him.

Captain Keevan was already waiting, centered in the grand space beneath the towering viewport, framed by the swirl of starlight beyond. She stood with arms loosely at her sides, but there was nothing relaxed about her stance; it was the posture of someone ready to plant their feet against a storm. Her gaze locked onto the approaching lieutenant, and the hum of the atrium seemed to vanish. The crew members nearby stilled. Even the guests who moments ago were pretending not to notice now found themselves watching, caught in the gravity of two opposing forces about to collide.

"This is how you seize control?" Keevan's voice cut through the atrium like a laser, carrying over the uneasy shuffle of the crowd. "Hiding behind stormtroopers, barking orders, and intimidating the people you claim to protect? I thought the First Order prided itself on order and unity. What I see is fear and arrogance parading as authority."

Croy's smirk curved wider, but there was a flintiness in his eyes. "Order and unity, Captain, are not achieved through softness. They require discipline. The *Halcyon* is no exception. Under our protection, your passengers will be far safer than under your… idealistic oversight."

Keevan took a deliberate step forward, her voice gaining force with each word. "Safer? You call this safe? Stormtroopers in every corridor, guests herded like prisoners, children clutching their parents because they don't know what you'll do next. This isn't protection, it's suffocation. You can dress up tyranny in any uniform you want, but it's still tyranny."

Croy's tone dropped into a cold, dangerous register. "Careful, Captain. Defiance is not bravery; it's a spark for rebellion. And rebellion, as you know, is treason. The First Order does not tolerate treason… or those who encourage it."

Keevan didn't flinch. If anything, the golden eyes set in her vivid blue Pantoran skin seemed to blaze hotter in the atrium's light, locking onto Croy with a steady, unblinking challenge.

"What you call insubordination," she said, her voice slicing through the murmurs with surgical precision, "I call integrity. My loyalty is to this ship and the souls aboard her, not to your hollow promises of protection that serve only your own grip on power."

A ripple of unease moved through the gathered passengers. The stormtroopers at Croy's side stiffened, fingers flexing near their holsters.

Keevan stepped forward, her height and poise commanding the space as though the *Halcyon* itself stood behind her. "I've seen what your kind calls 'protection,' Lieutenant. I've seen it scorch worlds, starve cities, and strip entire cultures bare, all while claiming it's for their own good. The First Order doesn't unite; it breaks. And then it takes."

Her words struck the atrium like a shockwave. Guests craned their necks from balconies, others peered nervously from behind columns, drawn to the confrontation like ships to a gravity well.

I slid among them quietly, the shimmer of my cape dulled in the half-light, listening with every sense attuned. This was more than an argument; it was a fault line forming under the voyage, and I intended to be standing in exactly the right place when it cracked open.

Croy's smirk thinned into something colder. "Careful, Captain," he said, his tone dropping into a level, dangerous register. "Defiance edges quickly into treason. And treason, " he leaned in slightly, letting the word hang, "is something the First Order does not forgive."

Keevan tilted her head, her golden gaze narrowing. "How long have you been with the First Order, Lieutenant?" Her tone was deceptively casual, but there was a weight behind it that made the air feel heavier.

Croy hesitated, just enough to betray that he hadn't expected the question. "Twenty years," he said at last.

One of Keevan's brows arched ever so slightly. "Twenty years… and still a lieutenant." She let the words drift between them like a dropped datapad, her meaning impossible to miss.

Croy's jaw tightened. "The First Order rewards loyalty. And competence, Captain."

"Does it?" Keevan countered, taking a deliberate step closer. "Because twenty years is a long time to be overlooked. Or… maybe they don't promote anyone who doesn't fit their ideal." Her voice sharpened, every word precise and deliberate. "You know, Lieutenant, I almost feel sorry for you."

"Watch your words, Captain," Croy snapped, his calm veneer beginning to crack.

"Why?" she pressed, her voice rising, not in volume, but in force. "Because the truth stings? You've spent two decades enforcing their rules, believing loyalty and fear would earn you a seat at their table. But you'll never be anything more than a pawn. Twenty years, and they still see you as disposable."

Everyone in the atrium went utterly still. Even the hum of the ship seemed to fade. Passengers froze mid-step, heads turning toward the confrontation. The stormtroopers themselves hesitated, their helmets tilting almost imperceptibly, as if unsure whether they'd just heard correctly.

I felt my own breath catch. For all my bluster and flair, I knew a line like that could draw blood, and Keevan had just driven it straight into the heart of the First Order's pride.

Croy's face darkened, the muscle in his jaw flexing. His lips pressed into a thin, unforgiving line. "You may think you have the upper hand, Captain," he said, his voice low and deliberate, each word edged with frost. "But let me remind you, I am in command now. Defiance will only make things harder for you… and your crew."

Keevan didn't flinch. She held his gaze with the same unshakable poise she'd worn since the moment he marched into the atrium. "You may have taken the ship, Croy," she said steadily enough to cut through the silence, "but you will never command it. Not in the way that matters."

Croy stepped back, his expression carved in ice, and gestured sharply to the stormtroopers. "Secure the passengers. Confine the crew to their quarters. I will not tolerate further disruption."

The command cracked through the atrium like a blaster shot. Armored figures moved at once, their boots striking the deck in a grim, mechanical rhythm. Croy turned his attention to his datapad, scrolling through whatever intelligence he had at hand, but his gaze kept sweeping the crowd, a predator scanning for the first sign of prey. Every lingering glance felt like the tip of a blade, searching for weakness.

The passengers huddled in uneasy knots, their conversations dissolving into whispers and darting looks. Even those who moments before had been merely curious now shifted with palpable fear.

In the middle of it all, Gaya and Raithe slipped through the crowd toward the exit, and Ouannii made her way through the crowd, joining them in the chaos. Raithe held Gaya's stage bag tight under his arm. It looked, to anyone watching, like a performer's kit, props, costumes, maybe an instrument or two. But I knew better. Inside that bag was the Hayananeya, the stone that meant everything to her people on Ryloth. A relic of unity. A symbol of resilience. A hope they had been denied for generations.

If the First Order laid so much as a finger on it, that hope would be gone, shattered as surely as if they'd crushed the stone itself. And from the way Croy's gaze cut across the atrium, sharp and unyielding, I knew he was only moments away from finding an excuse to take it.

26
SANDRO

The stone was in the bag. I knew it. Gaya knew it. Raithe definitely knew it. The only thing that mattered now was making sure Lieutenant Croy did not know it.

Unfortunately, fate, or perhaps the galaxy's questionable sense of humor, put him directly in their path.

"Miss Gaya," Croy said, his tone slipping into something dangerously close to reverence, though tangled with suspicion, "you're leaving so soon?"

I felt my pulse spike. The ship was on lockdown. No one was coming or going without a good reason. The only reason Croy would wave someone through right now was if…

Ah! There it was.

He was looking at her not like an officer screening a potential security breach, but like a fan standing in the glow of his favorite holostar. His stance softened, his voice tried to carry authority, but the edges were fraying under the weight of awkward admiration.

"I was hoping… " he continued, "to hear another song before the evening was out. Perhaps… a private encore?"

Gaya smiled the kind of smile that could launch a thousand smuggling runs, tilting her head just enough to make her lekku sway. "Another time, Lieutenant. I've… an urgent matter to attend to for a dear friend."

Croy hesitated, clearly torn between orders to keep the ship sealed tight and the once-in-a-lifetime chance to impress the galaxy's most renowned Twi'lek performer.

"Of course… of course," he stammered, smoothing the front of his uniform like it might help him regain composure. "Your… ah… service to morale aboard this vessel has been invaluable. Truly. But… " His tone strained to sound official. "Might I trouble you to inspect your bags before you go? Merely protocol. A formality, you understand."

My heart lurched up into my throat.

"Of course, Lieutenant," Gaya said, her voice smooth as silk. "Though I promise you there's nothing inside but my costumes, makeup, and a few notes for future songs."

Croy nodded, looking almost apologetic, before leaning down and plucking the bag right out of Raithe's hands.

"Well… I'll have my troopers carry this to your shuttle. A star of your caliber shouldn't bother with such trivialities."

Raithe's jaw tightened so hard I half expected to hear enamel crack, but he said nothing.

"Lieutenant," Gaya purred, her charm dialed up to eleven, "you're too kind."

Oblivious to the bag's true contents, Croy turned to order his troopers to escort "Gaya's luggage." The seconds ticked like detonator beeps in my head. We needed a distraction… now.

And the galaxy, in its infinite mischief, delivered.

From the edge of the atrium, Sandro Almander, lute-like instrument slung at his side, sprang onto the small performance platform with a flourish.

"This one… " he called, his young voice cutting through the crowd like a hyperspace beacon, "is about the greatest hero I've ever known… Montgomery Starstalker!"

Every head turned toward him.

Including Croy's.

Including the stormtroopers.

Including the Lieutenant's gloved hands, one holding the datapad, the other still clutching the bag.

Then Sandro struck the first triumphant chord.

From the edge of the void to the farthest bright star,

He'll find you and save you, no matter how far!

His cape ever-dazzling, his moustache so fine,

With Monty in charge, the First Order's decline!

The passengers, caught somewhere between amusement and admiration, began clapping along. Even the stormtroopers, momentarily disarmed, shifted in place, their helmets tilting in curiosity.

Croy, visibly irritated by the ridiculousness of it all, let the bag slip ever so slightly from his grasp. Gaya, moving with all the grace of a headliner stealing the show, caught it neatly before it could hit the deck, her smile never breaking.

With style and with grace, with a wink and a flair,

Montgomery Starstalker, beyond all compare!

By now, the clapping had become rhythmic, infectious. Sandro was milking it for all it was worth. Even a few crew members were tapping their feet. Croy's smirk had twisted into something darker, his datapad momentarily forgotten as the atrium's energy swirled entirely around me.

I'll admit it, my chest puffed just a touch. There's something about an entire room chanting your name to a jaunty tune that makes you momentarily forget you're in the middle of an operation that could get you thrown in a First Order cell.

The atrium's lights seemed to glint off my cape at exactly the right moments, as if the ship itself had joined Sandro's performance. I gave the crowd a small bow, nothing too ostentatious, just enough to fan the flame.

And there it was… the window.

While Croy's attention was fixed on me with the expression of a man being forced to swallow something sour, Gaya, Ouannii, and Raithe drifted backward toward the corridor, the bag… the bag, now slung casually over Gaya's shoulder. Her gait was perfect: unhurried, elegant, utterly unremarkable to the untrained eye.

I took another deliberate step toward Sandro, clapping along with the audience, and felt the subtle shift in the room as they neared the exit.

Raithe was nearly at the threshold. Gaya caught my gaze for half a heartbeat, just enough to confirm the precious cargo was still safe, before vanishing into the corridor.

I kept smiling, even as my mind raced. The song was almost over. Once it ended, Croy's focus would snap back like a rancor on a chain. And when that happened, we'd better be ready.

With courage and charm, and a moustache of might…

Montgomery Starstalker will win the fight!

The last chord rang out, Sandro striking a triumphant pose while the crowd erupted into applause and cheers. I gave a sweeping bow, long enough for Gaya, Raithe and Ouannii to vanish completely.

When I straightened, Croy was already blinking as if waking from some absurd daydream he'd been tricked into. His jaw tightened, and the sour expression returned with interest.

"Well… " he said, snapping his datapad shut, "that was… distracting." His gaze swept the atrium, hawk-like, hunting for whatever he'd just missed.

I stepped into his line of sight, letting the sequins on my cape flare under the lights like a miniature supernova. "Oh, I wouldn't call it distracting, Lieutenant. I'd call it morale building. You wouldn't want to be known as the officer who crushed morale, would you?"

The faint muscle twitch in his temple told me he would if it served the First Order, but it bought a few precious seconds before his mind caught up with the fact that Gaya and her entourage had vanished.

Passengers began to scatter in the wake of the performance, a noisy enough dispersal to mask the sound of Croy's boots as he moved away, barking quiet orders to his troopers.

I let out a slow breath. One more round won, but the match was far from being over.

Across the atrium, Captain Keevan stood with her arms folded, still holding the aftershock of her earlier exchange with Croy. Her golden Pantoran eyes tracked his movements like a predator watching a rival.

I crossed to her, lowering my voice, "He thinks he's in control," I murmured, "but the First Order won't win the day… not while you're captain, and certainly not while I'm aboard."

For a moment, her stern expression softened, just slightly. "You have more confidence than most," she said quietly.

"Confidence," I replied, "… is the first weapon in any battle. And the most contagious."

The corners of her mouth twitched, almost a smile. But then her gaze hardened again, following Croy as he disappeared down the corridor. "Then let's hope it's contagious enough."

I straightened my cape, gave my moustache a practiced twist, and decided a drink was in order. Aerobics of the heroic variety was thirsty work, after all… and I deserved nothing less than a perfectly stirred cocktail to toast yet another victory.

I'd barely taken three steps toward the nearest bar when a familiar voice called out behind me.

"Monty! Wait up!"

Turning, I saw Sandro Alamander bounding toward me, his lute slung over one shoulder, his face glowing with the kind of pride usually reserved for award ceremonies or marriage proposals.

"Well, if it isn't the bard of the hour," I said, offering him my most magnetic smile.

He skidded to a stop in front of me, slightly out of breath. "I've gotta ask, what did you think of the song? Was it… I mean, was it great?"

I paused, letting the moment stretch as I stroked my moustache with deliberate gravity. Sandro's wide eyes fixated on mine, starving for approval.

Finally, I placed a hand on his shoulder, giving it a solemn squeeze. "Sandro," I began, "your song was… inspired."

"Really?" he breathed, half-disbelieving, half-hopeful.

"Inspired," I repeated, "in the way a comet streaking across the night sky is inspired. You captured the grandeur, the charisma, the sheer heroism that defines me, and wrapped it all in a melody that stirred the hearts of everyone in that room."

His face split into a grin so wide I feared it might require medical intervention.

Sandro's face lit up like the Corellian sky on Empire Day.

"Monty, I… thank you. That means so much coming from you."

I lifted a finger, stopping him mid-gush. "But… if I may offer some advice."

"Of course. Anything."

I leaned in, lowering my voice as though sharing a closely guarded secret. "Never underestimate the power of the encore. A hero like me deserves a sequel, perhaps something about my moustache, my capes, or my uncanny ability to outwit stormtroopers without so much as a bead of sweat."

Sandro nodded so vigorously I feared for his neck, already plucking absent chords on his lute. "A sequel about the moustache... that's brilliant. I'll start working on it immediately."

"And one more thing," I added, letting my tone soften, "you did more than write a good song tonight. Whether you realize it or not, you helped save the day. That little distraction of yours gave Gaya and Raithe the moment they needed to slip away."

He blinked. "Wait... what? I helped with... ?"

"Let's just say your talents extend far beyond music," I cut in with a wink. "Keep playing, Sandro. The galaxy needs more songs like yours."

For a moment, I thought he might actually cry. "Monty... I don't even know what to say."

"Say nothing," I replied, waving a hand with regal finality. "Just keep singing about me.

Sandro straightened, eyes shining. "Then I swear, from this day forward, Montgomery Starstalker will be my muse."

I gave a gracious nod, as though accepting a royal title. "A wise choice. History is written by the victors, Sandro... but the legends? They're sung about me."

With that, I turned on my heel and resumed my quest, cape billowing behind me like the wake of a starship. Somewhere aboard this vessel, there was a perfectly stirred cocktail waiting to be graced by my presence, and after all, heroism was thirsty work.

27

THE FORCE
BETWEEN US

I wasn't looking for adventure. In fact, I was looking for a drink.

After the chaos of Captain Keevan and Lieutenant Croy's explosive argument and Sandro's perfectly timed ballad that let Gaya and Raithe slip away, a quiet corner with a stiff glass of Hoth Icebreaker seemed like the perfect retreat.

But as with most things in the life of Montgomery Starstalker, what I planned and what the galaxy provided were rarely the same thing.

I wandered the *Halcyon's* corridors, my cape swishing with just the right degree of elegance, hunting for the nearest cantina. Unfortunately, the First Order lockdown had turned most of the ship's social hubs into ghost towns. No laughter, no clinking glasses, just the faint hum of the ship's systems and the occasional stormtrooper stomp.

Left turn. Right turn. Another left… confidently, of course, and I was certain I'd found my haven. The ornate double doors before me screamed private bar. I pictured plush seating, dim lighting, and an impressive wall of rare spirits awaiting my expert critique.

The doors slid open with a soft hiss.

No bottles. No bar. No Hoth Icebreaker.

Instead, the air was thick with the hum of focused energy, the serene scent of incense, and the unmistakable presence of the Saja. They sat in a loose circle, their calm expressions a sharp contrast to my sudden (and, frankly, heroic) entrance.

"Not a cantina," I muttered, adjusting the fall of my cape.

At the center stood Master Tal'Veren, a Pantoran whose golden gaze could probably outshine the blade of a lightsaber. His eyes found me immediately, and something about the way he studied me suggested that my unexpected arrival was… not unexpected at all.

"Montgomery Starstalker," Tal'Veren said, his voice low and resonant, filling the chamber like the hum of a starship's engines at idle. "You are here."

I paused, one hand instinctively drifting to my moustache. "Yes, well… here is a bit of a stretch. I was actually looking for a drink. But since I've arrived… " I swept a hand around the room, "… what a lovely meditation chamber you have. And what is that smell? Very calming. Spice? Candied root?"

Tal'Veren didn't smile, but I caught the barest flicker of amusement in his golden eyes. "The Force brought you here."

I arched a brow. "The Force, you say? Not my impeccable sense of direction?"

"The Force," he repeated, with a firmness that could sand down a durasteel hull, "often guides those who do not yet realize its presence."

I blinked, caught off guard by the weight of his words. "Are you implying there's a… suggestion… that I'm Force-sensitive?"

Another Saja, a Mirialan named Keryn, stepped forward, her expression thoughtful. "The way you move. The way you act. It is as though the Force guides you without your awareness."

"Well," I said, stroking my moustache, "that would explain why I always land on my feet. And here I was thinking it was all charm."

Keryn's eyes searched mine. "The stone… it's truly gone from the ship?"

I gave a small, satisfied nod. "Gone and, if the galaxy has a sense of humor, well out of the First Order's reach by now."

Tal'Veren inclined his head, as if weighing my words. "Then that part of the current has passed. Whatever its purpose, it will have to unfold far from here."

"Fine by me," I said. "Frankly, I prefer my priceless relics well beyond arm's length—usually someone else's arms entirely."

The Pantoran's golden gaze sharpened. "And yet, the greater danger remains. The First Order has taken a foothold aboard this vessel. That cannot stand."

I swept my cape into place with mock solemnity. "Their décor alone is reason enough to toss them out the airlock."

"This is no jest," Tal'Veren said, though a flicker of amusement touched his eyes. "What you witnessed in the atrium was only the beginning. They will want more than a demonstration of power. They will want control over every passenger, every crew member, every corridor."

"Let me guess," I said, "they don't plan to leave politely after tea?"

"Captain Keevan will stand against them," Tal'Veren replied. "But a captain is only one voice. The ship will need others, people who can move unseen, and bend the enemy's attention elsewhere."

I caught the pointed look. "Ah. You mean people with a talent for… theatrical distraction?"

"That is one way to call it," Keryn said, a smile playing at her lips.

I straightened, moustache twitching with pride. "Well then, I suppose I've found my next drink order: one part cunning, two parts charm, shaken over ice, and served with a First Order defeat on the side."

Before I could respond, the doors hissed open again, and a young human in grease-stained overalls stumbled inside. It was Sammie… the *Halcyon*'s ever-enthusiastic mechanic… hair skewed, a wrench clutched like a lifeline.

"Captain Keevan sent me," he blurted, words tumbling over each other in a rush. "The First Order's locking down the bridge and life-support systems. If we don't act now, they'll have full control of the ship."

The Saja exchanged calm, deliberate glances, their serenity at odds with Sammie's urgency. Tal'Veren's golden gaze shifted back to me, grave and unyielding.

"The Force brought you here for a reason, Montgomery Starstalker."

I straightened, adjusted my cape, and rose to my full… and objectively heroic… height. "Clearly. And what, exactly, might this reason be?"

Keryn stepped forward, her voice urgent. "The First Order's grip grows stronger with every passing moment, but the Force resists them. It flows through the ship, through all of us, pushing back against their oppression. We've sensed it since they arrived."

Tal'Veren nodded. "The Jedi of old relied on the Force to overcome impossible odds. Tonight, we must do the same."

I gestured toward Sammie, who was watching the exchange with wide eyes. "And where does our young grease-smeared champion fit into this grand strategy?"

Sammie flushed but lifted his chin. "I know the maintenance corridors better than anyone. I can get us to the bridge, or at least close enough to disrupt their systems."

I studied him for a beat, then flicked my cape over one shoulder with a smile. "Well, Sammie, it appears your wrench and my moustache are about to save the galaxy. Again."

Tal'Veren's golden eyes fixed on me, unblinking. "You've arrived at the moment we need you most."

Sammie seized the opening. "The First Order's locking down the bridge… navigation, comms, and even life support. If we don't act now, they'll have total control."

Keryn knelt by the central holo-display, a starfield flickering between her hands as she traced a series of glowing corridors. "They've sealed the main routes to the bridge. Stormtroopers in both primary turbolifts and forward stairwells. But here… " she highlighted a narrow, twisting line, "this maintenance artery bypasses their patrols. Tight, dark, and deafening from the ship's core, but it leads straight to a service hatch beneath the bridge."

Sammie tapped another point on the projection. "From there, I can splice into the auxiliary systems. If we cut power to the forward control stations, Captain Keevan can retake the bridge before Croy even realizes we're there."

Tal'Veren studied us like a general preparing troops for battle. "This path is dangerous, and the First Order will not yield easily. But the Force moves with you tonight. Let it guide your steps."

I tipped him a two-fingered salute. "The Force, a good cape, and a moustache… they'll never see us coming."

With a quick flick of his wrist, Sammie closed the holo-map on his datapad, the glowing starfield vanishing. Keryn touched my arm before I could move. "One more thing, Starstalker. The Force stirs in more than just us. There is another presence aboard… a friend to the Resistance. If fate is kind, your paths will cross before the night is done."

I arched a brow. "Mysterious, cloaked in secrecy, and presumably taller than me. Sounds intriguing."

Keryn's lips curved in a knowing smile. "Taller, yes. And loud enough to shake the bulkheads when angered. May the Force be with you."

I swept my cape in a dramatic bow. "And with you. Now… let's go liberate a bridge.

28
WOOKIEE MAINTENANCE

The hatch slid shut behind us, sealing the Saja in their quiet sanctum and locking us back into the *Halcyon's* dimly lit corridors. Gone was the meditative calm; in its place came the hum of power couplings and the distant, echoing cadence of stormtrooper boots somewhere above.

Sammie moved like someone who'd been born in these maintenance passages, half crouched, weaving around conduit junctions, ducking under low-hanging coolant pipes. I followed, my cape swishing in a far less practical manner.

"Maintenance corridors run the whole length of the ship," Sammie whispered over his shoulder. "We stick to these, we can get close enough to the bridge without them knowing we're coming."

A thrum of the engines vibrated through the deck plates beneath my boots, the sound as familiar to me as my own heartbeat. Somewhere beyond these walls, the passengers were being herded and contained. Every second we delayed, Croy's grip tightened.

I caught Sammie glancing back, probably checking if I could keep up. I adjusted my moustache just to reassure him. "Don't worry, my boy. I've navigated tighter spots than this. Once, on the Smuggler's Moon… "

"Monty," Sammie hissed, "less story time, more not-getting-caught time."

We pressed on. The air grew warmer as we passed near the engine manifolds, and the lighting flickered in an almost conspiratorial rhythm. Somewhere ahead, the corridor split, one path angling toward the starboard service lifts, the other toward the upper command junction.

Sammie slowed, pulling out a battered datapad and calling up a schematic. "Bridge access is two levels up from here," he said. "But I've got one more stop in mind before we climb."

I arched a brow. "Detour? During a First Order coup? Bold choice."

"It's not a detour," Sammie replied. "It's insurance. And trust me, you'll want to meet who's waiting there."

The way he said it made the hair on the back of my neck stand on end.

We slipped into another narrow passage, this one smelling faintly of lubricants and ozone, and came to a hatch that looked… at best… like it had been pried open by something very large and very determined.

Sammie tapped the panel twice in a strange rhythm, then ducked inside.

I followed, and the first thing that hit me was the sound.

Not boots. Not blaster fire.

A low, resonant growl that rolled through the compartment like distant thunder.

Before I could ask what sort of creature Sammie had stashed away, a towering shape emerged from the shadows, ducking to avoid the overhead pipes. Brown fur. Broad shoulders. A bandolier that looked older than some planets I'd been to.

And then… those eyes. Fierce, intelligent, and very much assessing me.

"Monty," Sammie said, his voice somewhere between awe and pride, "meet Chewbacca."

Chewbacca rumbled something deep in his chest, tilting his head as though I were an especially questionable menu item.

I straightened my cape, smoothed my moustache, and offered what I hoped was an appropriately diplomatic bow. "An honor, my… very tall friend. I've heard stories."

Another growl… this one with the distinct tone of I've heard stories.

"Why," I began, "do I feel as though I've stumbled into the middle of a very large and very hairy secret?"

"Because you have," came a familiar voice from behind.

Reginald Starjammer straightened from where he'd been crouched, grease smudges on his jacket and a spanner in one hand, and a crate next to him. "Nice of you to finally join us, Monty."

I arched a brow. "You've been hiding in the maintenance corridors with a Wookiee while I've been out risking my neck? How dreadfully unfair."

Reggie ignored the jab, tapping the crate. "Keevan sent for him. Quietly. The First Order locked down the bridge, but they also crippled our hyperdrive by removing the regulator. This… " he rapped his knuckles against the crate "… is the replacement."

Chewbacca gave a confirming growl and shoved the lid aside, revealing a gleaming hyperdrive regulator cradled in foam. Even I could tell it was important, and I generally measure importance by whether it can be worn as an accessory.

Sammie crouched beside it, practically vibrating. "Once we slot this in, we'll have control over the ship's main power grid again. Without that, we're dead in the water, and the First Order knows it."

I looked between them. "And I assume there's a very narrow, very dangerous window to get this installed without Croy finding out?"

Reginald smirked. "Exactly. Which is why you're here."

I blinked. "Oh? And here I thought I was just the decorative mascot of the rebellion."

Chewbacca let out a sharp bark that I chose to interpret as, less talking, more helping.

Reggie pointed to a schematic glowing faintly on his datapad. "We've got to move through maintenance junctions D-14 to F-22. That keeps us out of the main corridors, but it means we're in tight spaces, and we'll be passing dangerously close to one of the First Order security posts."

I tugged my cape tighter. "So, in summary: crawl through cramped, greasy tubes with a Wookiee, sneak past heavily armed stormtroopers, all while carrying the single most valuable piece of equipment on the ship."

"Exactly," Reginald said.

A slow grin spread across my face. "Splendid. Let's make it look effortless."

Chewbacca gave another rumbling growl, shouldered the crate like it weighed nothing, and started toward the hatch.

We slipped into the maintenance corridor, the hatch sealing behind us with a metallic thud that sounded far too final for my liking. The air here smelled faintly of ozone and machine oil, and the lighting was little more than the occasional flicker from strips recessed into the bulkhead.

Chewbacca lumbered ahead, the crate balanced easily in his arms despite being the size of a small speeder. Reginald followed close behind with the datapad, occasionally glancing over his shoulder to make sure I was keeping up.

"I do hope," I whispered, "that this heroic crawl will not scuff my boots. These are a limited edition from Corellia."

Reggie didn't even look back. "If we fail, your boots will be floating in a debris field so that I wouldn't worry about scuffs."

Sammie, bringing up the rear, tapped my arm and pointed ahead. We'd reached the first junction… D-14… where the corridor narrowed even further. The passage beyond was barely wide enough for Chewie's shoulders.

The Wookiee rumbled something low, and Reginald translated without looking up from the datapad. "He says to keep quiet from here on. We're about to pass within twenty meters of a First Order checkpoint."

Ah. The fun part.

We dropped into a crouch, our footsteps now a careful shuffle against the grated flooring. Chewbacca moved with surprising grace for someone his size, setting the crate down as gently as a jewel merchant. I found myself holding my breath as faint voices filtered through the bulkhead… two stormtroopers chatting about rations and some betting pool they had running.

Reggie signaled for us to wait. Thirty seconds passed. Forty. Then a muffled clank came from above, and the voices on the other side cut off mid-sentence. My pulse quickened.

Sammie leaned toward me, whispering so softly I almost didn't catch it: "One of them's moving. We need to go now."

Chewbacca slung the crate back up, and we slid along the corridor's curve, our shadows stretching across the bulkhead in the dim light. A sudden sweep of illumination… the white beam of a trooper's helmet lamp… slashed across the grate in front of us. I froze, my cape brushing the wall with the faintest whisper.

The light paused.

Then moved on.

We exhaled in unison and pushed forward until the checkpoint sounds faded. Reggie finally stopped at an intersection marked F-22 Access, and Sammie immediately popped a panel off the wall, revealing a ladder descending into the ship's guts.

"That's the service pit for the hyperdrive housing," Sammie said. "Once we're down there, we'll have to work fast."

I peered into the opening. "Fast? My dear boy, I've made a career out of fast. But if I'm climbing down there, someone had better promise me a drink when this is done."

Chewbacca growled low and approvingly, which I decided meant deal.

The ladder groaned under Chewbacca's weight as he descended into the pit, the crate cradled against his chest. I followed next, my boots finding each rung with deliberate precision, no sense risking a tumble into a tangle of high-voltage conduits.

The hyperdrive chamber spread out before us like the beating heart of the *Halcyon*… a cathedral of humming coils and plasma feeds, its soft blue light reflecting off the polished housings. In the center sat the failed hyperdrive regulator, the edges scorched from what looked suspiciously like deliberate sabotage.

Reginald was already on the deck below, tool kit spread open like a surgeon's tray. "All right, Chewbacca, on my mark, we lift the old one free. Monty… ” he fixed me with a pointed look, “… you're on stabilizer control.”

I arched an eyebrow. “You trust me with something as delicate as the ship's stabilizers?”

“No,” Reggie replied, “but Sammie needs both hands free for the coolant lines, and you're the only one left.”

I chose to interpret that as a vote of confidence.

Chewbacca grunted, and together he and Reginald heaved the damaged regulator from its housing. The sound it made coming loose was like a sick animal's last breath. Sparks cascaded down as Sammie killed the remaining power feed, and for a moment, the chamber went eerily quiet… too quiet for a vessel in motion.

“Monty, now!” Reggie barked.

I slammed the stabilizer override just as the replacement regulator cleared the housing. The ship gave a low shudder beneath us, but the deck stayed mercifully steady. Chewbacca was already lowering the new unit into place, his massive hands surprisingly precise as he aligned it with the couplings.

From above, the distant thump of boots echoed… stormtroopers moving through the adjacent corridor.

Sammie's voice was tight. “They're heading this way.”

Reggie cursed under his breath and dove for the coolant seals. Chewbacca locked the clamps with a decisive twist, and I held my breath as a deep, rising hum filled the chamber.

Then, the sweetest sound in the galaxy, the hyperdrive's core spun up, its glow brightening to a healthy cerulean.

"Regulator's stable," Reginald announced, wiping his hands. "We're back in business."

Chewbacca rumbled a note of satisfaction and gave the bulkhead an approving slap.

But before we could savor the moment, a sharp metallic clack came from the access ladder; someone was opening the hatch.

Without missing a beat, I swept my cape around my shoulders and straightened, ready to play the bewildered passenger who had absolutely no business being here. "Gentlemen," I whispered, "allow me to be the face of confusion."

The hatch swung open, white armor glinting in the light. "What's going on down… " the trooper began.

I didn't think. I acted.

Snatching the nearest thermal blanket from a wall rack, I whipped it over Chewie's head and shoulders in one sweeping motion.

"Don't just stand there!" I barked at Reginald and Sammie, shoving them forward. "Get him to the med shuttle… now!"

The trooper's vocoder crackled. "What's going on here?"

I turned to him with my most urgent, over-enunciated concern.

"Severe plasma burns, trooper! Third-degree… maybe fourth! Poor fellow took the brunt of an exhaust backfire while repairing the auxiliary relays."

I lowered my voice to a confidential hiss.

"If he doesn't get off this ship and into a bacta tank immediately, you'll be writing the longest incident report of your career. Trust me, you don't want that."

Chewbacca, bless him, groaned in perfect, pitiful agony under the blanket.

Sammie added, "And the smell's only gonna get worse the longer we wait."

The trooper froze, likely imagining singed fur, and took an involuntary step back.

"Uh… right. Med shuttle's in the forward bay. I'll, uh… clear a path."

"Good man!" I said, clapping his plastoid shoulder so heartily I nearly knocked him sideways.

"Now, team… every second counts!"

We hurried down the corridor, Chewbacca shuffling awkwardly under the blanket like a very tall, very hairy ghost. Every time his head brushed the ceiling, he let out a moan worthy of an amateur dinner-theatre performance.

"Bit over the top," Reginald muttered.

"Rubbish," I whispered back. "If anything, he's underplaying it."

By the time we reached the forward bay, the trooper had run ahead to shoo away a pair of curious passengers.

Chewbacca ducked into the concealed shuttle alcove, tearing the blanket off with a relieved roar.

"See?" I said, dusting off my cape as though the entire charade had been a matter of routine.

"Just a perfectly normal medical emergency. Happens all the time on luxury cruises. Though usually it's less 'mystery burns' and more 'someone overindulged at the buffet.'"

We quickened our pace, the corridor lights flicking off Chewbacca's blanket like we were smuggling a very large, very furry festival float. Ahead, the cargo bay doors loomed… the promise of freedom for our towering patient.

At the cargo bay, the freighter Captain Keevan had arranged was already waiting, its lights dimmed to keep from drawing attention. The ramp lowered with a soft hiss, spilling just enough light to catch the faint gleam in Chewbacca's eyes.

As we walked him aboard, Sammie darted ahead to the control console. "Just a few tweaks," he said, fingers flying over the panel, "and this bird will drop you exactly where you need to be."

Chewbacca gave a low, rumbling growl that seemed to vibrate in my chest. Sammie grinned over his shoulder. "He says… he owes you one."

I stepped forward, reaching into my satchel. "There's no need for debts between old friends," I said warmly. "But before you go, allow me to offer you this."

From the bag I produced a small tin, holding it aloft as if it were a priceless relic. "Montgomery's Wacky Wookiee Wax™. The premier grooming product in the galaxy."

Chewbacca tilted his head, issuing a curious, questioning growl as he stepped closer to inspect it.

Sammie smirked and translated. "He says… most of his people already use it. Swears by it, actually."

I blinked, caught entirely off guard, then broke into a slow, satisfied grin. "Well, of course they do. Good taste runs deep in Kashyyyk culture." I held the tin a little higher. "But this… " my voice dropped to a conspiratorial tone, "… is the deluxe blend. Extra shine, added volume, and a hint of sandalwood essence. Perfect for a Wookiee of your legendary stature."

Chewbacca accepted the tin with a short, approving rumble, then clasped my forearm in a grip that nearly dislocated my shoulder.

The ramp began to rise, the hatch sealing between us. I gave him a last two-fingered salute. "Safe travels, my friend. May your mane forever catch the starlight."

And then he was gone, taking the faint scent of engine coolant, sandalwood, and adventure with him.

Sammie and I turned to leave, the quiet hum of the cargo bay still in our ears, when the ship's comms system crackled to life.

"Starstalker. Sammie. Report to me in the Sublight Lounge. Immediately."

It was Croy's voice… cold, clipped, and entirely too close for comfort.

Sammie groaned under his breath. "We're doomed."

I adjusted my moustache with a deliberate flourish and gave him my most unflappable grin. "Nonsense, my good man. We're simply… in demand. Adventure awaits."

With that, I swept into the corridor, cape trailing behind us like the opening curtain of a drama, leaving only the faint scent of sandalwood… and the echo of a Wookiee's laughter lingering in the air.

29
HIGH STAKES SABAAC

Reginald, walking just behind us, tilted his head. "Sublight Lounge? With Croy? Sounds like a trap."

"Which… " I said, halting dramatically and pointing at him, "… is precisely why you're not coming. I need you elsewhere."

He raised an eyebrow. "Doing what, exactly?"

"Find R2–DPR. No one's seen him since before we went down to Batuu. The ship feels… too quiet without him."

Reginald gave a slow nod. "So, I wander the ship looking for our missing droid while you stroll into whatever this is?"

"Exactly. And if I don't make it back, remember… keep my moustache wax in a temperature-controlled environment. It's artisanal."

Before he could answer, I pivoted sharply, letting my cape swish in just the right way as Sammie and I set off toward the Sublight Lounge, leaving Reginald to disappear down another corridor on his own errand.

***

The Sublight Lounge was far from its usual self. Normally, it was a sanctuary of soft lighting, low laughter, and the cheerful click of sabacc chips sliding across the table. Tonight, it was stripped bare of all charm.

205

No music. No guests. Just an empty, echoing room that smelled faintly of stale lum ale and impending trouble.

Lieutenant Croy sat dead center like a spider in the middle of his web, his posture rigid, his dark grey officer's coat immaculate. A squad of stormtroopers flanked him in perfect formation, their blank visors fixed forward as if daring anyone to twitch the wrong way.

Sammie and I had been summoned, just the two of us, and from the way Croy's smirk tugged at the corner of his mouth, I had the distinct feeling he'd been rehearsing whatever was about to happen.

"Well," I murmured to Sammie as the lounge doors hissed shut behind us, "either we've been invited to an intimate sabacc tournament… or this is the part where he feeds us to a rancor."

Sammie shot me a nervous glance. "I don't think there's a rancor on board."

"There's always a rancor, Sammie. Sometimes it just wears better tailoring."

Croy didn't rise to greet us; predators rarely do. Instead, he gestured lazily to the empty chair opposite him, the way an emperor might motion to a supplicant. I took my seat with the sort of casual grace one adopts when pretending not to notice the four stormtrooper blasters within arm's reach.

And then I saw it.

At his side, sitting obediently on the floor like a loyal pet, was R2–DPR. *My* R2–DPR. The little droid's dome swiveled toward me, and I could swear the faintest, most apologetic beep escaped him.

Oh. So this was the game.

"Starstalker," Croy said as we stepped into the lounge, his voice rolling across the empty room like distant thunder. My cape caught the low light just so naturally, casting a dazzling emerald ripple as I moved.

"So good of you to join us. I was beginning to think you were avoiding me."

"I assure you, Lieutenant," I replied, adjusting my moustache with a flourish only years of practice could perfect, "I'd never miss an opportunity to bask in the... glow of your hospitality."

Croy's eyes narrowed, the faintest smirk playing at his lips before he let them settle into a line of calculated disinterest. His gaze slid past me to Sammie, who had been hovering behind like a schoolboy summoned to the headmaster's office.

"And your mechanic friend," Croy said, voice cool enough to frost glass.

Sammie swallowed hard and stepped forward, grease-streaked hands twitching at his sides. "Here, sir."

"Good," Croy said simply, turning his back on us as though confident we'd follow. He returned to the sabacc table and settled into his seat with the unhurried grace of someone who already believed they'd won.

"Sit," he ordered, gesturing to the chairs opposite him.

The tension pressed in as we obeyed, the silent stormtroopers flanking the walls like statues with rifles.

With a deliberate calm, Croy began dealing the cards, each flick of his wrist a display of surgical precision. The shhhk of cardboard on felt echoed unnaturally loud in the hollow room.

"I must say, Starstalker," he began, his tone smooth but soaked in insincerity, "your presence aboard the *Halcyon* has been... colourful.

Though I can't help but notice…" he paused to place a card in front of me, "… that wherever you go, chaos seems to follow."

I crossed one leg over the other, letting my cape drape like I owned the place. "Lieutenant, chaos doesn't follow me… it tries to keep up."

If he was amused, he didn't show it. His gaze flicked to R2–DPR, parked beside his chair like a prisoner of war, dome tilted down. "Your astromech was caught meddling in restricted systems. We can't have that."

"Oh, I'm sure it's all a misunderstanding," I said smoothly, leaning forward. "He's a curious little fellow. Artistic temperament. Sometimes he hears the word 'restricted' and assumes it's an invitation."

Croy ignored me, shuffling the deck with surgical precision. "I'm a reasonable man, Captain. So I'll offer you a chance to keep your droid… functional."

Sammie, sitting stiffly at my side, blinked. "Functional?"

Croy didn't break eye contact with me. "We play. One-on-one. Sabacc. If you win, the droid goes back to you, free to… improvise, as you call it. If I win…" His smile was the kind that didn't reach his eyes. "… the First Order will deactivate him and recycle the scrap before the day is out."

Sammie inhaled sharply. "That's…"

I raised a hand to silence him, still locked on Croy. "You want to gamble for my droid's life? Lieutenant, I'll have you know that's monstrously unfair."

Croy's smirk widened. "Then don't lose."

I let the pause stretch just long enough for Sammie to start fidgeting, then leaned back and gestured for the deal. "Fine. But don't be surprised when my moustache and I send you home empty-handed."

The cards began to fall, each one crisp against the table, the stakes hanging heavy in the air. This wasn't just a game… it was a duel. And I intended to win.

The first few rounds were cautious… Croy played like a predator circling his prey, every bet deliberate, every draw measured. I matched him with bold wagers and the occasional theatrical flourish, just enough to keep him guessing.

Sammie, bless him, managed to avoid looking completely out of his depth, though I could practically hear the sweat forming under the lieutenant's glare

"You know," Croy said as he slid more credits into the pot, "I've been on this ship long enough to spot a liar. And you, Starstalker, reek of deception."

"Deception?" I let out a scandalized laugh, tossing a credit chip onto the growing pile. "Lieutenant, you wound me. I'm as transparent as a Hoth snowdrift."

Croy's brow furrowed. "What does that even mean?"

"I don't know," I admitted cheerfully, straightening my cape. "But it sounded convincing when I said it."

Sammie choked back a laugh, which earned him a sharp look from Croy.

"Then," the lieutenant pressed, his tone turning cold, "you won't mind explaining why your droid was accessing restricted systems."

"He was probably lost," I said with an easy shrug. "Much like myself, he has a terrible sense of direction."

The game ground on, the tension coiling tighter with every hand. I kept up my steady stream of banter, batting away Croy's probing questions with the ease of a man who's been dodging inquiries his entire life.

The pile of credits in the center of the table grew higher—along with the lieutenant's smirk. His fingers tapped the edge of the deck, a rhythm of quiet confidence that made Sammie shift uneasily beside me.

Sammie's boot nudged mine under the table. "Monty," he breathed, barely audible, "he's setting us up."

"Of course he is," I murmured back, without taking my eyes off Croy. "But so am I."

We slid into the final round, the stakes ratcheted up so high the air in the lounge felt electric. My pulse matched the thrum of the ship's engines. One hand… one card… would decide it all. The fate of R2-DPR was balanced on the edge of a sabacc deck.

Croy, ever the picture of smug superiority, leaned back in his chair, steepling his fingers. "Your move, Starstalker."

I rested my hand on the table, letting the moment stretch because if you can't win on cards, you win in theatre.

I glanced at my cards, then at Sammie, whose wide-eyed expression practically shouted, 'we're doomed.' Taking a slow, deliberate breath, I set my hand face-down on the table.

"I'm all in," I said, pushing the last of my credits forward with the kind of flourish a man reserves for his final toast before the firing squad.

Croy's smirk widened like a crack in durasteel. "Bold," he drawled, flipping over his cards. Pure sabacc.

The room seemed to tilt. My eyes locked on his winning hand, the heavy reality sinking like a stone in my gut.

"Well," I said, rising to my feet with as much dignity as I could muster, "looks like the game is over. And so, I suspect, is your…"

A sharp burst of static cut me off. Croy's comm crackled to life.

"Lieutenant," a voice blurted, hurried and tense, "we've got a breach in the cargo bay. Possible resistance activity."

The lieutenant's smirk froze, the win forgotten in a flash of suspicion.

Croy's smirk froze, his eyes narrowing at the comm.

"On my way," he snapped, standing so abruptly his chair scraped the deck.

Two stormtroopers moved with him, boots pounding toward the door. He jabbed a finger at the last one… the one left behind.

"Secure the droid. I'll deal with it when I return."

The trooper turned toward R2–DPR with mechanical obedience… then his helmet tilted ever so slightly when his gaze flicked toward me.

The trooper planted himself a few steps away, blaster in hand, clearly under orders to watch us until Croy returned. His visor turned toward me, lingering just long enough for me to sense the awkward familiarity.

"You… " he said slowly. "You're… Captain Montgomery Starstalker."

I allowed a modest smile. "I suppose I am, yes."

"I saw you on Batuu. That… that autograph? Best day of my rotation."

"Well, I'm glad to have improved your otherwise dreary service record."

He shifted on his feet, almost embarrassed. "Look, I'm just here to keep you put. No funny business."

"Of course," I said, gesturing to my perfectly still posture. "Do I look like a man capable of mischief?"

Before he could answer, his comlink crackled: "Unit Thorn… report to Cargo Bay immediately. Priority one."

The trooper hesitated, clearly torn between orders. "Uh… I'm not supposed to… "

"Go," I urged, lowering my voice conspiratorially. "The galaxy calls. I'll keep the lounge exactly as you left it."

He glanced at R2–DPR. "I'm just… I'll slap a restraining bolt on him so it's not on me if anything happens. Don't… don't take it off… Please."

He clipped the bolt in place, looking almost guilty. "Alright, Captain… don't make me regret this."

I placed a hand over my heart. "My dear boy, I regret nothing."

With one last nod, he jogged out, leaving Sammie, R2–DPR, and me alone in the suddenly quiet lounge.

Sammie gave me a flat look. "You're going to take it off."

"Absolutely," I said, crouching beside the droid. "But in a way that would make a lawyer proud of the technicalities."

R2–DPR let out a sly beep-whirr, already turning his dome as if he'd been waiting for this all day.

I knelt beside R2–DPR like a surgeon about to attempt the most delicate operation in the galaxy.

"Now, my little friend," I murmured, "this will be tricky, but I've faced worse. Once, on a drifting casino liner, I dismantled an explosives rig while blindfolded and being serenaded by a tone-deaf Rodian. This will be nothing."

I pulled a small multi-tool from my satchel, flicked it open, and prodded the restraining bolt. It didn't budge.

"Hmm. Stubborn little thing, aren't you?"

I tried again, this time with a gentle twist. Nothing.

"All right, perhaps a firmer touch."

I braced myself, gritting my teeth, and gave it a solid wrench. The bolt didn't so much as blink, but my knuckles did make an audible crack

R2–DPR gave a low, mournful boooop.

"Don't you start," I muttered. I switched grips, crouching low like a holo-drama action hero. I twisted, tugged, and even gave it a polite tap-tap-tap as though that might persuade it. Sweat began to bead at my temple.

"Right," I said through clenched teeth. "It's a battle of wills now. One of us will give in, and it won't be me."

Sammie crouched beside me, watching for all of ten seconds before sighing. "Monty... you're overthinking it."

"Overthinking? My dear boy, this is a dance. A contest of patience and technique. The restraining bolt must believe you are its friend before..."

Click.

I blinked. The bolt was gone. Sammie was holding it between two fingers. "You just... unscrew it. Quarter turn counter-clockwise. Done."

I stared at him. "That's it? No subtlety? No flair?"

"Monty," Sammie said, "it's literally designed to be removed for maintenance."

I rose slowly, adjusting my cape with dignity I didn't entirely feel. "Well. Yes. But you've robbed it of drama."

R2–DPPR let out a chipper beep-beep-beeeep, as if to say he didn't mind.

"Fine," I sighed. "But if anyone asks, we'll tell them it was a daring, five-minute battle of man versus machine. My legend must be preserved."

R2–DPR's lights flared back to life, blinking in rapid sequence as the droid shot upright with an almost panicked whistle.

"Whoa, slow down!" Sammie said, raising both hands like he was calming a spooked tauntaun. "What's he saying?"

I tilted my head, squinting in the way I imagine fluent droid-speak interpreters must. "Something about circuits... or was it circus? No, wait... he's talking about... "

"He says," Sammie cut in, his voice dropping to a tense whisper, "he has to send a message to the Resistance. The First Order fleet is moving into position."

I froze, my moustache twitching in alarm. "Fleet? As in multiple ships? With guns?"

Sammie nodded grimly. "If we don't unjam the comms, they can't get the warning out. We might be the only ones who know."

My hand flew to my chest. "You mean it's up to us to save the galaxy again? Oh, how tiresome," I said with mock exasperation, already

straightening my cape. "Very well. Tell the droid to send his message…
we'll hold the fort here."

R2–DPR gave an urgent, negative BWAAP!

Sammie's eyes darted to mine. "He says he can't send the message until
the First Order's signal jammers are taken offline. And those controls…
are three corridors away. Past at least two stormtrooper patrols."

A slow grin spread across my face. "Ah. So we don't just have to hold
the fort, we have to storm the fort, disable their precious toys, and make
it back before Croy notices his moustachioed nemesis is missing.
Excellent. This is shaping up nicely."

Sammie looked considerably less enthusiastic. "You realize, Monty, that
if we get caught, we're done. I mean… like, forever done."

I gave his shoulder a reassuring pat. "Nonsense. I've faced far worse
with far less at stake. Now…" I swirled my cape dramatically. "… let's
go unjam a communications array and ruin Lieutenant Croy's evening."

R2–DPR beeped in eager agreement and zipped toward the door,
forcing us into a quick jog to keep up. Somewhere down those dim
corridors lay the difference between warning the Resistance in time…
and being too late.

R2–DPR zipped out the door like a tiny blue-and-white missile, and
Sammie and I had no choice but to follow at a half-jog.

"Stealth, Sammie," I whispered as my cape brushed dangerously close
to a bulkhead lamp. "We must move like shadows in the night."

"You're wearing a luminous cape," he muttered back. "The only thing
you're blending into is a parade."

We rounded the first corner just as a pair of stormtroopers clomped past. I pulled Sammie into an alcove, my hand flying to my moustache in a protective reflex. The troopers paused, one glancing at his wrist com, the other shifting his blaster grip. I leaned in close to Sammie.

"Observe," I whispered, "the art of blending in."

Then I casually picked up a nearby crate, spun it around, and began loudly complaining to Sammie about "defective food rations" while marching directly past them. The troopers barely glanced at us. They'd been trained to ignore grumpy passengers. A valuable lesson: theatrics, properly applied, can be camouflage.

We reached the jammer control room with only one other near-miss, an incident involving R2–DPR, a tipped-over service cart, and Sammie's entirely unnecessary scream. Inside, the air was heavy with ozone, the jammers' indicator lights blinking in smug, mechanical rhythm.

"Two minutes," Sammie said, already at the console.

"Two minutes? My dear boy, I can disable this in one," I replied, flipping open a panel and pretending to understand the tangle of wires within. R2–DPR whistled impatiently and bumped me aside before expertly slicing into the system

The hum of the jammers died. The last jammer went quiet with a faint hiss, like a dying kettle. R2–DPR let out a satisfied chirp, his dome swiveling to me for approval.

"Well done, old boy," I said, giving him a dignified nod as though he'd just performed a particularly elegant violin solo.

"He's sending the message now," Sammie whispered, eyes darting between the door and the console.

"Good," I replied. "Once the Resistance knows, they can send help, and we can all go back to our normal lives. You back to fixing hydrospanners, me back to being devastatingly handsome and adored."

We slipped back into the corridor, my cape flaring just enough to clip Sammie in the arm. "Ow… could you not… " he hissed, but his complaint was cut short by a familiar voice ahead.

"Monty!" Reginald stepped out from a side passage, looking mildly annoyed, which for him was practically a bear hug. "There you are. I've been dodging patrols for twenty minutes, and all I find is you two wandering around like tourists."

"Not wandering," I corrected. "Heroically returning from a mission of utmost importance." I gestured toward R2–DPR, who was beeping in smug agreement

"Yes, well, heroic or not," Reginald said, glancing over his shoulder, "I just heard something on the comms. The bridge is in uproar. Something about 'containment measures' and 'disciplinary action.' And I doubt they mean giving us all a stern talking-to.

"Containment measures?" Sammie echoed. "That sounds… bad."

"It is bad," Reginald replied. "And it's moving our way."

We began heading toward the atrium, the three of us keeping to shadows where possible. Reginald whispered to Sammie, "Monty's idea of stealth involves tossing dramatic looks at every reflective surface we pass."

I stopped mid-stride, adjusting my moustache in the faint gleam of a polished wall panel. "Correction, Reginald," I whispered back with gravitas, "my idea of stealth involves ensuring the galaxy doesn't forget me even in shadow. If the First Order catches a glimpse, let it be a dazzling one."

At one point, we ducked behind a decorative column as two stormtroopers stomped past, mid-argument.

"… telling you, it was him!" the first insisted. "Cape, moustache, the works!"

"Oh, right," the second snorted. "Like the Lieutenant wouldn't have him locked in the brig by now."

I waited until their footsteps faded, then leaned toward Sammie and Reginald. "You see? My fame precedes me."

Sammie just sighed. "It's not fame if they're trying to arrest you."

By the time we reached the atrium's edge, the sound of raised voices carried across the space. Stormtroopers were corralling passengers into tight groups. Croy stood like a dark tower in the middle, his hands clasped behind his back, eyes scanning the room with the cold precision of a man about to make an example of someone

I stopped just short of stepping into view, my stomach sinking. "Well," I murmured to the others, "I think I've just spotted the evening's entertainment. And unfortunately, I suspect we're all in the front row."

30
CHAOS

It was too late. I had been spotted. Croy's eyes locked on me like a targeting computer.

"Starstalker," he said, each syllable dripping with contempt, "you've been a thorn in my side since the moment you boarded. And where there's one thorn… "

He turned his gaze to Sammie. "… there's usually another."

Sammie straightened, confusion and defiance warring on his face. "If you think I've been messing with the ship, it's because I've been fixing the damage your bucketheads keep doing."

The passengers shifted uneasily, a nervous ripple through the atrium.

"Take him," Croy ordered.

Two stormtroopers moved in, one of them the same trooper who'd once asked for my autograph on Batuu. I recognized him as my faded autograph was still on his armored forearm. His helmet dipped toward me for half a heartbeat before they grabbed Sammie by the arms.

"Monty… " Sammie started, but he cut himself off, forcing a shaky grin. "Don't do anything stupid. You've got more important things to… "

Croy's gloved hand lifted, silencing him. "Remove him from my sight."

They marched Sammie out toward a side corridor, their boots clanging against the decking. The last thing I saw was Sammie's face vanish behind the curve of the bulkhead. Then…

The blaster report echoed like a thunderclap, sharp and final. A few passengers gasped; one let out a strangled cry.

I stood frozen, the sound still ringing in my ears.

Croy let the silence stretch until it became unbearable. Then, with a thin smile, he said, "Let that be a warning. Defiance will be erased." No one could see down the side corridor where Sammie had been dragged, but the sound was enough. A ripple of gasps swept the atrium. My stomach dropped through the polished floor.

"Enough!

Captain Keevan's voice cut through the silence like a hyperspace rupture. She strode in, every inch the Pantoran commander, golden eyes blazing, posture straight as a durasteel girder.

"You dare?" she said, her tone low and precise, each syllable edged to wound. "This is my ship, Lieutenant, and you just murdered one of my crew in cold blood."

Croy stood unmoved, though a flicker of satisfaction danced at the corners of his mouth.

"I enforced order," he replied evenly. "Your mechanic violated First Order control of this vessel. The punishment was… appropriate."

"Appropriate?" Keevan's voice rose like a gathering storm. "You've just shown every soul aboard exactly what your 'order' means: fear, brutality, and the execution of the innocent. You haven't secured this ship, Lieutenant… you've poisoned it."

Murmurs ran through the passengers clustered at the edges of the atrium, eyes darting from Keevan to the white-armored wall of stormtroopers.

The two troopers who had executed Sammie finally reappeared from the corridor, returning silently to flank the room as if nothing had happened. Helmets down, rifles at the ready… they were just shadows in the First Order's machine.

Croy's gaze stayed locked on Keevan. "Control will be maintained. One way or another."

Keevan took a deliberate step forward, the tension stretching so tight I could almost hear it hum. "Not for long, Lieutenant."

I stood rooted to the spot, my pulse loud in my ears. Sammie was gone. Just… gone. And if Croy could do that to a ship's mechanic in plain sight, there was no telling what would come next.

Keevan's golden eyes never wavered, locked on Croy as if she could cut him down with the force of her stare alone.

"You can threaten me all you want," she said, her voice steady as durasteel, "but it won't change the fact that you're nothing more than a glorified errand boy for an organization that doesn't respect you."

Croy's lips curled, his smirk hardening into something far more dangerous.

"Careful, Captain. Your insubordination is walking a very thin line."

Keevan took a step closer, close enough that the air between them seemed to vibrate with tension.

"You think your words mean anything here? You preach control, but all you have is fear. Fear is the only language you know, and that's why you'll never truly command anyone's loyalty."

His eyes narrowed.

"Fear," Croy said, his tone dropping to a cold, deliberate growl, "is the only language this galaxy understands. And I will teach it to them, starting with you."

He turned sharply toward a nearby stormtrooper, his hand flicking in a wordless order. The trooper raised his blaster, the black muzzle swinging toward Keevan's chest.

And then…

"Fear is not the way."

The voice cut through the atrium like a ripple of light through shadow: calm, resonant, and impossible to ignore.

The crowd turned. Emerging from one of the side passages, the Saja entered with ethereal grace, their flowing robes untouched by the tension that gripped the room. Master Tal'Veren stepped forward, his golden eyes fixed on Croy, while two other Saja flanked him in silent solidarity.

"The Force binds us all," Tal'Veren said, his words carrying effortlessly to every corner of the chamber. "It is through unity, not oppression, that true strength is found."

For a moment, the air seemed to shift. Stormtroopers hesitated, the crowd leaned forward, and even Croy's rigid posture faltered ever so slightly, as though the certainty of his own narrative had been dented.

Croy's jaw tightened. "Unity," he repeated, his voice dripping with disdain. "A quaint sentiment, Master Saja. But unity without control is chaos. And chaos," he turned slightly, addressing the passengers now as much as the Saja, "is exactly what opportunists like Starstalker thrive on."

I raised an eyebrow. "Lieutenant, please. I thrive on well-mixed cocktails, rare scarves, and applause—not chaos. Chaos is just a... side effect."

A few nervous chuckles fluttered through the crowd, but Croy's glare snapped them into silence.

"This," he gestured sharply at me, "is the very man who's been a thorn in my side since he boarded. Always in the wrong place at the wrong time, always meddling. And I've been far too lenient."

Keevan stepped forward again, cutting the distance between them to almost nothing.

"You lay a finger on any of my passengers or crew, Lieutenant, and you'll answer for it, not just to me, but to the New Republic, the Resistance, and every soul aboard this vessel."

Croy smirked. "The New Republic is a dying ember, Captain. The Resistance is a rumor. And you... " he leaned in just enough for the nearest guests to hear, "you're standing in the way of the inevitable."

"Fear is not inevitable," Tal'Veren countered, his voice like tempered steel. "You will find that those united by trust and hope can resist even the most ruthless designs."

Something in Croy's expression shifted, calculation replacing irritation. His gaze swept the passengers like a predator choosing which prey to strike first.

"If you truly believe that," he said, "then let's put it to the test."

He pointed toward the gathered civilians.

"Bring someone forward. Someone who can pay the price for this ship's defiance."

A stormtrooper began to move, and my heart lodged somewhere between my throat and my cape clasp.

"Oh, now hold on," I said, stepping forward just enough to insert myself into the line of sight without making it too obvious I was doing something noble. "If you need a volunteer… "

Keevan's eyes flicked to me, warning me off, but I gave her the faintest of nods.

"… you might as well choose someone who looks good under duress."

Croy's eyes locked on me like a targeting computer settling in for the kill.

"Enough of this," he said coldly. "Starstalker, you've meddled in my operations for the last time. Execute him."

Gasps rippled through the atrium. Keevan started forward, but two stormtroopers, both from the squad that had dragged Sammie away, stepped in front of her, blasters raised.

I adjusted my moustache with a flick of my wrist. "Well… this seems rather final."

From somewhere behind the crowd, Reggie's voice cracked like a faulty comlink. "Monty!"

The stormtrooper on my right shifted slightly. "Lieutenant," he said, voice oddly measured through the helmet. "Perhaps we should reconsider… "

"Reconsider?" Croy snapped, his expression twisting. "Who do you think you are, questioning my orders? Execute him now, or I'll "

The trooper on my left moved in one swift, deliberate motion, unclasping his helmet and pulling it free. Gasps rose again as the face beneath was revealed.

Sammie.

Alive.

Grinning like a smuggler who'd just outbluffed a Hutt.

"Surprise!" he exclaimed.

Before the shock could settle, the second trooper yanked his helmet off, revealing the very young, nervous-looking face of a man I didn't recognize. His cheeks were flushed, his blond hair plastered down from the helmet.

"With respect, sir," he said to Croy, standing a little taller, "you don't give the kill order on Montgomery Starstalker. Not on my watch."

I blinked at him. "I'm sorry… have we met?"

"It's me, sir," he said quickly, pride swelling in his voice. "Batuu. Cantina. You signed my armour." He extended his arm to show me again what I had noticed only moments earlier.

Realization hit me like a misfired thermal detonator. "Ah! Forearm Autograph Enthusiast Number Forty-Seven. Of course."

A murmur swept through the passengers. Keevan's golden eyes blazed with sudden hope.

I took a slow, theatrical bow, my cape fanning behind me.

"Well," I said lightly, "it appears my public continues to surprise me."

Croy's jaw worked like he was chewing on molten durasteel. "You think this changes anything?" he snarled. "You think a stunt like this will stop me? I am in command here!"

Sammie stepped forward, blaster now leveled steadily at Croy, his face set with a determination I hadn't seen before. "The First Order has no power here, Lieutenant. Not as long as we stand together."

For the first time, a flicker of doubt crossed Croy's eyes.

Captain Keevan seized the moment. She stepped into the open, her voice ringing out through the atrium with all the force of a rallying horn. "Did you hear that?" she called to the passengers. "Together… as one!"

"Together as one!" a few voices echoed, hesitant at first.

Keevan's golden eyes swept the crowd, locking with individuals, willing them to join her. "Louder!" she demanded. "Together as one!"

The chant grew. Passengers in the balconies leaned over the rails, shouting it. Crew members emerged from doorways, adding their voices.

"TOGETHER AS ONE!"

The stormtroopers hesitated. The sound was deafening now, an unstoppable wave of defiance filling every corner of the atrium. The SAJA emerged from the meditation nook, their robes flowing, lending their voices to the chant, their presence radiating calm and resolve.

The crowd pressed in, not violently, but with sheer numbers, their unity a wall Croy could not push through. A few stormtroopers glanced at each other, unsure. And then… one lowered his weapon. Then another.

Even the fanboy trooper, standing at Sammie's side, raised his chin and joined the chant.

Croy spun in place, trapped, his voice lost under the thunder of the people he could not control. He slammed a fist against the nearest console in frustration.

I allowed myself a small, satisfied smile and murmured, "And that, Lieutenant, is what they call losing the room."

31
TOGETHER AS ONE

The tension in the atrium was stretched so tight you could almost hear it hum. Croy's jaw was locked, his finger twitching as he tried to work his datapad. Then…

BZZZT-CRACKLE

The *Halcyon's* comm system, which had been spitting nothing but First Order commands for hours, suddenly went wild. Static hissed… and then a voice, strong and urgent, burst through.

"This is Commander Lysa Marrek of the New Republic. Citizens aboard the *Halcyon*… hold fast. You are not alone."

Gasps rippled through the passengers. Croy's head snapped up toward the nearest speaker grille.

"The First Order's control of this vessel will not stand," the voice continued, unwavering. "We have your coordinates. Help is on the way."

The comm cut to dead silence.

For a single, fragile heartbeat, nobody moved. Then Captain Keevan stepped forward into the center of the atrium, her golden Pantoran eyes blazing.

"You heard her," Keevan said, her voice ringing out so that even the farthest balconies heard. "Help is on the way. But we will stand together until it arrives."

She turned slowly, locking eyes with the passengers, the crew, even a few stormtroopers whose stances had faltered.

"This ship belongs to all of us," she declared. "Not the First Order. Together… "

A voice from the crowd, trembling but loud, picked up the word: " … as one!"

Keevan nodded, her voice gaining strength. "Together as one!"

The shout rolled through the atrium like a shockwave. "Together as one! Together as one!"

And right in the middle of that swelling chant, the comm crackled again. This time it was a growl: deep, unmistakable, and more than a little smug.

Sammie's face lit up. "That's Chewbacca… "

Passengers surged toward the atrium's massive viewport, pressing against the glass like children at a fireworks show.

From the star-streaked black, a familiar shape tore out of hyperspace… the *Millennium Falcon*, hull scorched, engines roaring in defiance. A heartbeat later, the void lit up with a dozen more flashes as Resistance cruisers and starfighters dropped in behind her, forming a wall of durasteel and laser cannons between the *Halcyon* and the First Order blockade.

The comms crackled to life again, this time with a voice that needed no translation. Chewbacca's triumphant roar rattled the speakers.

Sammie, still half wearing his stolen stormtrooper armor, grinned. "He says the cavalry's here."

The fanboy trooper, helmet now under his arm, leaned toward me like we were sharing a pub secret. "That's Chewbacca! You know Chewbacca?"

"I know everyone worth knowing," I replied smoothly, tugging my cape into perfect drape despite the looming space battle.

Lieutenant Croy spun toward Captain Keevan, fury breaking through his mask of control. "This changes nothing, Captain. Your ship is still under…"

"… my command," Keevan cut in, her tone sharp and biting. She strode to the nearest control console, fingers flying across the keys as she bypassed the First Order's lockouts. The *Halcyon's* lighting shifted instantly, cool, elegant gold sweeping away the oppressive gray the First Order had imposed.

"All crew, to stations," she barked into the shipwide channel. "Target First Order weapons systems only. Disable their ability to fire. Protect the passengers."

The *Halcyon's* great engines rumbled beneath our feet, her inertial compensators struggling to keep up as the luxury liner came alive in a way few had ever seen. Turbolaser batteries slid from concealed housings along her sleek hull, pivoting toward the First Order destroyer.

The fanboy trooper gave a low whistle. "She's armed?"

Sammie patted him on the shoulder. "Oh, you have no idea."

Croy's eyes widened. "You wouldn't dare…"

Keevan turned to him, her golden eyes burning. "You threatened my passengers. I dare."

The first volley of the *Halcyon's* turbo lasers lit up the void, green streaks slamming into First Order shields just as the *Falcon* and a wing of Resistance X-wings screamed past, opening the battle in earnest.

The atrium shook with the roar of the engines and the cheers of the passengers. For the first time since Croy boarded, the *Halcyon* was hers again.

The deck rattled again as the *Halcyon* traded fire with the First Order. Guests ducked behind furniture, and crew members ushered them toward safe compartments.

Croy was barking orders into his comm, trying to rally his stormtroopers, but half of them were already hesitating, glancing toward the viewport as the *Falcon* and Resistance fighters tore through the enemy line.

Sammie grabbed my arm. "Monty… those passengers near the stairwell are boxed in. If the First Order pushes there… "

I swept my cape over one shoulder. "Leave it to me, my boy. Nobody boxes in Montgomery Starstalker's audience."

Before I could even make my dramatic approach, the fanboy trooper charged forward, blaster in hand, shouting, "Come with me if you're with him!", pointing at me like I'd just saved the galaxy single-handedly.

A ripple of confusion and then, astonishingly, a cheer went up from a group of passengers.

From across the atrium, Sandro Alamander leapt onto a table, lute in hand. "To battle!" he cried, and began strumming a raucous tune that, regrettably, rhymed "Starstalker" with "blaster blocker." The rhythm was infectious. Guests clapped, crew members joined in, and the stormtroopers found themselves dodging more flying dinnerware than blaster bolts.

"Is… is this a rebellion or a cabaret?" Sammie shouted over the noise.

"A bit of both," I said proudly, tossing a serving tray like a discus that knocked a trooper's blaster from his hands.

The fanboy trooper cuffed one of his former squadmates, shouting, "That's for trying to arrest my captain!"

Amid the chaos, Croy's voice cut through, ragged now, less commanding than desperate. "Hold the line! That's an order… "

A fresh volley from the Falcon slammed into the destroyer outside, and the atrium's viewports lit up with the sight of the First Order flagship peeling away, shields flickering. The rest of their ships began to break formation, retreating under the combined fire of the Resistance and the *Halcyon*.

Keevan advanced on Croy, flanked by two Saja, her voice carrying over the cheers. "Lieutenant… the day is lost. Your men are scattered. Your fleet is fleeing. Leave the *Halcyon* now, or I'll have you escorted to the brig in pieces."

The atrium fell silent. Croy's jaw clenched, his pride warring with the truth staring him in the face. Finally, with a curt nod, he lowered his datapad. "Very well. This vessel is yours… for now."

The fanboy trooper raised his fist. "Long live Captain Starstalker!"

The atrium erupted in laughter and applause, Sandro striking one last triumphant chord.

I gave a gracious bow, adjusting my moustache just so. "The galaxy," I said, "is simply safer when I'm aboard."

The cheering in the atrium swelled as the First Order's retreat became undeniable. The fanboy trooper pulled off his helmet for good this time, revealing a face far younger than I'd imagined, wide-eyed, but with a stubborn set to his jaw.

Keevan studied him. "You're First Order… and yet you turned your blaster on your own."

He straightened. "My name's Fen Ralor. I joined thinking I'd be serving peace… order. But all I've seen is fear. You… " he glanced at me with something approaching awe, "… you showed me there's another way."

I placed a hand on his shoulder, tilting my head so the light caught my moustache just so. "My boy, you have excellent taste in role models."

Reggie, who had been suspiciously absent during most of the ruckus, emerged from behind a toppled serving cart with Dapper at his side. "I see you've been busy while I've been… " he waved vaguely, "… strategically repositioning myself."

"Strategically repositioning," I repeated, "also known as hiding under the champagne table."

"Preserving my talents for the crucial moment," Reggie corrected, dusting himself off.

Dapper whistled, projecting a holo of the Resistance sigil. Fen's eyes lit up.

Keevan nodded toward the droid. "If you're serious about leaving the First Order, R2-DPR here can transmit your defection credentials to Resistance command. They'll know you switched sides before the battle."

Fen glanced at me. "If I do this… maybe I can actually make a difference."

I grinned. "Fen, you've already made a difference. You helped save this ship. And, more importantly, you've spared the galaxy the tragedy of losing me."

Sandro, still balanced precariously on his table stage, called down, "And I'll write you into the ballad! Fen Ralor, the trooper who fought for freedom!"

Fen flushed but didn't argue.

Keevan gestured toward the bridge. "Resistance recovery crews are docking now. Let's get you out of that armor before the Resistance mistakes your loyalty."

As Fen followed Reggie and Dapper toward the exit, I called after them, "And remember, a sequin cape goes a long way in making a strong first impression."

Dapper beeped approvingly.

As the last of the First Order forces filed onto their transport, the tension in the atrium loosened like a drawn bow finally released. I turned to Keevan, Reggie, Sammie, and Dapper.

"Well," I said, brushing an invisible speck from my cape, "that went better than expected."

Keevan smirked, her golden eyes catching the light. "You know, you're not half bad, Starstalker."

"Only half?" I feigned outrage, pressing a hand to my chest.

"Don't let her get in your head, Monty," Reggie muttered. "Or your moustache."

I grinned, adjusting said moustache with the kind of deliberate pride that could be seen from orbit. "The galaxy has a way of remembering moments like this. And if it remembers my moustache along with it, well, I won't complain."

Sammie laughed, and Dapper gave a pleased series of chirps, spinning his dome like a dancer finally free from the stage. For the first time in what felt like ages, the *Halcyon* hummed with something other than fear. Passengers whispered and smiled, children pointed out the viewport at the distant New Republic fleet, and the air felt… lighter.

Yes, I thought, looking out at the stars. The galaxy seemed a little brighter.

And just maybe, my moustache did too.

32

EPILOGUE

The *Halcyon* had been utterly transformed.

Where only hours before the atrium had been a stage for chaos and fear, it now glittered like a Core World gala. Bright banners draped from balcony to balcony, strings of glowing decorations wound around railings, and an extravagant buffet table stretched so far down the polished floor it felt like it was mocking the ship's actual dimensions. Captain Keevan had declared it a celebration in honor of our victory, though I had humbly suggested renaming it Montgomery Starstalker Appreciation Day. She'd smiled politely and declined. A clear oversight, but I forgave her.

Passengers mingled and laughed, the earlier terror swept away by the intoxicating mix of music, food, and freedom. The Resistance had escorted us to safety, and for the moment, the shadow of the First Order had been driven from our horizon.

As I moved through the crowd, shaking hands, nodding magnanimously, and accepting more compliments than I could count, I felt a warm swell of pride beneath my perfectly tailored cape. A few even asked for moustache photos. Naturally, I obliged.

Sandro Alamander was perched on the buffet table… on the table, mind you… plucking at his lute and debuting an all-new number: The Ballad of the Brave and Dashing Starstalker (and Some Other People). Reggie was across the room, trying to pretend he wasn't enjoying himself, though I caught him smiling when Dapper twirled in place to the rhythm.

Chewbacca himself had even sent a comm message from the *Millennium Falcon*, a low, rumbling roar that Sammie swore translated to, "Tell the little one with the moustache he's not half bad." I chose to believe "half bad" meant "galactic legend."

And so I basked in the glow of victory, the music, the laughter, and my own undeniable charisma. For now, the galaxy was safe. My cape shimmered. My moustache gleamed.

It was, in short, a perfect day.

The centrepiece of the celebration, however, was the dessert buffet, a monument to both culinary genius and, frankly, my own legend.

Captain Keevan had clearly gone above and beyond, collaborating with the ship's chef to create an entire lineup of treats inspired by my exploits. There were towering cakes shaped like my illustrious moustache, complete with edible gold trim that caught the light just so. "Starstalker's Galactic Gateau," they called it. Next to it stood a neat display of cookies modeled after my faithful droid, R2-DPR, christened Dapper Bites… each one featuring a tiny edible restraining bolt you could theatrically remove before eating. Even the drinks had been rebranded: Monty's Marvellous Moustache Mocha was a runaway favorite among the passengers, though I myself gravitated toward the "Reginald Rum Punch," an obvious nod to my dear friend.

"Impressive spread, isn't it?" I said, sidling up to Reginald, who was leaning against a column with a glass of punch in hand.

He took a slow sip and raised an eyebrow. "A bit self-indulgent, don't you think?"

"Self-indulgent?" I gasped, one hand to my chest. "This," I gestured to the cakes, the cookies, the entire decadent display, "is a carefully curated celebration of survival, bravery, and good grooming. These confections are history in edible form."

Reginald smirked. "Uh-huh. History. And the part where the cake has your face on it?"

"That," I said solemnly, "is educational. The galaxy's youth must learn their heroes' features."

Before he could reply, a pair of passengers passed by holding moustache-shaped cookies and giggling. One of them whispered, "I heard he signed one earlier." I offered them a gracious nod because the truth should never be denied an audience.

The celebration reached its peak when the doors slid open with a hiss, and a wave of murmurs rippled through the room.

Chancellor Mon Mothma herself entered, flanked by a pair of Resistance pilots in crisp flight suits and her personal guard, who looked as though they could take down a platoon of stormtroopers before breakfast. The crowd instinctively parted, forming a clear path through the atrium. Conversations faltered, laughter quieted, and even the clink of glasses seemed to fade into silence.

Captain Keevan stepped forward, her golden eyes gleaming with pride. She inclined her head in a respectful nod. "Chancellor Mothma, welcome aboard the *Halcyon*. It's an honor to have you here."

"The honor is mine," Mothma replied, her voice calm yet commanding, the sort of voice that could both soothe and silence a Senate chamber. "I've come to personally commend your crew… and one individual in particular for their bravery."

All eyes turned to me.

I took a single step forward, letting my cape sweep dramatically behind me, and offered my most dazzling smile, one I had perfected for holocams, magazine covers, and the occasional diplomatic gala.

"Well," I said, bowing just low enough to be gallant without risking any damage to my moustache, "if one must be singled out, one must be prepared to rise to the occasion."

A murmur ran through the passengers… part awe, part amusement. Reginald, standing somewhere behind me, muttered just loud enough for me to hear, "Oh, here we go… "

Mon Mothma's gaze settled on me, warm but assessing. "Captain Keevan has spoken highly of your… unconventional methods, Captain Starstalker. Your actions aboard this ship have not only safeguarded lives, but… " she allowed the faintest hint of a smile, "… apparently provided an unprecedented boost to passenger morale."

I gave a modest shrug that fooled no one. "I've always believed morale to be the true engine of any vessel, Chancellor."

She inclined her head slightly, as though humoring me. "Then consider the *Halcyon* very fortunate indeed."

The passengers applauded, and I resisted the urge to wave like royalty. Instead, I placed one hand over my heart and the other on the tips of my moustache, for history's sake.

The applause swelled, and I was prepared, naturally, to let it run its proper course (a full thirty seconds, by my count) when I raised a hand for silence.

"Chancellor," I said, adopting my most solemn baritone, "while I am deeply moved by your words, I must draw attention to another hero of this voyage; someone whose courage, loyalty, and admirable taste in personal role models deserves recognition."

From the back of the crowd, the young stormtrooper who had defected, now wearing civilian clothes, froze like a tooka in a spotlight. His cheeks flushed nearly as red as a Sith lightsaber.

"This," I declared, beckoning him forward with a sweep of my cape, "is Trooper… "

"Fen," he stammered.

"Yes, Trooper Fen," I continued, as though I had known all along. "Once a servant of the First Order, he saw the truth, cast off the chains of tyranny, and… most importantly, risked life and limb to protect not only this ship, but me personally. A wise decision on both counts."

A ripple of chuckles passed through the passengers. Mon Mothma regarded the young man with interest.

"Is this true?" she asked

"Yes, ma'am," Fen said, standing taller. "I couldn't… I couldn't follow them anymore. Not after what I saw here. I want to fight for something that matters."

Mothma gave a small, approving nod. "Then perhaps your place is with the Resistance."

Fen's eyes widened. "Truly?"

I clapped him on the back. "You heard the Chancellor. Welcome to the winning side, Fen. And remember, good posture, keep your blaster clean, and always respect the moustache."

The room erupted in laughter and applause as Fen was led away by the Resistance pilots, already looking ten years lighter without his armor. I allowed myself a proud smile. After all, what is heroism, if not inspiring the next generation… preferably one with excellent taste in personal heroes?

Mon Mothma's faint smile carried the weight of a thousand victories and just as many losses.

"Montgomery Starstalker," she said, her voice clear enough to reach every corner of the atrium, "for courage in the face of overwhelming odds… for ingenuity that turned the tide… and… " her gaze flicked deliberately to my moustache "… for a sense of style that can make all the difference… on behalf of the Resistance, it is my great pleasure to present you with this Medal of Honor."

One of her guards stepped forward, offering a polished medallion gleaming in the atrium's light. Mon Mothma placed it around my neck, and the room erupted into thunderous applause.

I turned to face them all, raising the medal high. "This isn't just for me," I declared in my best holodrama hero voice. "This is for all of us, for Captain Keeven, for Sammie, for Reginald, for the passengers… and especially for R2–DPR. Together as one, we achieved the impossible!"

The crowd's response was electric. "TOGETHER AS ONE! TOGETHER AS ONE!" they chanted, the sound bouncing off the atrium's walls until it felt as though the ship itself was joining in.

As the celebration continued, I found myself standing by the viewport, gazing out at the stars. The *Halcyon* glided through the velvet darkness, her lights twinkling against the void like a jewel that had survived the grasp of thieves.

Reginald joined me, holding another glass of rum punch. "Quite a spectacle," he said, his tone dry but not unkind.

"Fitting, wouldn't you say?" I replied, adjusting the medal around my neck. "It's not every day you save a starcruiser... and possibly the galaxy."

Reginald chuckled, shaking his head. "I've been onto you long enough to know you have a knack for... stumbling into success."

I put a hand to my chest in mock offense. "Stumbling? My dear Reginald, it was all precision and planning. Every moment. Every move. Perfectly orchestrated."

"Like when you nearly choked on your second moustache mocha?"

"That," I said with absolute dignity, "was part of the plan."

He laughed, and for a moment, we simply stood there in companionable silence, watching the stars drift past. Somewhere in the distance, a galaxy still full of danger, adventure, and opportunity was waiting.

I took a slow sip of my drink, savoring the moment.

"You know, Reg, the galaxy's a better place tonight... but it's far from perfect. Which means... " I swirled my cape dramatically. "It still needs Montgomery Starstalker."

R2–DPR rolled up beside us, letting out a proud little trill.

I raised my glass toward the stars. "To moustaches, capes, and the next impossible thing we're going to make look effortless."

And with that, I turned from the viewport, rejoined the laughter and music, and strode into the crowd, ready for whatever came next.

33

BLUE SKIES
AND OLD GHOSTS

T he Centax-1 Starfighter Exhibition was exactly the kind of event that demanded my presence. A grand display of aerial superiority, a celebration of piloting excellence, and, most importantly, a chance for me to bask in the admiration of the galaxy's finest pilots.

I had, of course, received a personal invitation. A very official-looking New Republic communique had arrived just weeks prior, addressed to Captain Montgomery Starstalker, Hero of the Rebellion, Legendary Ace Pilot, and Savior of Corellia (Unofficial).

Reginald Starjammer, my ever-loyal companion and occasional saboteur, was less convinced.

"You sure this wasn't another clerical error?" he muttered as he trudged beside me, hauling my satchel over one shoulder while subtly pocketing a vendor's credit chit.

I waved a hand dismissively. "Reggie, please. My reputation precedes me. Clearly, the New Republic wishes to honor me for my invaluable contributions to galactic freedom."

"You mean when you didn't fly at Scarif?"

I stiffened. "That was a mechanical issue."

243

"A mechanical issue that only existed because you let a cantina bartender talk you into trading out your stabilizer coils for a real conversation starter."

"Technically, it did start conversations," I said, adjusting my gold-trimmed flight jacket. "Mostly about how my X-wing wouldn't start."

Reginald sighed deeply. "Still, nice of them to invite you, considering you never actually made it into the battle."

"Well, I was standing by, wasn't I?"

"You were at a bar buying drinks for Blue Squadron."

I winced. That part stung. I had meant it as a celebration; one last grand toast before we launched for Scarif. I didn't know it would be the last time I ever saw them.

Reginald must have seen the look on my face because, for once, he didn't press.

Then, the announcer's voice boomed across the airfield.

"And leading today's demonstration of precision aerial combat maneuvers, we welcome back a true hero of the Rebellion, Commander Merrick Voss of the former Blue Squadron!"

I choked on my drink as I whirled toward the airstrip, and there he was, Merrick Voss, alive and thoroughly not dead.

He stood by his X-wing, tall, broad-shouldered, and radiating that infuriatingly rigid posture he always had. His flight suit was crisp, his expression perpetually unimpressed, and his moustache was much more symmetrical than I remembered.

I turned to Reginald, who was already rubbing his temples.

"Reggie," I whispered. "He survived Scarif."

Reginald gave me a long, suffering look. "Monty, you told me many times that he died at Scarif."

"I thought he did!" I hissed.

"You held a memorial toast. You gave a speech. You made me build a little shrine to honor him."

"And it was a very nice shrine, I said defensively. "Very tasteful. I even included the tiny model of his X-wing."

"You put his tiny model X-wing into your drink before finishing the eulogy."

"Well, in my defense, it was a very strong drink."

Reginald sighed deeply, watching as Merrick climbed into his starfighter. "I don't know whether to be relieved or horrified that your dead friends keep showing up."

As I stared, still processing the miracle of Merrick's continued existence, our eyes met across the tarmac.

For a moment, I expected some grand reunion, a moment of shared history, of gratitude for having both survived the war against impossible odds.

Instead, Merrick's face twisted into pure, unfiltered fury.

I frowned. That was not the look of a man overwhelmed with joy at seeing an old friend.

"Montgomery," he growled, his voice crackling over the comm system as he strapped into his X-wing. "You… "

Oh dear.

I shot Reginald a quick glance. "Do you think he's angry because of the fond memories or the unresolved tension?"

"I think," Reginald said, rubbing his temples, "that he blames you for something."

"Preposterous!" I waved a hand dismissively. "I have done nothing but be an inspiration to my fellow pilots."

"You did miss Scarif."

"I wanted to fly!" I snapped, then lowered my voice. "I wanted to be there. But my X-wing was grounded, and… "

"And instead, you spent the day getting drunk."

That part stung, and Reginald knew it. I had meant well. It was supposed to be a celebration - one final round of drinks before the mission. But they had left, and I had stayed behind, stuck with an X-wing that refused to start and a hangover that felt like a direct punishment from the Force itself.

They never came back. And now, apparently, Merrick had. Before I could explain any of this, the air show began. Merrick, unfortunately, was leading it.

Which meant that I… the beloved, heroic, and officially invited guest, was expected to participate.

And so began a display of aerial acrobatics in which Merrick:

1. Tried to embarrass me with high-level maneuvers.
2. Became increasingly infuriated when I accidentally pulled off better ones.
3. Finally, snapped and decided this was an actual dogfight.

I, of course, was completely unaware of this. What followed was a highly dramatic aerial duel, in which:

- I unintentionally dodged his laser fire by spilling my tea in the cockpit and flailing for a napkin.
- I accidentally pulled a perfect evasive spin because my cape got caught in the throttle.
- And in the grand finale, I "defeated" Merrick by forcing him into a controlled crash landing by accidentally hitting his stabilizer with my landing gear.

Let me explain how this happened. I, of course, had not planned on flying that day. Oh, don't misunderstand me; I had every confidence in my abilities as a pilot. One might say I was a natural, though certain bureaucratic entities (New Republic Flight Command) and unfair regulatory agencies (Starfighter Safety Compliance Board) had differing opinions on the matter.

My plan had been simple: graciously accept applause, perhaps deliver a rousing speech, and then retire to the VIP lounge to sip a delicately mixed Corellian Sunset while basking in my own legend.

Instead, I found myself sitting in the cockpit of an X-wing, the comms buzzing with Merrick's barely-contained rage.

"Starstalker," he said in that clipped, precise tone he used when barely restraining the urge to kill me. "You are flying in today's demonstration."

"Ah, about that," I began, adjusting my gold-trimmed flight gloves for dramatic effect. "I'm more of a guest of honor, really. I don't want to upstage… "

"You are flying," Merrick repeated, his voice the same as it had been before, except somehow more murderous.

Reginald's voice crackled into my cockpit. "Monty, I strongly advise against this."

"Nonsense," I replied cheerfully, flipping a few unnecessary switches to look competent. "What could possibly go wrong?"

A lot, as it turned out.

The demonstration was meant to be a synchronized aerial display, showcasing the finest precision flying in the New Republic.

Naturally, I assumed this meant I was the star of the show.

We began with a tight-knit formation flyby, a display of discipline and control. The other pilots kept their ships within meters of each other, their movements fluid and exact.

I, on the other hand, misheard the instructions.

Instead of a steady flyby, I thought we were starting with evasive maneuvers, so I barrel-rolled directly through the formation.

The comms erupted in a mix of horrified gasps, shouted expletives, and one pilot who simply began screaming and had to land due to their "mental health".

"STARSTALKER!" Merrick bellowed, his professional composure utterly shattered.

"Ah, sorry about that," I said, steadying my ship. "Thought I saw a Mynock. False alarm!"

Merrick cursed in three languages.

The next phase was a mock dogfight, intended to be a non-aggressive, staged skirmish for the audience's enjoyment.

I misunderstood the word *mock*.

Merrick and I were paired for a one-on-one engagement, meant to be a choreographed exchange of laser fire with pre-arranged "hits" to make it look exciting.

Instead, I took it as a genuine fight.

I dodged, weaved, and counterattacked with reckless abandon, completely ignoring the agreed-upon choreography. The resulting exchange went something like this:

Merrick: "What are you DOING?"

Me: "Winning, obviously."

Merrick: "It's not a real fight!"

Me: "You should've said something sooner!"

"I DID!"

I spun into a hard right turn, avoiding Merrick's scripted shots by sheer accident.

In retaliation, Merrick broke the script as well, abandoning the pre-planned routine to actually try to outmaneuver me.

This turned out to be a terrible mistake.

Now, let's be clear: Merrick was a very good pilot.

Technically.

His maneuvers were precise, calculated, and executed flawlessly. Mine were pure, unfiltered chaos. At one point, I accidentally spun out of control, which just so happened to cause Merrick's carefully aimed shots to miss by centimeters.

At another, my cape got tangled in the throttle, forcing me to jerk the ship into a sudden evasive spiral, a move that looked incredibly intentional to the audience.

The crowd roared with approval.

Merrick's rage became palpable.

"You are NOT this good!" he snarled over the comms.

"I mean, the evidence suggests otherwise," I pointed out cheerfully.

Reginald's voice crackled in again. "Monty, you are not actually trying to kill him, right?"

"Reggie, please. That would be deeply unprofessional."

"Then WHY is he actually trying to kill you?"

That was a very good question.

Merrick, now fully committed to my destruction, looped behind me, preparing to force me into a surrender.

"Nowhere left to run, Montgomery," he growled.

"Ah," I said. "That's where you're wrong."

With absolutely no plan whatsoever, I cut my engines mid-turn.

Merrick, not expecting me to stop, overshot, his ship just barely missing my nose.

I reactivated my thrusters and instinctively jerked the controls right as he did the same.

We collided midair. Now, normally, this would be a catastrophic disaster.

Instead, due to what I assume was the Force deciding I am its favorite, I managed to knock Merrick's stabilizer at exactly the right angle to send him into a controlled spin.

He spiraled downward, his ship landing in a perfectly intact, but utterly humiliating crash.

I, on the other hand, landed flawlessly. The audience erupted in applause. To them, it looked like I had just outflown one of the greatest pilots in the Republic.

Merrick stalked toward me, seething.

I removed my aviator visor, giving him my most magnanimous grin.

"Ah, Merrick," I said, clapping him on the shoulder. "No need to thank me for making you look good out there."

He just stared at me.

Reginald sighed, shaking his head. "Monty, you really don't know when to shut up, do you?"

Merrick cracked his knuckles.

I suddenly remembered that I had a very important appointment elsewhere, possibly in another star system.

If there was one thing I had learned in my illustrious career, it was this: a hasty retreat is often the wisest course of action, particularly when an enraged ace pilot is stalking toward you with the singular focus of a man about to commit a court-martial-worthy offense.

Fortunately, my strategic foresight (read: instinct for self-preservation) had anticipated this very scenario. That is why I was already halfway toward the nearest exit when I heard Merrick's voice cut through the applause.

"Montgomery."

I froze.

Now, one might assume that a reasonable person, when confronted with an infuriated rival, would respond with caution and diplomacy.

I, however, was not a reasonable person.

I turned with an easy, charming grin. "Merrick! What a day, hmm? You really gave them a show out there."

He took a measured step forward. "You… "

I pointed at him before he could continue. "Ah, hold that thought… quick question: did I win?"

Merrick's right eye twitched.

Reginald, already standing off to the side, pinched the bridge of his nose. "Monty, for the love of the stars."

But to my great surprise, Merrick did not immediately punch me in the face. Instead, he exhaled sharply, his posture relaxing just slightly.

"You know," he said, shaking his head, "I used to think you were the worst thing to ever happen to the Rebellion."

"Oh, Merrick," I said, placing a hand over my heart, "that's one of the nicest things anyone's ever said to me."

Reginald muttered something about letting him punch me just once.

Merrick crossed his arms, regarding me with a long, unreadable expression. Then, to my utter shock, his lips twitched, just slightly, in something that might have been the beginning of a smirk.

"You're insufferable," he said finally.

"That's Captain Insufferable to you," I corrected.

He sighed. "But, you're not a coward."

This time, I froze for an entirely different reason. It was a small thing, an offhand remark, but it hit something unexpectedly deep.

I'd never told Merrick or anyone, really, how much it had haunted me that I hadn't been able to fly at Scarif. That my last moments with Blue Squadron had been buying them drinks, laughing, and making promises we never got to keep. That was when the battle had started. I'd been stuck on the ground, unable to help, watching the feeds as one by one they disappeared on the screens.

I pushed the thought away, forcing a grin. "Ah, Merrick. You're finally seeing the light. Any moment now, you'll admit you admire me."

"I will never say that," he said immediately.

But you thought it," I said.

"No, I did not."

Reginald leaned toward him. Just tell him he's a hero and get it over with."

Merrick scoffed. "He's not a hero."

I gasped. "You wound me."

You're a menace," Merrick corrected. Then, after a beat, "But, I wouldn't have wanted anyone else up there with me today."

It was, I realized, probably the closest thing to a compliment I would ever get from him. Which meant it was my duty to ruin the moment immediately.

I clapped him on the back, beaming. "Ah, Merrick! Such sentiment! If I didn't know better, I'd think you were getting soft on me."

Merrick took a deep breath, as if seriously contemplating murder.

Reginald took my arm before I could press my luck further. "Monty, let's go before you die."

***

The *Dashing Resolve* was exactly where we had left her, docked at the far end of the exhibition landing bay.

The moment we stepped on board, the familiar hiss of the airlock sealing was a welcome sound. I peeled off my flight gloves, tossed my jacket over the captain's chair, and collapsed into it with great theatricality.

Reginald, on the other hand, strode past me without ceremony, heading straight for the cockpit.

"Reggie," I said, stretching. "What's your hurry? We should celebrate! Perhaps a toast to old friends?"

Reginald paused. That was enough to make me sit up.

He turned, expression unreadable. "Blue Squadron."

I frowned. "What about them?"

"Did you ever check?" he asked quietly. "To see if there were any others?"

I hesitated. The truth was, I hadn't. Because some part of me had assumed that, if Merrick had survived, maybe the others had too. Maybe.

But Reginald had checked.

And when he didn't immediately say anything… The *Dashing Resolve* suddenly felt too quiet. I forced a grin, though it felt too tight on my face. "Well. That's…" I exhaled sharply, shaking my head. "That's war, isn't it?"

Reginald didn't say anything.

Neither did I… for once.

Then, with a slow nod, Reginald turned back toward the controls. "Coordinates set?" I asked after a beat.

Reginald nodded. "Heading back to familiar ground."

I adjusted my collar, rolled my shoulders, and smiled.

"Reggie," I said, leaning back into my seat. "You ever think about what it'd be like if we lived normal lives? Just… respectable traders or something?"

"Not even once," he said.

"Good. Because I have an idea."

"Absolutely not."

"Oh, come now, you haven't even heard it yet."

Reginald flicked a switch, and the engines hummed to life.

The *Dashing Resolve* lifted from the landing bay, the planet shrinking below us as we ascended into the sky.

As the stars stretched before us, Reginald leaned back in his chair, sighed, and muttered the same words he always did at the end of a mission.

"Congratulations, Monty. Another successful mission."

I grinned.

And for once, I didn't argue. I removed myself from the *Resolve's* bridge and headed to my quarters. The door to my quarters slid shut behind me, sealing away the familiar hum of the Dashing Resolve.

The laughter, the bravado, *the mask* I always wore, stayed outside.

Inside, there was only silence.

I stood there for a long moment, staring at nothing, feeling everything.

Then, without a word, I crossed the room to the small, locked cabinet in the corner. My fingers hesitated on the latch. It had been years since I'd opened it.

Not because I had forgotten.

But because I hadn't.

The lock clicked open, and I reached inside, pushing past old relics of past misadventures until my hand closed around a dust-covered bottle of Corellian whiskey.

I pulled it out, turned it over in my hands.

I had bought it the night before Scarif.

A celebration bottle. Something special.

We were supposed to drink it after we came back. Blue Squad. After we laughed about how close we'd cut it. After we toasted to another mission survived.

But there had been no "after." Only a list of names.

I swallowed hard, setting the bottle on the table, as a flicker of movement in the doorway caught my eye.

R2-DPR had rolled up silently, his polished dome tilting as he watched me.

He didn't chirp. Didn't beep. He just waited.

I let out a slow breath. "Guess you're wondering why I'm standing here like a man contemplating his life choices."

Dapper let out a soft, inquisitive whistle.

I huffed a tired laugh. "Don't worry. I'm not about to do anything dramatic."

I grabbed two glasses from the shelf, setting them down on the table.

One for me.

One for *them*. *All* of my fallen comrades.

The whiskey poured smoothly, its amber liquid catching the dim cabin light.

I picked up my glass but didn't drink. Not yet. I turned toward the empty glass across from me.

"To Blue Squadron," I said softly.

My voice sounded strange, like it belonged to someone else.

"To Merrick, who lived. To the rest, who didn't… And to you, Thea."

The words sat heavy in the air.

I raised my glass, hesitated. Then I drank.

It burned all the way down, but the ache in my chest burned worse. A quiet beep pulled me from my thoughts. I looked up.

Dapper had projected a holo-recording.

A bar. Laughter. A handful of pilots, all in Blue Squadron jackets, arms slung around each other, grinning at the camera. And there I was, in the center, flashing that same reckless, carefree smile, the kind I used to believe in.

The image flickered, and then it was gone.

I clenched my jaw, staring at the spot where it had been.

Dapper didn't say anything. Didn't need to.

I reached for the bottle and poured another glass. I didn't drink it. Didn't touch it. I just left it there. A toast for those who weren't here to drink it. A silence for those who never would. And in that silence, for the first time in a long time, I let myself remember.

The door slid open behind me, but I didn't turn.

I heard the familiar weight of Reginald's boots against the floor - measured, unhurried. He stopped just inside the room, standing there for a moment. Watching. Then, a quiet clink as he set a glass on the table beside mine.

I didn't say anything.

Neither did he.

But I felt him there, steady as always.

I stared at the second glass, then exhaled.

Reginald didn't sit across from me, like he normally would. Instead, he lowered himself into the chair beside me, close enough that I could feel the quiet weight of his presence.

Not intruding. Not asking. Just there.

He reached for the bottle, poured himself a drink, and then, after a brief hesitation, poured a third.

One for them.

One for me.

One for him.

I let out a breath I hadn't realized I'd been holding.

Reginald didn't speak, didn't offer condolences, or reassurances, or any of the things that would have made it harder instead of easier.

He just sat there.

A quiet presence in the dim light of my quarters, an unspoken "I know" in the way he settled beside me.

And for the first time in a long time, I wasn't carrying it alone.

34

A HIGHLY CLASSIFIED, INCREDIBLY DANGEROUS, ABSOLUTELY MIND-BLOWING ACCOUNT

Well, every food unauthorized autobiography needs a chapter of salacious gossip and tantalizing revelations… preferably the kind that causes gasps at dinner parties and gets you banned from certain core world casinos.

Consider this… that chapter.

Few beings in the galaxy have the privilege, nay, the honor, of learning the truth behind what transpired in the Top Secret, Highly Sensitive, and Utterly Thrilling events leading up to the Battle of Endor.

Many have speculated, few have dared to ask, and none, not even the most elite spies of the Rebellion, have been entrusted with the details you are about to witness. What you hold in your hands is a revelation so shocking, so daring, so utterly classified that it has been kept hidden from the galaxy… until now.

Prepare yourself! Breathe deeply! Make sure you are seated (or reclining dramatically) with a strong drink in hand for what you are about to read!

It started with ██████████. I had received a communication from ████████████ ████████████. It appeared that Dastar lee was only too happy to ██████████

It took three rotations for Reginald to understand what was happening. It turned out that ████████████████ ████ ████ ████████████ ████████████████████. Chief Chirpa had ████████████ ████████████ Mon Mothma, ████████████████ ████████████████████████████ ████████████████████████████████████ Three Twi'leks ████████ ████████████ ████████████████████████████████. Six whole standard days! I had to act fast! Grappling with the ████████████ ████████████████████████ only made things worse. The rash spread ████████ only four fingers ████████ ████ █!!!!!!!!

The pain in the ████████████████████████, oozed out slowly, and I knew it was only a matter of time that ████████████████████ ████████████. Reggie exclaimed, " ████████████ ██ ████████████!!!!"

It was pulsating with expectation.

"Don't worry, old friend," I said, reassuring him that ████████████ ██ ██ ██ ██ ██ ██.

And by some miracle, it worked!

Chief Chirpa began to wander into the restricted ▮▮▮▮▮▮▮▮
▮▮▮▮▮▮▮▮▮▮▮▮▮▮▮▮▮▮▮▮▮▮.

"Are you sure?", Reggie queried.

"It's our only chance for Princess Leia to ▮▮▮▮▮▮▮▮
▮▮▮▮▮▮▮▮▮▮▮▮▮▮▮▮▮▮▮▮▮▮▮▮▮▮▮▮▮▮▮▮
▮▮▮▮▮▮▮▮▮▮▮▮."

The room fell silent. My moustache was ▮▮▮▮▮▮▮▮ and my
cape ▮▮▮▮▮▮ gleaming as the glitter was ▮▮▮▮▮▮
▮▮▮▮▮▮▮▮▮▮▮▮▮▮▮▮▮▮▮▮▮▮▮▮▮▮▮▮▮▮▮▮
▮▮▮▮▮▮▮▮▮▮▮▮▮▮ laser panache ▮▮▮▮▮▮▮▮
▮▮▮▮▮▮▮▮▮▮▮▮▮▮▮▮▮▮▮▮▮▮▮▮▮▮▮▮▮▮▮▮
▮▮▮▮▮▮▮▮▮▮▮▮▮▮▮▮▮▮▮▮▮▮▮▮▮▮▮▮▮▮▮▮
▮▮▮▮▮▮▮▮▮▮▮▮▮▮▮▮▮▮▮▮▮▮▮▮▮▮▮▮▮▮▮▮
▮▮▮▮▮▮▮▮▮▮. A sense of dread filled the observation deck.

It was time.

Holding back the ▮▮▮▮▮▮▮▮▮▮▮▮▮▮▮▮▮▮▮▮
▮▮▮▮▮▮▮▮▮▮▮▮▮▮▮▮▮▮▮▮▮▮▮▮▮▮▮▮▮▮▮▮
▮▮▮▮▮▮▮▮▮▮. It went wild.

The next day, we were alerted to ▮▮▮▮▮▮▮▮▮▮▮▮▮▮
▮▮f Thrawn s▮▮▮▮▮▮▮▮▮▮ four holds full. ▮▮▮▮▮▮▮▮
▮▮▮▮▮▮▮▮▮▮▮▮▮▮▮▮▮ moustache wax ▮▮▮▮▮▮▮▮
▮▮▮▮▮▮▮▮▮▮▮▮▮▮▮▮▮▮▮▮▮▮▮▮▮▮ globs of
▮▮▮▮▮▮▮▮▮▮▮▮▮▮▮▮▮▮▮▮▮▮▮ thrusting upwards to
▮▮▮▮▮▮

Unexpectedly, tearing off [REDACTED]

[REDACTED]

Mon Mothma was breathing heavier now as she ▮▮▮▮▮▮▮▮

"Oh Monty," she ███████████████████████████████ one that size before. ████ Chief Chirpa now joined ████████████

[CLASSIFIED BY ORDER OF THE NEW REPUBLIC]

The moustache wax also served as a makeshift emergency lub███ ████████████████████ giggling as it tickled her ████████ ████████████

[SECURITY LEVEL OMEGA-MOUSTACHE]

Panting heavily, ████████████████████████████████████

Reggie exclaimed, "Well done, Monty. ████████████████ mission!!!

[ALL DETAILS REMOVED FOR READER SAFETY]

****

Ah. Well. That is unfortunate.

It appears that certain parties (glares in the direction of New Republic bureaucrats) have deemed this account too explosive for public consumption.

And so, dear reader, you must simply trust me when I say: it was magnificent. Truly, a tale for the ages. You would have gasped. You would have wept. You would have questioned everything you thought you knew about intergalactic history.

I can sense your disappointment, dear reader. You were prepared - perhaps even trembling with anticipation - to uncover the untold, highly classified events preceding the Battle of Endor. And yet, through a cruel twist of bureaucratic meddling, the entire account has been REDACTED. Tragic. Infuriating. Deeply suspicious.

35
DASTAR-LEE

No memoir of a galactic legend would be complete without mentioning one's nemesis. For every dashing hero, there must be a villain, a shadowy figure lurking in the background, plotting revenge, and, more importantly, being utterly envious of said hero's incredible success.

For me, that nemesis is Dastar-Lee.

Dastar-Lee is, tragically, a TIE pilot of some renown. By "renown," I mean he's known for crashing into things, losing dogfights he started, and being the subject of several Resistance jokes involving improperly calibrated targeting computers. But what truly makes him my nemesis isn't his poor piloting skills or his dogged attempts to shoot me out of the stars.

No, it's his moustache.

The Hideous Moustache of Dastar-Lee

Dastar-Lee's moustache is, frankly, an affront to the galaxy. If my moustache is a beacon of hope, his is a black hole of despair. Imagine, if you will, two uneven tufts of wiry hair, desperately clinging to his upper lip like frightened porgs. It's patchy. It's crooked. It's the sort of thing that makes you want to hand him a trimmer and say, "It's time, Dastar. Let it go."

I have it on good authority that his moustache is so offensive, it's listed as a health hazard on several Outer Rim stations.

But does Dastar-Lee shave it off? Of course not. Instead, he grooms it in the most laughable ways possible. He once tried to braid it. *Braid it.* Needless to say, the results were catastrophic… not unlike his flying.

Dastar-Lee's jealousy of me is as vast as the galaxy itself. How could it not be? I have the *Dashing Resolve*, a ship so elegant and well-maintained that it practically hums with sophistication. He has a standard TIE fighter that rattles like a malfunctioning food processor.

I have a wardrobe of capes and suits tailored to perfection. He wears the same poorly fitted pilot uniform that smells vaguely of engine oil and despair.

I have a moustache that has inspired Resistance pilots to volunteer for missions, while his moustache has inspired… nothing… except maybe pity.

Oh, don't misunderstand me, dear reader, Dastar-Lee *has* tried to best me. There was that one time in the Arkanis sector when he actually managed to tail the *Dashing Resolve* for several minutes before losing control and spinning into a cargo freighter full of nerfs. The resulting explosion sent nerfs drifting through space, mooing indignantly.

Or the time on Batuu when he confronted me in Oga's Cantina, challenging me to a duel. He knocked over two tables, spilled someone's hyper-rye, and tripped over his own boots before I even had to lift a finger.

And yet, he persists.

Here's the thing about Dastar-Lee: He simply doesn't understand what it takes to be truly great. It's not just about skill (though I have plenty of that) or courage (I positively ooze it). It's about presence. It's about panache. It's about looking danger in the eye while your moustache gleams under starlight and saying, "Not today, my friend."

Dastar-Lee lacks all of that. He's a try-hard with bad grooming habits, and while he may take the occasional potshot at me from his sad little TIE fighter, he'll never truly measure up.

The last time I saw Dastar-Lee, he was floating in space, his TIE fighter spinning lazily after a particularly one-sided encounter near the Anoat system. I could've finished him off, but instead, I opened a comm channel and said, "Dastar, I'd offer you some grooming tips, but frankly, I think it's a lost cause."

His response was garbled, likely by rage, but I heard enough to confirm my theory: Dastar-Lee will always be my lesser.

Now, some might say it's unkind to mock a nemesis so thoroughly. To them, I say this: The galaxy needs to know the truth. Heroes like me don't just inspire others; we also highlight the follies of those who dare to oppose us.

So, Dastar-Lee, if you're reading this: Thank you for being an example of what not to do. And to the rest of you, dear readers: May you never encounter a moustache as hideous as his.

36
THOUGHTS ON THE FORCE

By now, dear reader, you've likely gathered that I am many things. A pilot. An adventurer. A hero. A man of impeccable taste in capes and facial grooming. But if there's one thing I am not, it's an expert on the Force.

Oh, I've heard the stories. The mystical energy field that binds the galaxy together. The chosen few who wield its power to move rocks, trick stormtroopers, and deflect blaster bolts with glowing sticks of plasma. All very impressive, yes… but also very confusing.

For me, the Force has always been less about destiny and more about dumb luck. Some might say it's *suspiciously* lucky how often I stumble into solutions, narrowly avoid catastrophe, or emerge from a firefight without a single scorch mark on my cape.

I say, why question it?

There was one moment, however, that sticks out. A Saja, one of those wise Force-mystic types, approached me after our victory aboard the *Halcyon*. They were calm, serene, and, frankly, far too serious for my liking.

"Montgomery Starstalker," they said, their voice like a gentle breeze, "you are more connected to the Force than you realize."

I gave them my most charming smile. "Oh, I realize it. I just call it being extraordinary."

The Saja tilted their head, clearly unimpressed. "The Force works through you, even if you do not understand it."

"Ah," I said, stroking my moustache thoughtfully. "So you're saying the Force is responsible for my impeccable fashion sense and irresistible charm?

They blinked, clearly not expecting such wisdom.

"You may quip," they replied, "but your connection to the Force is real. Even your moustache may serve as a symbol of unity and inspiration."

Now, I'm not one to argue with a Force mystic, but that seemed a bit far-fetched even to me. A moustache? A symbol of unity? Ridiculous.

But then, later that day, a young pilot approached me in the lounge. Wide-eyed and clearly nervous, they stammered out, "Captain Starstalker, sir, I just wanted to say that… well, your moustache gave me the courage to volunteer for the next mission."

I stared at them, unsure whether to laugh or cry. "My moustache?" I asked.

"Yes, sir," they said earnestly. "It's so… bold. So confident. I thought, if you can wear that and save the galaxy, then I can do my part too."

Well, reader, what could I say to that? I clapped them on the shoulder, gave them my warmest smile, and said, "You're absolutely right. And don't forget the cape."

Now, do I believe I'm some secret Jedi or Force prodigy? Of course not. But I do know this: the galaxy is full of mysteries, and maybe, just maybe, the Force is one of them.

Perhaps it's luck. Perhaps it's destiny. Or perhaps it's simply the power of believing you can do the impossible, even if you're doing it while tripping over your own feet or getting your cape caught in a blast door.

If the Saja are right, and the Force really is guiding me, then I can only assume it has an excellent sense of humor. After all, it chose *me*.

So, dear reader, if you've taken anything from these memoirs, let it be this: Life is unpredictable. The galaxy is vast. And sometimes, all it takes to make a difference is a little luck, a lot of heart, and a moustache so magnificent it could inspire a pilot to volunteer for the Resistance.

37

MERCH

As a galaxy-renowned hero, pilot, adventurer, and symbol of everything extraordinary, I've come to realize that my greatness cannot be contained within mere stories or legends. It must be *shared*.

And so, I have done just that by launching the Montgomery Starstalker Galactic Collection™, a comprehensive line of products designed to bring a little bit of my brilliance into your daily life. After all, why should *I* be the only one to benefit from my remarkable taste, ingenuity, and, of course, my moustache?

Allow me to walk you through the collection. You're welcome.

For the Daring Gourmand

Start your day like a hero with Monty's Star Crunch™ Breakfast Cereal. Featuring adventure-shaped marshmallows (X-wings, moustaches, blasters, and capes), this is the breakfast that powered me through many a daring mission. Plus, every box includes an inspirational quote from yours truly, because a well-fed stomach deserves a well-fed mind

For snacking on the go, try Monty's Galactic Nougat Bar™, available in three heroic flavors: "Hyperdrive Hazelnut," "Cosmic Caramel," and "Victory Vanilla." Each wrapper features my face (of course) and a collectible quote about my many triumphs.

And for the discerning drinker, there's the Starstalker Swizzle Stick™ Collection. These intricately designed swizzle sticks, shaped like my legendary moustache, are perfect for stirring cocktails while looking fabulous. A must-have for your next cantina soirée!

For the Fashion-Conscious Adventurer

My Hero's Cape Collection™ remains the pinnacle of galactic fashion. Whether you're attending a diplomatic gala or sneaking onto an Imperial base, there's a cape for every occasion. Highlights include:

• The Daring Resolve Cape™, lined with starship-grade reflective fabric, because safety and style go hand-in-hand.

• The Smuggler's Sweep™, with hidden compartments for storing… well, anything you'd rather not declare at customs.

• The Starstalker Original™, featuring a dramatic collar and enough flair to stop a stormtrooper in their tracks.

And don't think I've forgotten the little details. For the fashion-forward pilot, there's Monty's Star Covers™, luxurious seat covers for X-wings, Y-wings, and beyond. Available in faux Wookiee fur, Bantha leather, or my personal favorite, embroidered silk featuring miniature capes.

For the Grooming Enthusiast

Greatness starts with grooming. My Marvelous Moustache Wax™ is made from the finest ingredients sourced across the galaxy. Whether you're facing down a Sith Lord or attending a royal banquet, this wax guarantees that your moustache will stay impeccable.

For those without moustaches, fear not, I've got you covered with Monty's Legendary Locks Pomade™, perfect for keeping your hair battle-ready, even in zero gravity.

And, of course, there's Wacky Wookiee Wax™, my best-selling product for the furrier beings among us. It's so effective that even Chewbacca gave it a roaring endorsement. (He also took six jars, which I'm billing him for.)

For the Star-Faring Hero

Every hero needs the right tools, and my Galactic Survival Kit™ delivers. It includes:

- A collapsible cape that doubles as a thermal blanket.

- A pocket-sized hologram of myself offering words of encouragement.

- A portable moustache grooming kit (because survival doesn't mean neglecting style).

And for those who dream of piloting their own ship, there's **The Dashing Resolve Experience™**, a fully immersive starship simulator modeled after my legendary vessel. It comes with customizable capes for your avatar, a holographic Reginald as your sarcastic co-pilot, and a "Nemesis Encounter Mode," starring none other than Dastar-Lee.

For the Younglings

Even younglings deserve to be inspired by greatness, which is why I'm proud to offer **Monty's Galactic Adventure Playset™**. This set includes a miniature Dashing Resolve, tiny capes for action figures, and a moustache applicator kit for those who dream of heroic facial hair.

For rainy days, there's the Montgomery Starstalker Holo-Coloring Book™, filled with scenes of my most daring exploits. Younglings can color me in with holo-pens while learning about bravery, style, and the importance of a well-timed quip.

And don't forget Monty: The Animated Series™, now streaming on all major holo-networks. Featuring slightly exaggerated (but mostly accurate) versions of my adventures, it's a must-watch for young and old alike.

Now, you might wonder, "Monty, why go to such lengths to create all these products?" The answer is simple: the galaxy deserves access to the tools, inspiration, and brilliance that have defined my life.

Every cape sold, every swizzle stick stirred, every nougat bar unwrapped is a way for me to bring a little bit of Starstalker magic into your lives.

So, dear reader, as you close this memoir, I invite you to join me in celebrating all that makes life extraordinary. Be bold. Be brave. Wax your moustache, wear a cape, and always, always choose the swizzle stick that matches your drink

The galaxy is vast, but with a little style and a lot of heart, you can leave your mark on it, just as I have.

You're welcome.

38

ACTIVITIES

I don't know about you, but there are times I need to challenge my searching skills. Here's a special reward for you, readers: Monty's Marvellous Word Search!

You're welcome!

```
C E Z J Y O R T A U C A P E B R R M Z P E R F E C T I O N Z
X Q E L J P A I A N Z Z C A P T A I N F W S M I S P C Y T Y
J V W P P K G V K F E N C D B C W E D A S H I N G D X K J N
P R F H D F W B G C Y J J J H L C T A L P T G L Q G Y W K B
A Z V R E G I N A L D S T A R J A M M E R H I B B O E P W E
R Z M E D A L S X P B G O K R D A P P E R C U R L Y C F F I
S O C P A Q F T T I L P R I N C E S S L E I A N B I A V V Z
E M W I D A P B I L M E K D D P R E P G G X Q I P M H L P K
C D I C D B S Z X O J O V T J M J I D G L D I U I A L G B M
A I A D H W U Q A T D H U P N Y P I B U I U M R O N Z X V O
X G N S X Y F P P F J R Z S R M X G J D T J P I N Z Q S F N
I R K F H S P O P E L D O E T U W O O W T X Z F T J B W B T
H Y D A L I I E R U B M R I B A B K R O E W H L R I B X A G
P O N W V I N D R C O M O Z D P C E H Z R O E Y A V T B T O
P Y L N R A G G C D E Y D U H X I H E X R O U I I C D L J M
I O R O U G Z H R N R S O C S D X D E M L K C N L Q E U I E
D C R B N T N J T E W I E U Y T L Z O D W I W G O Z F E O R
A H L Y B E J W E S S B V N R K A Z V S V E M A T C Z F S Y
S Y G I O W T K L O U O F E S E R C C F P E V C H J W O J S
T P S E N D I V W A Y I L D E I W I H J Z B H E N X J U G T
A R I O U U A Z Q N S M T V A B T E T E O V R R C S K R G A
R B N F A Z I D A C I E F M E I F I L P W I E V L F U M G R
L Y P U P S A J A R Y I R W I Q N F V C L A K R K P D K A S
E X Z H D U I S L B D H Y P T H Z R H E O E X C G P J M L T
E B N W C O W U L P H N I E A Q P N M I K M X O V S D V A A
R D G M M B M O N M O T H M A N I I J D H J P E G U B S T X L
J E D I A D J A C A N T N E W R A W M E D W Z M T Q P R Y K
A Z I B L U E S Q U A D R O M B I C N R S T A B U D X A E E
U C A P T A I N K E E V A N D Q U F H O X E D Z M K N X K R
S M A R E B E L B A S E V U H A V G T E I A F K P O N P D J
```

Words

MONTGOMERY STARSTALKER

REGINALD STARJAMMER

CAPTAIN KEEVAN

PILOT

PRINCESS LEIA

LASER PANACHE

FORCE SENSITIVE

DASHING RESOLVE

CURLY

MOUSTACHE WAX

JEDI ADJACENT

PERFECTION

HERO

FLIGHTSUIT

MON MOTHMA

REBEL BASE

YODA

MOUSTACHE

CAPE

HYPERDRIVE

DASTAR-LEE

FLYING ACE

ION TRAIL

BLUE SQUAD

SAJA

DASHING

R2 DAPPER

WOOKIEE

TEA

GLITTER

CAPTAIN

GALAXY

IMP

MEDALS

WIZARD

BLUE FOUR

COG

DROID

PARSEC

HOLONET

39
CONCLUSION

And so, dear reader, our tale concludes… at least for now.

The First Order has retreated. The *Halcyon* sails on, her decks once again alive with music, laughter, and the reassuring swish of my cape through the atrium. The passengers will dine out on the story of "that time Montgomery Starstalker saved us" for years to come, and frankly, who could blame them? I've dined out on lesser triumphs myself.

But I know the galaxy well enough to understand that peace is a fleeting guest, never one to overstay its welcome. Somewhere out there, trouble stirs. Somewhere, a scoundrel sharpens his blaster skills, a tyrant drafts new edicts, and a daring pilot… me… prepares to be summoned. The galaxy will call, and I, Montgomery Starstalker, will answer.

Now, before we part ways, allow me to leave you with a few invaluable lessons, pearls of wisdom polished through years of harrowing escapes, narrow victories, and immaculate grooming:

1. Always dress for the moment. A man in the right cape can turn suspicion into admiration, and admiration into distraction. Bonus points if the cape catches the light just so.

2. Maintain your equipment. Whether it's your starship's hyperdrive or your moustache wax, neglect is the enemy of greatness. My own line of grooming products, Montgomery's Majestic Moustache Wax™, is now available in Core Worlds and select Outer Rim boutiques.

3. Confidence is the best weapon. (Though a charged blaster doesn't hurt.) Step into every room as if you own it, even if stormtroopers are currently trying to arrest you. Especially then.

4. Surround yourself with exceptional people. Reginald, Sammie, Gaya, R2–DPR… they've all played their parts. And while it's true they're lucky to know me, I'm wise enough to admit I'm lucky to know them too.

5. Pilot like you mean it. If you're going to fly, fly. With style. With daring. Preferably while looking devastatingly handsome in the cockpit.

Remember: heroism is not just about blaster bolts and bravado; it's about leaving a lasting impression. Not just on the galaxy… but on the galaxy's mirror.

Until the next crisis, I remain,

Your friend, your guide, your savior,

Captain Montgomery Starstalker

P.S. Keep your cape pressed and your moustache sharp. You never know when adventure might knock.

40
CONCLUSION
THE REAL ONE

B y now, dear reader, you've walked with me through the winding corridors of my life, my daring childhood escapades, my glittering career in Blue Squadron, the bittersweet tragedy of Scarif, the dizzying highs of galactic heroism, and even the unutterable heartbreak of losing the great love of my life.

You know my triumphs, my heartbreaks, my capes. You've learned of my impeccable piloting, my impeccable moustache, and the fact that yes, I am devastatingly photogenic from every conceivable angle.

And through it all, one constant remains: my friendship with Reginald Starjammer. Steadfast, unflappable, occasionally grumpy, and yet somehow always there when the galaxy demands a well-timed intervention. If I have any wisdom to impart to you beyond my encyclopedic knowledge of cape fabrics, it is this: find yourself a Reginald. Ideally my Reginald, but as I'm not inclined to share, you'll have to make do with your own.

I extend my gratitude to him here, publicly, in print, in a manner that will be legally binding if he ever tries to deny that I'm the best friend he's ever had.

And so, here at last, we reach the final page... the end of the journey... the ultimate conclusion to the definitive chronicle of Montgomery Starstalker.

Or perhaps not.

You see, there's something I didn't tell you. Something I've been saving. A tale so bold, so grand, so utterly Starstalker that it demands its own conclusion… a second conclusion. Because really, does one conclusion ever suffice for a man like me?

No. No, it does not.

So close this chapter, dear reader. Take a moment. Compose yourself. And when you are ready, mentally, spiritually, and sartorially… turn the page.

Montgomery Starstalker has one more ending for you.

41
CONCLUSION PART THREE

S o, here we are again.

I can see the puzzled look on your face.

"Montgomery," you're saying, "didn't we just conclude your book?"

And to that I say: Yes. But so what? Do you think Han Solo only flew the Kessel Run once? Did Luke Skywalker stop after blowing up one Death Star? Of course not. Legends deserve encores.

Besides, after finishing my "first" and "second" conclusions, I found myself in a reflective mood… reflective both in the contemplative sense and literally reflective, as the light from the viewport caught my cape at just the right angle.

It occurred to me then that perhaps the galaxy could benefit from a few final pearls of Starstalker wisdom before I send you back to your undoubtedly less glamorous lives.

First, fashion is not optional. It is the armor we wear into the world. A properly chosen cape can defuse a tense negotiation, blind an enemy under stage lights, or conceal a thermal detonator in a pinch. Never underestimate a man who looks this good under fire.

Second, invest in quality grooming products. Whether it's my signature Montgomery's Magnificent Moustache Wax™ or my soon-to-launch

Reginald's Regrettable Hair Tonic™ (patent pending), presentation is key. The galaxy notices the details… makes them dazzling.

Third, and perhaps most important: never underestimate the power of your allies. From Reginald's dry wit to Gaya's soaring voice, from Sammie's ingenuity to the unshakable loyalty of a certain astromech, I have learned that while one man can be remarkable, a team can be unstoppable.

Even I… yes, I… am not above admitting that some of my finest hours came not from solo heroics, but from standing shoulder to shoulder with those I trust.

And finally, should the galaxy ever call on you to rise to the occasion, rise spectacularly. Leave no doubt in the minds of those watching that they are witnessing something extraordinary.

So, dear reader, I bid you farewell… for now. The galaxy is vast, its perils many, and I can assure you this will not be my last chapter… not in print, and certainly not in life. When destiny calls, Montgomery Starstalker answers… Always with style.

And to that, I say… you're welcome.

THE END

EDITOR'S DISCLAIMER

D ear Reader,

The following pages are unauthorized additions to this already unauthorized autobiography.

The author, Captain Montgomery Starstalker, is entirely unaware of their inclusion.

While the Captain's own account offers… shall we say… a unique perspective on his life and exploits, the inserts you are about to read have been sourced from ship logs, eyewitness statements, and the occasionally unfiltered commentary of certain long-suffering associates.

They are presented here in the interest of providing additional context, and perhaps a touch more substance… to the larger-than-life figure at the heart of this memoir.

Whether these glimpses serve to further burnish his legend or gently puncture it… Well, that is for you to decide.

A Note for the Inquisitive: You will also find a Glossary of Terms at the back of this volume, which may assist in deciphering certain phrases, stylistic flourishes, and grandiose references unique to Captain Starstalker's storytelling. We assure you, it's worth the read.

Respectfully,

—The Compilers

APPENDIX A:
MONTGOMERY STARSTALKER'S GLOSSARY OF ESSENTIAL GALACTIC TERMS

A Touch of Flair

A phrase I use frequently to describe my approach to life, problem-solving, and starship maintenance. Reginald insists it usually means a recipe for disaster. Ignore him.

Blue Squad

A group of extraordinary pilots who were my family in the stars. Heroes all. I wasn't there when they needed me most, and that's a regret I'll carry to my last flight. This book is for them.

Brooding Smuggler

A highly sophisticated stance, perfected during a particularly tense mission on Zalvex-9. Reginald and I were outnumbered, and with no immediate plans for escape, I leaned against the dark walls of the hangar, arms crossed, one leg bent, and stared dramatically into the distance. It serves no tactical purpose, but it is essential for morale.

Cape

A tactical garment designed for elegance, intimidation, and the occasional emergency use as a parachute. Not merely an accessory, but a lifestyle choice. Anyone who says otherwise lacks imagination and style.

Capesonia

A fictional planet I invented to bluff my way past an Imperial blockade. Not to be confused with Ghorman, the actual planet of capemakers, which I'm currently banned from visiting (long story).

Captain Keevan

A commanding presence and the captain of the *Halcyon*, known for her sharp mind, steady hand, and absolute refusal to let nonsense interfere with her ship's operations. She is a Pantoran and as cool under pressure as she is adept at handling unruly guests.

Monty's Notes: Keevan is the kind of captain who can handle a First Order invasion while sipping a cup of tea and still have time to scold you for wearing a cape to dinner. She doesn't suffer fools gladly - unless, of course, the fool happens to be me. I suspect she secretly admires my ingenuity, though she'd never admit it.

Chewbacca

A legendary Wookiee warrior and part-time critic of my grooming products. Surprisingly good at sabacc. Known for his growls, loyalty, and ability to throw me across a room when irritated.

Dashing Resolve, The

My personal starship, as dashing as its captain. Some say it's held together by dura-plast and optimism, but Reginald assures me it's technically spaceworthy.

Dashing Resolve, The Drink

A drink as bold as a hyperspace jump and as smooth as a Corellian cape swish.

Ingredients:

- 2 oz Spiced Rum (for that hint of daring escapades)
- 1 oz Velvet Falernum (because only a fool neglects a touch of refinement)
- ½ oz Blue Curacao (to match the twinkle in Monty's eye and the glow of his moustache wax)
- ¾ oz Fresh Lime Juice (for that necessary zest of unpredictability)
- ½ oz Honey Syrup (sweet, like the whispers of admirers left in his wake)
- 2 dashes Aromatic Bitters (for the complexities of a well-traveled man)
- A splash of Sparkling Ginger Beer (a subtle fizz, much like Monty's charm)

Garnish:

- A flamboyant orange twist (to mimic his unnecessarily extravagant cape)
- A Luxardo cherry (because Montgomery insists on at least one accessory at all times)

Instructions:

1. In a shaker filled with ice, combine rum, falernum, curacao, lime juice, honey syrup, and bitters.

2. Shake as if dodging a blaster bolt in a high-stakes sabacc game.

3. Strain into a chilled coupe glass.

4. Top with a splash of sparkling ginger beer for that final flourish.

5. Garnish with an audaciously long orange twist and a cherry on top because Montgomery believes in going the extra parsec.

Serving Suggestion:

Best enjoyed aboard The *Dashing Resolve* while recounting exaggerated tales of adventure, ideally to an audience that finds Monty's escapades both impressive and slightly dubious.

Monty's Notes: If someone tells you this drink is "too much," just remember: so is life, old boy! And we drink to life!

Dastar-Lee

My so-called nemesis, though I hesitate to use the word worthy in his case. A self-proclaimed ace pilot whose skills are, let's say, subpar at best. Known for his embarrassingly uneven moustache (seriously, I've seen Wookiees with better grooming habits), an overuse of hair gel, and his penchant for dramatically shouting, "Curse you, Starstalker!" every time I outwit him.

Monty's Notes: While Dastar-Lee is mildly amusing as a villain, he's hardly what you'd call a challenge. His catchphrase is uninspired, his piloting skills are questionable, and his attempts to defeat me have all ended in either complete failure or his own humiliation. Still, I'll give him this: he tries really, really hard. It's almost endearing.

D3-09

The *Halcyon's* logistics droid, programmed to assist passengers with information, navigation, and other practical needs. D3-09 is polite, precise, and surprisingly good at bedtime storytelling.

Monty's Notes: Ah, D3-09, proof that even droids can appreciate greatness. During my stay on the *Halcyon*, D3-09 recounted a tale of how I heroically saved Captain Keevan during a tense standoff with the First Order. I may have embellished the details when I told the story originally, but D3-09's version was truly inspiring. I think even the droid was impressed with my brilliance.

Fear the Stache

A state of awe and intimidation, inspired by my exceptional moustache. Many have underestimated its power… fewer lived to regret it. When properly groomed, it doubles as both a weapon of charm and a shield against foolish questions.

First Order

A group of uptight, humorless villains dedicated to oppression, bad uniforms, and stomping out joy. Easily confused by a confident speech or a cape twirl. I've escaped them so many times that they probably have a poster of me in their break rooms. Also, what do you do when you make it to the local cantina before anyone else?

Force, The

A mystical energy that binds the galaxy together, moves objects with willpower, and sometimes makes me look extremely lucky. I've been told I'm not Force-sensitive, but I suspect otherwise. (How else do you explain my impeccable sabacc instincts?)

Frostfang Clan, The

A nomadic group of Kelvinarian warriors known for their stoic demeanor, impressive fur cloaks, and tendency to throw newcomers into the nearest glacier for fun. Fortunately, they have a deep respect for moustaches, which is why I was able to negotiate peace and even a temporary leadership role (brief as it was).

Grand Admiral Thrawn

A legendary tactician, brilliant strategist, and master of unsettling calmness. Known for his ability to predict enemy movements by studying their art. Frankly, it's impressive and mildly terrifying.

Monty's Notes: A brilliant mind, yes, but I can't help wondering: what would Thrawn think of my cape collection? I like to imagine he'd say something like, "Fascinating, yet an unparalleled display of reckless bravado and artistic hubris." I could live with that.

Hyperdrive Malfunction

An occasional hiccup in faster-than-light travel, often blamed on faulty parts. In my experience, it's usually caused by spilled drinks, unsanctioned capes stored in the engine room, or Reginald overreacting. (Reginald disagrees with this definition.)

Ice Arachnids

Terrifying multi-legged predators that thrive in the frozen caves of Kelvinar Prime. They can grow up to three meters tall, have venomous fangs, and are extremely difficult to bargain with (trust me, I tried). Weakness: loud noises and fire.

Imperial Bureaucracy

A labyrinthine system of rules and paperwork designed to crush the soul. Fun fact: Most officers will let you pass a checkpoint if you distract them with a long enough monologue about hair care.

It's a Small Galaxy (Ride)

A slow-moving, animatronic-filled ride at the Ziroplex Galactic Amusement Emporium that celebrates galactic unity by featuring poorly-synchronized singing droids from various planets. The song is catchy in the worst possible way and has been known to haunt the dreams of riders for weeks.

Monty's Notes: Reginald once dared me to endure it twice in a row. I survived, but I swear I still hear that blasted tune in quiet moments. The real terror isn't the ride, it's trying to get the song out of your head.

Kelvinar Prime

An ice-covered wasteland of a planet where survival depends on sheer willpower, ingenuity, and a good pair of thermal boots. Known for its treacherous blizzards, labyrinthine ice caves, and aggressive native wildlife, most of which seem to have far too many teeth.

Monty's Notes: I once spent an entire week on Kelvinar Prime after an unexpected crash landing. (Reginald insists it was because I ignored his warning about flying into a storm, but I prefer to think of it as fate.) During my stay, I bravely evaded an army of ice arachnids, single-handedly negotiated peace with the Frostfang clan, and discovered the galaxy's best recipe for snowberry cider. Some might call it a disaster, but I call it my finest hour. Reginald, of course, calls it unbearable.

Laser Panache

An advanced combat enhancement that blends artistry and firepower. Definition still under debate. Even I don't know what it truly means, but trust me, it's brilliant.

Lieutenant Croy

An ambitious First Order officer who takes his job far too seriously. Known for his rigid posture, overuse of the word protocol, and relentless pursuit of Resistance activity aboard the *Halcyon*.

Monty's Notes: Croy is everything I despise about the First Order: humorless, unimaginative, and utterly convinced of his own importance. His greatest weakness? He underestimates me every single time. (Also, his cape is atrocious. Truly an affront to galactic fashion.)

Monarch of Mustafar

Unofficial title I once claimed after negotiating a ceasefire during a lava dispute. Technically, no one acknowledged it, but that's beside the point. For three glorious hours, I was royalty.

Mon Mothma

The face of the Rebellion and the best-dressed politician in the galaxy (besides myself, naturally). A woman of incredible poise, vision, and restraint, she only rolled her eyes at me once. Quite the accomplishment, considering I did accidentally spill Corellian whiskey on her speech notes.

Montgomery Starstalker

A daring adventurer, fearless pilot, and occasional genius. Known for his wit, charm, and impeccable cape collection. Some call me reckless, others call me lucky, but I like to think of myself as inevitably heroic. (Disclaimer: opinions may vary.)

Ouannii

A Rodian musician and Gaya's trusted assistant aboard the *Halcyon*. Ouannii's talent for creating beautiful music is matched only by their sharp wit and unwavering loyalty to the galactic pop star.

Monty's Notes: Ouannii is the true genius behind Gaya's performances. Their music has been known to reduce grown beings to tears (or, in my case, inspire dramatic cape twirls). I once offered Ouannii a partnership in my burgeoning line of musical capes that hum melodies when you spin. Sadly, they declined. I remain hopeful.

R2-DPR

My highly stylish and extremely resourceful astromech droid. While not as appreciated by the galaxy as he should be, his ability to look dignified under pressure is unmatched. Not only does he repair the ship faster than Reginald (don't tell him), but he also keeps my cape collection impeccably organized. Once saved my life using a tray of cocktails as a diversion.

Raynolph 7 (District on Chandrila)

A modest little district on the otherwise serene and idyllic planet of Chandrila. Known for its colorful markets, friendly locals, and creative approach to urban planning (if you can't find your way out of Raynolph 7's winding alleys, don't worry, you're not the first). It's where I grew up, learned to fly, and perfected the art of charming my way out of trouble.

Monty's Notes: While most Chandrilans are known for their diplomacy and good manners, Raynolph 7 added a bit of spice to my upbringing. If you can survive a Raynolph 7 street festival (and the occasional runaway bantha), you can survive anything.

Reginald Starjammer

My loyal mechanic, confidant, and frequent wet blanket. A genius at fixing things and at pointing out when I've broken them. Don't let his sarcasm fool you; he admires me deeply (probably).

Sabacc

A high-stakes card game of skill, strategy, and sheer audacity. Also, an excellent way to bankrupt yourself if you don't have my talent for bluffing while wearing a sequin cape.

Saja, The

A mysterious group of Force-sensitive guides aboard the *Halcyon* who train others in the ways of the Force. They are wise, patient, and deeply dedicated to understanding the Force in all its complexity.

Monty's Notes: The Saja are an intriguing bunch. I suspect they're still trying to figure out if I'm secretly Force-sensitive or just ridiculously lucky. (Hint: it's both.)

Sammie

The *Halcyon's* mechanic, a bright-eyed, eager young man who loves ships almost as much as I love capes. Sammie dreams big, works hard, and has a knack for being in the right place at the right time.

Monty's Notes: I like Sammie. He reminds me of a younger version of myself: idealistic, clever, and occasionally a bit too enthusiastic. Of course, he lacks my sense of flair (and my moustache), but he's learning. One day, he might even graduate to cape-worthy status.

Sandro Alimander

A budding musician and Resistance sympathizer with a flair for melody and a passion for justice. Sandro dreams of inspiring the galaxy with his music while quietly aiding the cause against the First Order.

Monty's Notes: Sandro is a good kid with a lot of heart, and, frankly, far too much idealism for his own good. He once serenaded a room full of stormtroopers as a distraction, and somehow it worked. I'm not sure if that says more about his talent or the troopers' lack of musical standards, but either way, I respect it.

Snowberry Cider

A delicious, warming beverage made from the elusive snowberries of Kelvinar Prime. Perfect for surviving an ice storm or impressing hostile locals. Recipe remains classified, as I promised the Frostfang chieftain I wouldn't share it with the galaxy. (Well, unless someone offers a really good price.)

Tantor Coaster

A high-speed, stomach-turning roller coaster at the Ziroplex Galactic Amusement Emporium. Famous for its sharp drops, unexpected twists, and tendency to malfunction at the worst possible moments.

Wacky Wookiee Wax

A revolutionary grooming product for discerning Wookiees (and anyone else with unruly fur). Not yet a galactic bestseller, but Chewbacca himself used it.

You're Welcome

My signature catchphrase, delivered with just the right amount of charm, timing, and cape flourish. Sometimes, said before I actually do anything because let's face it, my mere presence is a gift to the galaxy.

Ziroplex Galactic Amusement Emporium

A sprawling theme park and one of the galaxy's most over-the-top attractions, boasting rides, games, and overpriced snacks from dozens of star systems. Official motto: Bringing Joy Across the Stars! Unofficial motto: Don't Look Too Closely at the Safety Features.

Monty's Notes: It's where heroes are made. Or at least that's what I told myself after I saved a group of terrified children on the infamous Tantor Coaster.

INSERT 1
BY REGINALD STARJAMMER, CHIEF MECHANIC OF THE DASHING RESOLVE

Well, you made it. You've journeyed through the misadventures, the capes (so many capes), and the near-disasters disguised as victories. And if you're still reading, I assume Montgomery Starstalker has left you as simultaneously bewildered and impressed as he's left me.

Now, I'll be the first to admit, being Montgomery's mechanic isn't what you'd call straightforward. Between his penchant for extravagant cape choices (one of them had sequins that blinded an entire room during a negotiation) and his ability to

turn minor inconveniences into galaxy-wide events, most days feel like an exercise in patience.

And then there was the day he tried to "enhance" his blaster with something he called laser panache. To this day, I don't know what that actually meant, and I'm fairly certain neither did he. All I know is, by the end of it, the blaster had glitter in the barrel, the safety switch was missing, and I was the one who had to explain why the ship smelled like burnt cologne for a week.

Still, there's more to Monty than his ridiculous ideas and his inability to resist adding "a touch of flair" to everything he touches. There's a reason I've stuck around all these years.

Take Blue Squad, for example.

Monty flew with them, a squadron of reckless, talented pilots who weren't just his friends; they were his family. And there was Blue Four, his fiancée. She was sharp, brilliant, and could outfly anyone in the galaxy. They had this way of looking at each other like they were already planning their next adventure, or their next argument.

But Monty wasn't there for the mission that took them all. He wasn't there because he spilled a drink in his cockpit, a ridiculous accident, caused by one of his infamous, over-complicated "cocktail innovations." The resulting system malfunction grounded him just long enough for Blue Squad to head into the fight without him. And they never came back.

I was there when he got the news. Monty didn't yell or cry, at least not in front of anyone. He just stood there, holding Blue Four's insignia, staring at it like he could will her back. Later, when he thought no one was listening, I heard him whisper, "They needed me and I wasn't there."

That's the thing about Montgomery Starstalker. For all his flamboyance, his absurd schemes, and his questionable decision-making, he carries his losses deeply. He doesn't show it often; he masks it with jokes and capes and wild adventures, but he remembers every name, every face, and every failure. And somehow, he keeps going.

That's what sets him apart. For all his flaws, Monty doesn't give up. Not on people. Not on the galaxy. Not even on himself.

I've seen him do the impossible: convince a bounty hunter to lower their blaster with a speech about hair tonic, escape a Wookiee's wrath by inventing a proverb about friendship and fur, and somehow win over an Imperial officer by sheer force of absurd charm. But behind all the antics is someone who never stops trying to make the galaxy a little better, even when the odds and his own plans are against him.

So, if you've made it this far, you've seen both the absurdity and the brilliance of the man I call my Captain. Yes, he's flawed. Yes, he's baffling. But Montgomery Starstalker is also the bravest, kindest, most ridiculous hero I've ever had the honor of serving.

And if you don't believe me, well, stick around. There's always another adventure.

Reginald Starjamme

PREFACE TO INSERT 2 (As issued by the Office of Historical Records, New Republic Archives)

To the Esteemed Readers of The Noble Record of Montgomery Starstalker's Legacy,

The following document was not included in the original manuscript provided by Montgomery Starstalker. In fact, it is highly probable that he remains unaware of its existence.

As archivists of the New Republic Historical Records, it is our duty to present a complete and accurate account of galactic history, and in doing so, we have taken the unprecedented step of including this personal correspondence, discovered within the private effects of Commander Starstalker following the liberation of Coruscant.

The letter, written by Thea "Blue-4U" Lorne, a decorated pilot of the Rebel Alliance and founding member of Blue Squadron, was never opened.

Commander Starstalker's known recollections of his service are grand, theatrical, and deeply self-assured. His memoir, while an invaluable historical document, does not dwell on loss, personal sacrifice, or the cost of heroism. This is, in many ways, what makes him the legend he is.

However, to exclude this letter would be to ignore a critical piece of his story.

It is a truth known to those who served under the banner of the Rebellion:

Some heroes chose their battles. Others had their paths chosen for them.

It is our belief that this letter deserves to be read.

It is a rare and unfiltered moment of truth, not about the greatness of Montgomery Starstalker, but about what was lost to ensure that he would survive to become the hero he is today.

We recognize that its inclusion may be met with objection by the Commander himself. However, history must be honest, and sometimes, even the greatest legends must face the reality of the sacrifices made in their name.

We leave it to the reader to determine what weight this letter carries.

Office of Historical Records,

New Republic Archives

[Issued 12 ABY, Coruscant

INSERT 2

[THE FOLLOWING IS THE FINAL KNOWN CORRESPONDENCE OF LIEUTENANT THEA "BLUE-4U" LORNE, WRITTEN PRIOR TO HER DEPLOYMENT TO SCARIF. THE LETTER WAS FOUND AMONG THE PERSONAL EFFECTS OF COMMANDER MONTGOMERY STARSTALKER, UNOPENED.]

My Dearest Monty,

I know you'll hate me for this. You'll storm around the hangar. You'll curse and rant about cowards and conspiracies and how it is a crime against heroism to leave Montgomery Starstalker grounded while the rest of us fly into battle. You'll insist that only a fool would dare keep the finest pilot in the galaxy from taking to the stars.

I know, because I know you.

And because I know you, and I also know you will live.

You'll live because I made sure of it.

Yes, Monty. It was me.

I did it.

I sabotaged your X-wing. I made sure that, when the time came, you wouldn't be able to launch.

I need you to understand; I did not do this because I doubt you.

I did not do this because I think you are incapable or unworthy or anything less than the legend you were born to be.

I did this because I love you.

And I could not… I would not… watch you die.

They say there's a weight that comes with war.

We all carry it in different ways; some of us in our hands, some of us on our backs, some of us in the quiet spaces of our hearts.

I have carried you.

From the moment we met, I have carried your fire, your impossible charm, your boundless, maddening, ridiculous belief that you are untouchable.

I carried it through every dogfight, every mission, every time we barely made it out alive.

But this time, Monty, I could not carry the risk of losing you.

I won't lie to you. This battle is different.

We all feel it. Even the commanders… especially the commanders. This isn't just another skirmish.

It's a turning point.

A fight we cannot afford to lose.

And that means we're not all coming home.

I need you to listen to me, Monty.

You must survive.

Not for me, but for the galaxy.

For the stories you will tell, for the victories still waiting to be won, for the dream of what we are fighting for.

You will live. You will fight another day. And when that day comes, the Rebellion will need you.

The galaxy will need you.

Because you are Montgomery Starstalker, and your legend is not meant to end in fire.

I don't know if I'll make it back from Scarif.

I hope I do. Stars above, I hope I do.

I hope I walk through that hangar bay and find you leaning against your broken X-wing, arms crossed, waiting to give me that smug, infuriatingly charming smirk as you scold me for ruining your ship.

I hope I get to tell you this in person.

I hope I get to spend every day for the rest of my life arguing with you about who is truly the better pilot.

I hope for all of that.

But if hope isn't enough, and if this is the last thing I ever give you…

Know that I love you.

I love you with the same reckless, wild devotion that you give to the stars.

I love you in the way that you fly; all fire and speed and impossible joy.

I love you in the way that you stand, always taller than the fear, always braver than the odds.

And I will love you, even if the stars burn out before we meet again. And as you often say to me, I now tell you… "You're Welcome," my love.

Yours, always,

Thea (Blue-4U)